RUNS
IN THE
FAMILY

Thirteen Stories

RUNS IN THE FAMILY

Thirteen Stories

Sandy Rogin

RayDan Books
Oakland, California

Runs in the Family
Thirteen Stories

Published by RayDan Books
Oakland, California

Runs in the Family is a work of fiction but is based on the lives of real
family members, years of conversations with family and friends, and
thorough research into family documents, historical records, and
newspaper accounts.

Print ISBN: 979-8-9902593-0-0
E-Book ISBN: 979-8-9902593-1-7

Printed in the United States of America

FICTION/Literary; Fiction/Historical
1. Family farm. 2. Family relationships. 3. Sibling relationships.
4. Suicide and family. 5. Iowa farm experiences. 6. Family history.
7. Rural life in the 1900s. 8. Challenges of farming.

Cover photo from Shutterstock, Siekierski.photo
Cover and interior design by Gilman Design, Larkspur, California

For Dan

CONTENTS

Introduction

I GREW UP IN rural Iowa, on a farm six miles from the nearest town, with siblings so much older than I that four of them had left home by the time I was a toddler. Seeing them rarely, I got to know them well only when I was older. Then I became fascinated by how different each of us was and wondered how we arrived at those differences.

These thirteen interlinked stories, based on the ten members of my family, began with the one I've called "Abandoned," which I started thirty years ago. I've long tried to understand what led to that tragic episode on our farm. The events around that calamity have stuck with me since I was fourteen years old.

I knew that one brother, whom I look at in "God's Plan," had left our family when he was only fifteen but only learned later the details of what drove him away. I idolized my oldest sister, who started her own fashion-design business in San Francisco, to such an extent that it took me years to admit the selfishness at the core of her glamorous life. I was vaguely aware that my dad had been a professional boxer but didn't know that some of his bouts had drawn huge crowds. Wondering how my seemingly incompatible parents ever got together, some twenty years before I was born, I tried to understand what made an educated city girl and a poorly schooled farmer and professional boxer decide to make a life together.

The stories in *Runs in the Family* reflect years of exploration: of my own memories and experiences; conversations with family members and childhood friends; family-written letters and notes; local newspaper stories from Iowa, Indiana, and North Carolina; and institutional and genealogical records. What emerged was a long-held family secret, as well as the predilections of some of my family members to alcoholism and mental illness.

In these thirteen stories, I've stayed with the known facts

as much as possible—I wanted this book to convey my family history. Where I've created situations, conversations, and inner thoughts I could not have known, I sought a maximum of authenticity and the truth of each character as I came to understand him or her. Call it fact-based fiction.

Through these stories, I want to honor the lives of my parents and siblings, to describe their struggles and accomplishments and, in particular, the unique life led by each. In a sense, by delving into their inner worlds, I've brought my family back to life and gotten to know them all over again.

Sandy Rogin
Oakland, California
May 2024

New Growth

D AD RAN TOWARDS ME from the barn, the denim shirt-sleeve on his right arm rolled up to his shoulder. His arm was wet and streaked with blood. Dirty straw clung to his overalls, and his forehead was caked with mud and sweat.

"Sandy, where's Dale?" he yelled at me, then paused for a breath. "And Danny."

"Just left for town," I said, clutching the handle of my flannel-lined wicker egg basket and letting the screen door of the chicken coop bang shut.

"Shit." He waved toward the barn. "Come and help me."

I dropped the basket and heard eggs crack. Yikes! Mom would kill me if I broke too many, egg sales being her only source of pocket money. But my two brothers were away, and Dad needed my help. I ran after him, past the machine shed with its two tractors, around the side of the faded red barn, and through the wide-open double doors. Straw and hay bales were stacked against the left wall. Narrow beams of light from the four small windows under the high, peaked roof illuminated one of the stalls on the right, where a milk cow lay moaning on grimy, matted straw, struggling to get up.

"Hold the head down so she can't move," Dad said, kneeling behind the cow. "The calf's stuck. I can't get the damn thing out."

Crouching down, I braced my shoulder against the animal's neck, my body weight holding her against the floor. Her wailing, a low-pitched, drawn-out sound, was almost human in its distress. The cow's terrified eyes rolled back in her head as I stroked her, and I heard Dad grunting as he worked to birth the calf. The floor around us darkened for a few seconds as a flock of sparrows flew out of the hayloft, frightened by the noise.

Dad grabbed the calf's legs and slowly pulled out the baby's wet, floppy head, then its slippery brown body. The cow jerked, and I felt a piercing pain in my shoulder as the mom struggled to her feet, a bag of fluid hanging out of her. She gazed at her lifeless newborn, while I massaged my sore shoulder and looked at the calf in the bloody straw.

"Damn," Dad said as he wiped his forehead with a red bandana. "We lost it." He took hold of the cow's halter to help her stand up. "Good work, though."

My eyes widened through my tears. Not only had Dad let me help him with actual men's work, he'd given me a compliment.

Head high, I walked back to the chicken coop to retrieve my basket and got some straw from the henhouse to clean away the broken eggs. I hoped Mom wouldn't notice the haul was less than usual.

The next day, I stood outside the fence around the pigpen, with its usual odors of pig poop mixed with mud that smelled like rotten eggs. Dad, Dale, and Danny were clamping metal rings in the animals' snouts to keep them from rooting under fences. Our Appaloosa horse, Champion, chomped on the grass near me, his leather reins dangling on the ground. Dad hated spending money on anything that wasn't land or farm machinery, but maybe he figured that having cattle required a horse, and he'd probably gotten him cheap.

Dale, the oldest of us eight children, was my favorite brother. He drove Danny and me to Saturday-afternoon movie matinees in Lake Park and gave us money for candy and popcorn. In the summer, he took us swimming at the gravel pit two miles away, where he'd constructed a diving board from which we'd do belly flops into the water.

But he was thirty-two, with two years of college, and he still lived at home. And he and Dad were arguing way too much. Some of their squabbles seemed silly. Should we replace the rickety old pickup truck? No, it could still go a few hundred miles. Had Dale picked up the new cultivator shovels yet? Why not? Hurry, or they'll sell them to someone else. When I was a grown-up, I'd never be stuck at home like Dale was, with Dad always bossing me around.

"Sandy!" Dad yelled above the din of screaming animals. He was straddling a pig and gripping it with his knees. "Get another box of hog rings from the bench in the workshop. Move."

This was Dad's usual idea of a task for me. He didn't think a twelve-year-old girl could wrestle a fifty-pound pig to the ground, while Danny, a head shorter and a year and a half younger, qualified for the job. Dad never gave me any serious farm chores. What I wanted was to milk the cows, not hold their mucky tails out of Dad's face while he milked. What I wanted was to drive our new 1954 Farmall tractor, which Dad let Danny do, even though his feet barely reached the clutch.

What I didn't want was women's work: chopping vegetables, gathering eggs, pulling weeds in the garden.

That evening, the five of us sat around our circular kitchen table. As usual, we didn't talk much or even look at one another as we ate our fried chicken, mashed potatoes, and sliced tomatoes from the garden. Mom tried to try to fix interesting meals, looking for recipes in newspapers and magazines. Dale's black hair flopped over his forehead and below his dark eyebrows; his hazel eyes were fixed on his plate. Danny fidgeted in his chair, his wavy brown hair tousled from constantly running his hands through it. The three of us sat ready to bolt at any sign of conflict—even Dale, who, I thought, after so many years, must be used to my parents' quarreling, which was mostly about money and Dad's drinking. Mom had slept downstairs on the couch for so long that on overnights with friends, I marveled if I saw that their parents shared the same bed.

As usual, Mom slammed Dad's plate down on the table. She sat as far as she could from him, her lips set in a straight line.

"What are you so sullen about?" Dad asked her. He gulped the first of the two or three bottles of beer he usually drank at supper.

Otherwise, only the sounds of chewing, slurping, and an occasional request to pass the butter disrupted the quiet. This drama was happening more and more often, so I should have been used to it.

I tried to screen out the supper scene and focus on my doings. Our accordion band was set to perform on KICD, the local radio station, and I'd made several baskets in our after-school basketball scrimmage against Okoboji. Mom attended my games and musical performances whenever she could. Dad never acknowledged any of my activities, his concerns only farm-related.

When we finished eating, I cleared the table, then rushed through washing the dishes. Dale and Danny were long gone, Dale up to his room and Danny out to ride his bike. Mom had disappeared into the living room, probably to read or crochet. Dad still sat, slumped in his chair, nursing a beer.

A few nights later, we didn't wait for Mom to finish serving before we began eating, hoping to gobble up our food before any argument erupted. As Dad wolfed down a second helping of fried potatoes and pork chops, grease dribbled onto the gray stubble on his chin. Then, his plate clean, he shoved it away and picked up his cigar stub from an ashtray.

"So, Dale, should we ship some cattle to Georgia? Vern have any good ideas?" Dale had just returned from a trip to Atlanta, where my second-oldest brother lived. The two were always discussing ways to make raising cattle more profitable. This time, it was whether to ship the animals to Georgia pastureland, then bring them back home for a final fattening up in our feedlot.

After a few minutes, I heard Dad addressing me.

"Sandy, it's high time you helped out around here," he said. "And that nag of yours has gotta start earnin' its keep, or we have to get rid of him." I cringed whenever he called Champion names or threatened to sell him to a glue factory. "The cattle aren't gainin' enough weight in the pasture. You need to start bringin' 'em to the feedlot every day." Between puffs on his cigar, Dad drained his bottle of beer and wiped his mouth on the sleeve of his brown flannel shirt. "You know the pasture we're talkin' about?"

I nodded. Champion and I had often explored the roughly sixty acres where the cattle grazed.

"There's a hundred head. Make damn sure you don't lose any. And start after school on Monday."

Mom collected our plates and filled the sink with water as I sat, stunned. "Yes," I said in a loud voice. "I won't lose any."

I suddenly had trouble breathing. Bringing in the cattle! Dale had never been relaxed on a horse, and after Danny fell off Champion a couple times, he didn't want to try again. At sixty-three, Dad was too old to ride comfortably on the rough and swampy pasture ground. I rode several times a week and in the last year had been on a thirty-mile-long overnight trail ride with teenagers and adults. I was sure I could bring in the cattle.

I stood up and crossed my fingers behind my back. My legs felt wobbly, from both pleasure at my new job and relief we'd had a calm meal. Dale and Danny even lingered at the table, perhaps so dumbfounded at the noncombative atmosphere, they couldn't move.

I sneaked a look at Mom. She'd turned around from the sink and was looking at me, her dishtowel, with its orange-and-black appliqué of a rooster, hanging over the shoulder of her floral housedress. Her tiny smile hinted she was happy for me. But then she frowned.

"Now, Sandy," Mom said, shaking her finger at me. "Don't you run Champion in the pasture. There're gopher holes all over. He could break his leg. You almost fell off Oscar's horse, remember? Maybe you shouldn't do this. It's too dangerous."

A wealthy neighbor had recently let me ride his spirited animal in his pasture. One day, the horse raced back to his barn, and I couldn't rein him in, then he jerked to a sudden stop at the barn door, throwing me onto his neck. Clutching his mane, I'd barely hung on.

"Please, Mom," I pleaded. "I'll be careful."

In bed that evening, all I could think about was how to round up a hundred cattle and drive them in from the pasture. Cattle are basically stupid and can suddenly bolt in all directions. Could I keep so many animals together and herd them where they had to go? If I lost a steer, it would cost us money, and Dad would get rid of Champion.

On Monday, I ran into the house as soon as I got off the school bus, dumped my books, then dashed to the barn. I saddled Champion and tightened the cinch under his belly, but as I slid the bridle over his head, my hand slowed and trembled slightly. We were ready to go, but was I prepared?

As I rode the three miles to the pasture, I sat up straight and balanced in the saddle. In the calf-length brown-leather boots with a pink-and-blue zigzag design I'd gotten for my last birthday, my feet fit snugly in the wooden stirrups. The reins dangled from my hand and rested on Champion's neck. I could do this job.

The pasture was dotted with small hillocks, tufts of grass, several clumps of trees, and numerous hidden gopher holes. In their tunneling, the rat-size critters pushed the dirt above ground into small piles, but the mounds were often concealed by grass.

I rode around looking for cattle and did rough counts, steering Champion away from any gopher holes. If he broke a leg, it was all over. At first, I saw only ninety steers. After a half-hour search deeper in the pasture, I found the ten stragglers half-hidden in a clump of trees. Then a steer stumbled in a gopher hole and went down on a knee. Climbing down off Champion, I approached it, not knowing what I'd do to help the animal stand up. Dad would have to find someone else to bring in the cattle, and he'd sell Champion. Then the steer struggled back up. I let out the breath I'd been holding.

The cattle, Champion, and I moved slowly through the pasture, then along a half-mile-long narrow lane lined with barbed wire. At the muddy feedlot, Dad and Danny were distributing large squares of fresh salt licks around the area. Dale was scooping silage, a mixture of ground-up and fermented corn stalks, from the silo and bringing it to the wooden feed troughs.

Turning around to go back to the barn, I felt a satisfied tiredness. High above the ground atop my horse, I gazed for miles across the rolling pasture, separated by fences from ankle-high corn in neat rows, with unplanted pathways for tractor and cultivator to plow out the weeds. In the far distance, I saw our field of green alfalfa plants; when dried, they provided hay for our cattle and Champion.

As I rode along, I felt powerful, managing this thousand-pound animal with a gentle nudge from my boot heel or a slight tug of the reins. I couldn't control what happened between my parents, or my dad and Dale, or whether Dad would trust me with more real farm work. But here on Champion's back, I had it all together.

Each day over the next few weeks, Champion and I corralled the cattle into one big bunch and moved them slowly through the pasture toward the feedlot. I always found any stragglers.

But one sunny afternoon, I was daydreaming about basketball practice. The day before, I'd lofted the ball to the hoop and made six baskets in a short drill. Charging around the court in my mind, I suddenly felt a sharp pain in my knee. I yanked the reins and jerked Champion away from the barbed-wire fence; then, gripping the saddle horn, I leaned forward to look at the damage. Blood seeped out of a long rip in my jeans, and through the tear I saw a deep gash. I untied the red bandana from around my neck and pressed it on the wound. I tried to ignore the throbbing while chasing a few dawdlers back into the main bunch.

At the feedlot, I turned Champion around and began the ride home before Dad or my brothers could see my injury. I'd not give the men a chance to call me a sissy. We galloped across the pasture toward the slough, my body bouncing painfully in the saddle. Usually, we rode around this scary bog, an extra quarter mile, but my knee pulsed with pain, and I was in a hurry.

When we waded in, Champion sank to his knees in the stagnant water and mud. Slogging through the waving cattails and tall grass, his hooves made sucking sounds with each step. He stumbled twice, and both times I fell onto his neck, halfway out of the saddle, my face inches from the smelly muck.

At Champion's stall, soaking in sweat, I unsaddled him and fed him hay and water. Then, having ignored the pain for the past half-hour, I pulled the bandana away and looked through my torn jeans at a deep, bloody cut that extended almost three inches below my kneecap. Then, for the first time, I looked at the patch of dirty straw just ten feet away and remembered how it had been covered in a different kind of blood only a month earlier. I was now a part of real farm life, hard as it was. Delivering a dead calf. Bringing in the cattle.

As I limped to the house, my bandana stuck to the wound, and the aching kicked in again. I bit my lower lip and stumbled into the kitchen.

"What happened?" Mom called out.

My words came tumbling out as she helped me into a chair. She eased the bandana off, tore the fabric away, and gently washed the bloody gash with warm water.

"This looks bad," she said. "It's really deep. We better get you to Doctor Pell." She dabbed mercurochrome on the cut, then bandaged it. "I told you this was dangerous. You have to stop."

"No," I said, jerking my knee away. "I'm okay. Really. Dad will be mad if I can't bring the cattle in. And Dr. Pell costs too much."

"Get in the car," Mom ordered. While she drove, I studied the blood-soaked bandage. Maybe I was getting used to the sight of blood. A few weeks earlier, I'd been so eager to show I was more than just a girl, I'd asked Dale to load our 30-30 rifle. He showed me how to line up the V-shaped sight on a target, then engage and release the safety before pulling the trigger. Then he went to finish his chores.

I'd stood at the edge of our two-acre lawn, leaning against a tree and watching for movement, until I finally glimpsed a jackrabbit among the wild grapevines. I placed the rifle against my shoulder, sighted the animal in the V, and pulled the trigger. The kick of the gun knocked me backward, but I stayed on my feet. Luckily, Mom was gone. She would have had a fit.

But, suddenly ashamed, I couldn't bring myself to look at what I'd done. I'd killed a poor jackrabbit just to keep up with the men. I picked up the weapon and plodded to the workshop. I never wanted to shoot another gun.

Now, slumping against the car seat, I was worried. What if I had to give up riding and bringing in the cattle? Or stop playing basketball? My whole world would be over.

Doctor Pell sewed up the cut with eleven stitches and told me there would be about a two-inch-long scar. He said I had to give up basketball for at least two weeks. As I held my breath, he added that I could still ride, if I kept the knee bandaged. Yeah! I thought. I can hide any limp from Dad.

IN SPITE OF THE real men's work I was doing, I had a pesky girl problem that was making school difficult.

"Hey, what're those little bumps?" an older boy at school taunted, pointing at my chest and laughing with his friends. In the locker room after basketball practice, a girl on the team jeered, "Gonna be wearing undershirts in high school?"

The teasing had increased in the last few weeks, and to avoid it I spent many recess periods sitting in a stall in the girls' bathroom, staring up at a skylight so dirty, I could barely see the sky. Although I was the tallest girl in eighth grade, the others were a year older, and most of them wore bras.

Mom appeared totally unaware that my body was changing. I couldn't talk to her about it. The previous year, when I'd gotten my first period, I'd run to her, scared.

"Clean yourself up," she'd said, handing me some toilet tissue. "I'll get you something later."

The next day, I came home to find sanitary napkins and safety pins on my bed. Surely Mom had dealt with bras and periods with my two older sisters, long gone from home. But she never said anything, and now she was probably preoccupied with Dad's drinking and their fighting. So I couldn't blame her for not suspecting what was going on with me.

Determined to take matters into my own hands, I went with Mom on her next shopping trip to Lake Park, the nearest town, six miles away. At the grocery store, I said I'd meet her at the car. At the cross street—no stoplight in our thousand-person, two-block-long town—I hurried past the drugstore on the corner, where Dale sometimes treated Danny and me to root beer floats at the soda fountain. I glanced down the side street at our one-room library, the back part of which was a jail, housing mostly drunks. My accordion band practiced in the front. I rushed past Art Wright's leather shop, where I often paused to peer through the dusty window at the new and refurbished saddles.

At the Five-and-Dime, I looked across the street to the John Deere machinery dealer, to see if anyone I knew was watching. Inside, I glanced at the cashier behind the counter. It was Doris, my classmate Ralph's sister. She'd graduated the year before, but I knew who she was. Surrounded by cornfields, our three-story, red-brick school housed all twelve grades.

Doris gave me a quick glance, then looked back down at her book. Whew! She either didn't recognize me or didn't care. Though the only customer, I tried to appear casual, strolling along the two long aisles, glancing at the displays of stationery supplies, kitchen utensils, and cosmetics. After peeking once more at Doris, who was still engrossed in her book, I studied the measly selection of women's underwear laid out in square wooden boxes, then fingered the two one-dollar bills of babysitting money in my jeans pocket. What size was I? There was no changing room, not even a bathroom. My body sagged, and I slunk out to meet Mom, sad and disgusted that I'd chickened out.

I needed another plan. A few days later, I grabbed the Sears Roebuck catalogue from the bookcase in the living room, ran to the bedroom I shared with Danny, and sprawled on my bed. Danny had just left with Dale on an errand in Lake Park. I had probably a half-hour of privacy.

All my friends' families had this three-hundred-page catalogue, since the nearest department stores were miles away, in Spirit Lake and Spencer, and had limited selections. My friends and I often ogled the clothing, jewelry, and shoes. (Our parents probably dreamed over the appliances, furniture, bedding, and farm machinery.) For my birthday, Mom had ordered a small red turntable, on which I played *Peter and the Wolf* and songs by the Sons of the Pioneers endlessly. Danny had gotten an erector set. The last few months, I'd been eyeing a red cowgirl shirt with white polka dots and appliquéd flowers below the collar. I took a quick look at it, but I was on a mission.

Hearing Mom's footsteps, I threw the catalogue under the bed, my heart hammering, until she passed my door. Was she looking for it? As her footsteps faded away, I clutched the heavy book, combing the index until I found Lingerie. I'd already measured myself at size 32 with a tape measure from Mom's sewing machine and guessed my cup size to be an A. I picked out two of the plainest white-cotton bras. Hands shaking, I filled out the order form, addressed the envelope I'd found among my mother's papers, pasted one of her stamps on it, and slid in two one-dollar bills. The next day, I stuck the envelope in the mailbox at school.

Before rounding up the cattle each day, I galloped Champion the half-mile down the gravel road to get the mail before Mom did. Each time I brought it in, I felt Mom studying me, wondering, "Why the rush to the mailbox?"

Ten days after I sent in the order, I arrived just as the postman did. He handed our mail to me, including a small package with my name on it.

As I raced through my herding duties that afternoon, I kept reaching behind my saddle to feel the bulge in my saddlebag. When I got back to my room, I tore open the package and tried on the two simple bras, which fit perfectly. I stood in front of the mirror admiring my new profile, the flatness replaced with a girlish rounded shape.

During the next month, I alternated wearing the bras, washing them in the bathroom sink when no one was around and drying them on hangers far back in my closet, hidden by a shirt or blouse. No one noticed my new shape under my loose blouses, but the taunting at school stopped, and I felt more grown-up and less lonely. In fact, I felt good. I'd gotten my bra and was still bringing in the cattle.

One Saturday morning in early June, Mrs. Erickson, my friend Rosemary's mother, came to visit. My dad and brothers were out doing chores. Mom and Mrs. Erickson sat in the kitchen drinking coffee. I was sprawled on the couch in the living room, reading a book and trying to tune out their chatter.

"Honestly, Mildred," Mrs. Erickson said, "it was so hard to find a bra for Rosemary." I jerked my head up. "She got big a lot quicker than I expected."

Sweat trickled down the middle of my chest. I always felt sorry for Rosemary, who was my age but had such large breasts, her body looked top-heavy. At school, standing in the lunch line, she usually crossed her arms in an X down her front.

"Hardly anyone carries a 32D," Mrs. Erickson continued. "I had to drive to Spencer."

My mother was quiet. What was she thinking? Was she embarrassed she hadn't noticed that I needed a bra, that I was growing up?

How is it that my friend's mother got it when my own mother didn't?

When I got home from school a few days later, I found a white box on my bed. Inside were two bras nestled in tissue paper, much prettier than the ones I'd ordered. These had pale pink-nylon lace covering the upper half of soft beige-satin cups. Where had Mom found them? Probably in Spencer. I tried on each one before the mirror. How pretty they looked on me. How balanced I looked in my body.

I placed my new bras in the tissue paper in my dresser drawer, musing on how Mom only recognized I needed a bra after her friend's visit. Thank you, Mrs. E, I whispered as I changed into jeans and boots.

As I walked to the barn, I passed Mom scattering corn at the chicken coop, white chickens flocking around her. I wanted to hug her, but at the thought, I felt my face flush, and I rushed past without a word, not even "thanks." I hoped she somehow knew how grateful I was. When it came to talking about personal issues,

Mom and I seemed to be at the bottom of a steep hill neither of us could climb. Maybe one day we'd reach the top.

———

MY PARENTS' FIGHTS WERE getting worse. Dad kept shouting at Mom about not keeping the house clean. She responded with sullen silences and walking away. I offered Mom more help with the housework, but that didn't help. At supper one evening, on his second bottle of beer, Dad yelled at Mom about bedbugs in his sheets. Who knew if there really were any, or if he was just trying to irritate her? When he shoved his dinner plate onto the floor, Dale, Danny, and I bolted from the room.

A few days later, Dad grabbed a basket of dirty laundry, marched outside toward the barn, and threatened to burn the clothes. Dale grabbed the basket as blue jeans, flannel work shirts, and Mom's flowered housedresses scattered on the ground. Then Dale slammed his hands into Dad's chest and knocked him down. As Dad got to his feet, Dale spread his legs and raised both fists. I held my breath. How would this end? Dad punched Dale in the shoulder, knocking him backward but not off his feet. Then he marched to his car and drove off. Dale piled the clothes in the laundry basket and took it back to Mom.

The morning he moved out, all Dad said to me was, "Keep after those cattle. You've done good, not runnin' 'em and gettin' 'em to the feedlot. We can keep that nag."

After Dad left, I felt dizzy from the change. Was I supposed to be glad or upset? Life in the house was more peaceful, and I could finally have girlfriends over without worrying about scary clashes at the supper table. But none of my friends had parents living apart. And of course, neither Mom or Dad talked to Danny and me about what was happening, and he and I didn't discuss it. I had trouble sleeping. Danny began to wet his bed and constantly picked at the skin around his fingernails.

However, one thing was clear: Dad's moving out improved my parents' relationship. Just weeks later, he drove out every morning to work the farm from his new place in town. They no longer argued. He stopped in first for morning coffee, and they talked in normal tones. Mom even addressed him by his name, "Charles," instead of just glaring at him. I knew he was only there to run the farm, not to be a dad to Danny and me. But that was okay. He'd given me a real job. I could forgive him for leaving and everything else he didn't do.

"We've got that empty bedroom upstairs," Mom said a couple weeks after Dad left. "Want it?"

"Yeah, Mom," I said, astonished. "Thank you!" I wiped away happy tears with the dishtowel. I couldn't believe I'd finally have my own space. Mom preferred to sleep downstairs, so she moved into the room I shared with Danny, and he went upstairs to our brother Bob's room. Nine years older than I, he was in the Navy and seldom home on leave.

Over the next few weeks, Mom helped me transform Dad's old bedroom into mine. We scrubbed the musty smell of stale cigars and chewing tobacco from the walls and dingy green linoleum. Fresh paint covered the outlines of where Dad's souvenirs had hung, his World War I rifle, bayonet attached, and his red boxing gloves, tattered and frayed from professional matches long before I was born.

We replaced Dad's iron bed frame with a double bed, so I could have girlfriends sleep over, and covered it with a light-blue chenille spread. I put my lacy underwear in the drawers of the dresser we painted bird's-egg blue. Finally, we added sheer white curtains at the two windows, where torn paper shades had dangled for years. In the bookshelf, behind my Zane Grey and Nancy Drew adventures and Mom's high school copy of *The House of the Seven Gables*, I'd stashed a couple issues of Dad's *True Crime* magazines, smudged with coffee and tobacco stains.

I'd sneaked them from his room and now hid them from Mom, who'd probably disapprove.

Thinking about those magazines, I wondered if Dad had hated paying for all my new things. Mom always had to wheedle cash out of him for household expenses her egg money didn't cover. Beyond farm equipment and land, it was always a question of what he could be persuaded to spend money on. Maybe in this instance he'd felt guilty about moving out of the house, and the purchases were a way for him to make it up to one of his younger children.

As I looked around the room, I thought that as much as I wanted to do boys' jobs, I liked being a girl.

"I love my new room," I told Mom as we sat on my new bed, eating fried-egg sandwiches. I wanted to put my arms around her, but I knew she'd be uncomfortable. I wasn't even sure I could do it.

"Are you glad Dad's gone?" I asked. The question just popped out of my mouth. Why had I asked her such an unkind thing, after all she had done for me? Hadn't I learned that we couldn't talk about anything personal?

I wanted to take the question back but didn't know how to express my shame. I tried to apologize but couldn't. I'd had no practice in being open with my feelings.

"I have to feed the chickens," Mom said in a hoarse voice. She stood up and left. From downstairs I heard a shuffling noise as she put on her rubber boots. Then the porch door slammed.

When I heard Mom come back in, I walked downstairs to the kitchen. She was at the sink. I took a deep breath and said, "I'm sorry, Mom. Thanks again, so much, for my great room." Then I rushed out to saddle Champion.

Runs in the Family

ILDRED JUMPED AS THE door slammed and Charles walked into the kitchen. Would the noise wake Dale? He was even grouchier when he hadn't slept. She shivered from the cold January air that trailed her ex-husband into the room and tugged her cardigan tighter over her housedress. Charles poured himself a cup of coffee and joined her at the table. For a few seconds, he sat, gazing up at the ceiling.

"Still not up?" he asked Mildred.

"He was walking back and forth most of the night," she replied. "Hard for me to get to sleep." As happened most nights lately, she'd heard the creaking of floorboards above her bedroom as Dale paced.

"What the hell is going on?" Charles asked. "I need him to help me run this goddamned farm. It's seven o'clock in the morning."

Charles slumped in his chair and gripped his coffee cup with both hands. "Somethin's haywire. All of a sudden, Dale's turned into Mr. Gloom. Not the cheerful boy he used to be. Or the hard worker! It's crazy." He thumped his cup on the table, and liquid splashed onto the oilcloth.

Crazy, Mildred thought. Her own cup trembled in her hand. Could it really be true? The total shift in his personality. All the night pacing. For weeks, she'd tried to suppress the thought. The very illness that had hospitalized her mother—had it shown up in Dale?

"I should get him up," Charles said. But he didn't move. "On second thought, better not. He'll be in a foul mood. Again. Christ! I don't have time for this bullshit." He set his cup down again and headed for the door.

"Aren't the kids up?" he asked, turning around.

"Sandy's at Nancy's. And Danny's out feeding his 4-H calf."

"If Dale gets up before the day is over, tell him he's gotta get back to work." He stormed out, and Mildred flinched yet again at the noise that might wake Dale. Making a fist, she kneaded her temple where her migraine headaches usually began.

As her ex-husband's steps receded down the sidewalk, she thought once again that she'd finally accepted the end of her marriage. And Charles's remarriage. After almost thirty-five years and eight children, only Dale and her two youngest, thirteen and fourteen, remained on the farm, though each morning Charles drove out from town to help work the land and feed the animals. Mildred was a bit fuzzy on his and Dale's financial arrangement. She had a vague idea the two had agreed that Dale would get forty percent of any profits but wondered now how Dale felt about that agreement.

At this moment, though, Mildred was grateful that she and Charles could talk civilly. Charles had his cranky side, but real fighting was behind them. Now it was just occasional minor spats, usually over money. But there were sure to be arguments about Dale.

She heard a noise. Held her breath. Then released it. Probably just the creaks and groans of a hundred-year-old farmhouse. Or her imagination.

For the last six months or so, Dale's moods had been all over the place—from cheerfulness to dejection to extreme irritability within minutes, exhausting those around him. He no longer tinkered with car engines in the workshop, where he used to spend hours, and wouldn't take calls from Alice, his longtime girlfriend. Lately, he wasn't even feeding the cattle and hogs or repairing farm machinery. Many afternoons he just lay on the living room couch, dozing or staring at the ceiling. Once he trailed his fingers through the neat lattice crusts of two freshly baked apple pies, just to irritate her. That was not Dale. Mildred had thrown a spoon at him, and he slunk away. She'd thought he'd done it to be mean. But maybe it was the stress—and frustration—of still working with his dad.

All these years of keeping her mother's illness a secret. Maybe it was time to tell Charles, if it could help explain Dale's behavior. If she told him now, though, after all this time, he'd probably be furious. Who could blame him?

The door opened again, and Danny came in, gently closing it but not stopping to brush the snow from his coat and felt cap.

"Mom, Dad's giving me a ride to school," he said, grabbing his schoolbooks from the table. "He's gotta go to Lake Park. Mr. Martin's always there early. And I have basketball practice after school." He waved goodbye and ran out.

Mildred smiled. Her youngest, and the fifth boy. It was tiring, at fifty-six, still having young children at home. But with only two, she had time to attend their athletic competitions and music recitals.

In the quiet of the kitchen, her thoughts returned to her own mother. As far back as Mildred could remember, her mother's moods had been as erratic as Dale's were now. Mildred would lie awake, listening to her mother march back and forth in the hallway as her father pleaded with his wife to come to bed. The next morning, bleary-eyed, he'd leave their home in Richmond, Indiana, for his job as an engineer with the Pennsylvania Railroad.

At bedtime, her father would tell her and her younger brother, Harold, about his railroad adventures. Their mother often sat with them, but sometimes, after a few minutes, she'd ruin the moment by yelling, "It's late, get to bed." Then she'd complain of a headache, massage her temples, and tell them to get away from her. At those moments, Mildred always felt a pit of despair open inside her. What was wrong with her mother?

She shook her head to banish such thoughts and remember the good times, such as when Ida would come to her high school basketball games. Ida always yelled a bit too loudly, which embarrassed Mildred, but at the same time, she'd loved hearing her mother cheering her on. Always interested in her daughter's schoolwork, Ida often peppered Mildred with questions about her classes in English, Latin, and geography. Mildred had loved that.

And her mom was a good cook. She'd begin to prepare a meal, chop vegetables in a frenzy but often wander off to play the piano, leaving Florence, their live-in cook and housekeeper, to finish. Sometimes, with his railroad job, Mildred's father would be gone for a week, so he'd hired Florence to cook and care for Ida and the children and manage the household.

Creak! She jerked in her seat. Was that Dale's desk chair? Was he finally coming downstairs? She tiptoed to the bottom of the stairs to listen, biting her lip. What mood would he be in? Angry or indifferent? She always felt Dale's looming presence, fearful he'd create a scene.

Likewise, as a teenager, Mildred never knew, when she got home from school, which mother she'd encounter: the one who paced back and forth in front of the house, talking non-stop as she greeted Mildred and her friends, flooding them with questions, or the one in a dejected huddle on the couch, barely acknowledging her children's presence. After a quick "hi," Mildred would hustle her friends into her bedroom, apologizing for Ida's conduct. She soon stopped inviting friends over.

But sometimes Ida was carefree and happy. The last trip the family took together was by train to New York City, when Mildred was sixteen. All smiles, Ida had climbed with her children up the stairs and into the arm of the Statue of Liberty, while their father remained below. Gazing out over the city, Mildred had marveled at its breadth: Richmond was a mere speck compared to this metropolis. Recently, she had read that visitors were no longer allowed to climb into the arm. But oh, how wonderful it had been to see her mother so joyful.

Dale, too, had mostly been in good spirits, driving his girl-friend to the movies, taking Danny and Sandy to a matinee or bringing them candy from town, and attending his Masonic Lodge meetings. On the farm, he was always busy with projects; until a few weeks ago, he'd been transforming an old wagon into a water tank for the cattle. He'd taught Danny how to play chess. Now the pieces sat jumbled in a corner of the living room.

What had Mildred missed?

And her mother: Sometimes when Mildred came home from school, she saw the piles of purchases Ida had made that day: cotton blouses with lace trimming, shirtwaist dresses for Mildred, sailor suits and knee pants for Harold. One day when her father came home, his face lined with his usual anxiety, it transformed with a rare smile when he saw Ida sashaying around the room in an ankle-length blue linen dress with cloth-covered buttons. He'd let her keep that one but grabbed the rest of the clothes, handing them to Florence to return.

Sometime during the summer before Mildred's senior year, Ida's erratic moods and compulsive buying must have become too much for Papa. That's when their family doctor had Ida committed to the Northern Indiana Hospital for the Criminally Insane. Mildred would never forget the diagnosis on the hospital admission form: "Acute mania; talkative, restless, exalted." How could being talkative be called criminal? Mildred would give anything for Dale to lose his sad and angry moods and feel exalted.

Mildred had stayed home from school to help her mother pack, tucking the blue linen dress with the covered buttons into the suitcase beneath underwear, nightgowns, and Ida's piano music. Ida had sat on her bed, knees drawn up to her chest, shaking her head from side to side. She must think her husband and children were abandoning her, thought Mildred. And weren't they?

"I don't want to go away," Ida said. "I'm not sick."

"I'm sorry, Mama, but you get too excited," Mildred said, echoing her father. "Papa says the people at the hospital will help you learn to calm down." Mildred couldn't meet her mother's eyes, with their dark pouches underneath. "And help you sleep, Mama. And you get sad so much—maybe the doctors can help you with that, too."

Most Sunday mornings, the family visited Ida at the hospital, just a fifteen-minute drive away. Mildred was nervous before each visit. Sometimes her mother would run and hug them, but on other days she would not even bother with a greeting. In good weather, they usually found her in the institution's farm colony, in the women patients' blue-and-white-striped dress and white apron, planting or harvesting crops, pulling weeds, and generally engaged in what the resident doctor called "occupational therapy."

"Your mother is helping the war effort," Papa told Mildred and Harold on one visit. "A lot of farmers have been drafted."

Mildred suppressed bitter tears. Helping the war effort or not, her mother didn't belong here. She tried not to be angry at her father. He was doing the best he could.

Mildred jerked upright. Oh, my God. She took a deep breath—just a sneeze from upstairs. They both had colds. She always had a tissue in the pocket of her housedress, and he carried a blue kerchief in his jeans.

Maybe her son's illness was Mildred's punishment for abandoning her mother. Mildred deserved any kind of punishment for that, and for not being honest with Charles. Would he have married her if she'd told him her mother had been institutionalized?

She looked at the clock: past time to feed the chickens. After a quick glance at the door to upstairs, she put on her wool coat, knit hat, gloves, and boots and headed out. Leaving the stuffy, dry heat of the kitchen, she felt the invigorating brush of cool air on her cheeks as she walked to the chicken house. Inside, she took in its dusty, ammonia-like smell. Above the wire-mesh-covered wood floor spread with poop-speckled straw, a hundred hens perched in two-tier rows of straw-filled nesting areas. Whenever she saw her white-feathered chickens on their roosts, Mildred pictured church ladies in pews wrapped in their cloaks. Grabbing the covered pail by the door, she scattered handfuls of corn kernels around. There was still water in the trough.

Walking slowly over the snowy ground back to the house, she again wondered how she, a relatively well-educated young woman from a decent-size city, had ended up in the middle of nowhere with a husband who rated farm work above learning. Maybe she had just wanted to get away from a community that knew about her mother.

Papa had taken her and Harold, sixteen, by train to Yuma, Colorado, to celebrate Mildred's high school graduation. It was late May 1918, about a month after Mildred turned eighteen. Ida had been in the institution for a little more than a year.

Yuma had a Wild West feel about it, and the mountains were beautiful. The first morning, on a walk with her father and brother to explore the town, Mildred noticed a large flyer pasted on a pole. She grimaced now, remembering words she had never forgotten.

Wrestling match at the Ideal Garage – 2 p.m.
Charles Rubel, 185 pounds, Champion of Central Iowa, against
Wenzel Landauer, 180 pounds, Yuma County's Pride.
Admission 50 cents, ladies free.
A dance in Petrie's Hall after the match. All invited.

What had jumped out at her was the similarity of names. Her own father's name was Charles Ruble. Had there been a misspelling? Could her family be related to this fighter?

Above the text was a blurry black-and-white photograph of each fighter, shirtless and flexing his muscles. She examined the hazy picture of Charles: his square face, dense eyebrows almost meeting over his strong, broad nose, and lips turned up at the corners as if barely suppressing a grin. Curious about wrestling, she was at the same time repelled at the fighting nature of the sport. But the resemblance of family names—and Charles— had intrigued her. Now she wondered why she hadn't pointed out the flyer to her father.

Later that day, she'd dragged Harold along while their father rested. She'd tell Papa where they'd been afterwards.

When they approached the garage, a half-hour before the bout, she saw Charles standing outside, not yet in his sporting clothes. She noticed his muscular shoulders, the way he filled out his plaid shirt and denim trousers. Sitting at the kitchen table, she felt her face heat up. How could she, a sheltered just- turned-eighteen-year-old, have been so forward?

"Hello, our last name is Ruble," Mildred blurted out, gesturing at Harold, who hung back, twisting his cap and rolling his eyes.

"We should leave," Harold said in a firm, low voice, shaking his head. "Papa will wonder where we are."

She ignored Harold's entreaty but introduced him to Charles. "Our name is similar to yours but spelled 'le' at the end, and my father's name is Charles, too, an amazing coincidence, so I was just wondering...."

He looked her up and down, studying her, until she had to turn away. What was she doing addressing a total stranger? And a wrestler yet.

He didn't look like any of the boys in her school, in their dress pants and stiff-collared shirts. He appeared worlds away from her boyfriend, Rainey, with his horn-rimmed glasses and skinny body. Rainey was usually absorbed in his trigonometry and chemistry books, although he did play baseball. In her high school yearbook, the caption under Mildred's senior photo read "Millie wishes all her evenings were Rainey."

"I'm honored to meet you," Charles said, bowing slightly. "You don't look like you go to sporting matches much." His smile involved his entire face, and his brown eyes under those thick brows bored into hers. "Stay and watch," he added. "Maybe you'll like it." He winked at her and grinned at Harold. "We'll get a soda afterwards."

Walking to their seats a few minutes later, perspiring in her calf-length gingham dress, Mildred wanted to disappear. The whole names thing must be a silly coincidence. Who cared, anyway? But it was too late to slip away.

What had happened to Rainey? she wondered. He'd been a year older than she, nice, if maybe a little boring. She remembered her mind drifting as he talked about wanting to design more efficient trucks and tractors. He'd gone on to study industrial engineering at Purdue University, a couple of hours from Richmond by train.

Restless now, she walked into the living room to the upright piano. *Tales from the Vienna Woods* was on the rack. With a few postcards, photos, and books, the piano and more than fifty pieces of sheet music were all she had left of her childhood home.

"I'm tired of lugging that damn monstrosity around," Charles had complained at every move. They'd hauled the piano on a horse- or tractor-pulled wagon from farm to farm, household belongings piled on top. One castor wheel was flat, the ivory had worn off several keys, and the others had turned yellow. But Mildred still had the piano tuned every six months, so that she could play her mother's music and Sandy could have lessons.

Arrayed on the piano top were framed photos of her children. Vern was married and lived in Hickory, North Carolina, some sixty miles from Charlotte, the largest city; he'd finished law school but had some kind of sales job. In San Francisco, Marguerite's coat-manufacturing business was going well, and Evelyn, also married, worked as a bookkeeper. Norman had an engineering job and five children. Bob had been in the Navy and was in his third year of college.

She sat down on the piano bench and touched the keys. After four years in the Navy, Dale could have made a new life elsewhere, too. He'd gone on to two years of college at the University of Minnesota. Majoring in agriculture, he was always bringing home new ideas for raising crops and different breeds of livestock. But Charles had convinced him to drop out. Was he feeling trapped? Maybe it wasn't like her mother's illness; maybe there was an external reason. Either way, could he get help outside an institution? After all, it was 1956, not 1918. Help must be available now. Wasn't it?

Mildred tensed. A scrape from upstairs—was Dale opening his window, cold as it was outside? She listened for several minutes, then crept upstairs to stand outside his door. If by any miracle he emerged, she'd say she wanted to see whether Danny had made his bed, in the room he and Bob shared. But he must have gone back to sleep.

Back in the kitchen, Mildred thought about the wrestling match in the Yuma car garage. She and Harold had sat in folding chairs a few rows back from the front. She had felt out of place among others so different from her: farmers in overalls, a few with their wives, cowboys, a scattering of wounded soldiers. She was probably the only one there with a high school diploma.

"Do you understand what's going on?" she had whispered to her brother.

"Both men have to stay in the circle on the mat," Harold explained, "and the idea is to pin the other guy down, both shoulder blades flat. Whoever gets two pins first within a certain time wins. If nobody gets two pins—oh, forget it, it's too complicated to explain. Just watch."

How did she ever think she could be happy with an uneducated man? She refilled her coffee cup, pausing again to look out the kitchen window. The snow had let up, and she could see the faded red barn in the distance. In happier days, Dale would be out there hammering the trim on the new corncrib or, once the snow melted, guiding Danny as he learned to drive the small, used Ford tractor bought especially for him. Dale had said that Danny needed his own tractor. Mildred's eyes filled with tears. Now he completely ignored his youngest brother.

Mildred couldn't remember what she'd expected on that first day, as she and Charles walked to a soda fountain after he won his match. Harold had gone back to the boardinghouse. She'd sneaked glances at the back of Charles's rough, sunburned neck, his solid jaw, the line of his collarbone and thick black hair. He'd placed his hand on the small of her back as they approached the drugstore. Accidentally brushing against him as they entered, she was breathless and felt a tingle in her belly. He appeared much older and worldlier than she, making her feel like the naïve young girl she was.

Charles told her that he was twenty-seven, the oldest of eleven children. His father was a demanding immigrant farmer who came from Bavaria, Germany. She knew her family was from somewhere further north near the Rhine River.

"Gosh," she said. "How was it growing up with ten brothers and sisters? I only have the one brother, so it's pretty quiet around our house." She wouldn't dwell on the fact that it was largely due to her mother's absence.

"It was wild," he said. "Mother seemed beaten down sometimes, but my sister Mary, she helped with the younger ones. Mother got started at seventeen, after she came over from Germany. My old man was forty-seven. His first wife died when she was in her fifties, I think. So I have six older half-brothers and -sisters, too. But they were almost all grown and gone when I came along."

"My goodness," Mildred said. "What a story."

"My old man was a slave driver," Charles said. He leaned forward and looked at her intently. "We worked from dawn to dusk. He seldom had a good word for us, kept us out of school a lot to work on the farm. I still spoke German when I started first grade." He looked out the window, his cheeks coloring a little. "I only got through the eighth grade." Mildred had told him her family's trip was to celebrate her high school graduation. "So I'm not educated like you," he said. "But I liked school when I had a good teacher."

He asked her what she liked to do when she wasn't in school. She had probably told him she loved traveling and reading and would like to be a teacher. Hard to remember what they talked about. But she had liked his curiosity about her life.

"I played basketball all through high school; in fact, my team went to the championship in Indianapolis last year. But we lost."

He raised his eyebrows. "Guess I was wrong about you not bein' the sportin' type. Where I went to school, they didn't have sports for girls. There wasn't much for boys, either, except rough-housin' in the schoolyard and maybe some boxing. Sometimes a little football."

He said he hoped to win a few wrestling matches traveling around the western states, supporting himself by doing farm work. But he wanted to own his own farm someday.

"I bet you didn't know there're quite a few wrestling and boxing matches goin' on in Richmond. In fact, a few months ago I hired a boxing trainer here. I think I'm better at boxing. And there's more money to be made in that sport."

Between sips of soda, Mildred took in his calloused palms and the dirt under his fingernails. What was she doing here? She loved weekends and summer vacations on the farm her aunt and uncle owned, outside Richmond. She and her cousin Raymond would herd the milk cows from the pasture into the barnyard; she raced his pony on nearby dirt roads and scattered corn to Aunt Grace's chickens, all while trying to avoid having to use the wasp-infested outhouse. So she thought she understood a little about farming. But she also read newspapers and knew agriculture was dependent on the weather and fluctuating product markets.

Could she live in the country? No, her sights were set higher, on someone like Rainey. With him, she'd have a well-off life like the one she'd led, meaning more trips to New York, a decent public library, a chance for college, and maybe a job teaching school.

Now she knew that those occasional stays on her aunt's farm were the easy part of farm life. She hadn't anticipated moving to six or seven different homesteads over thirty years and suffering through drought, tornado threats, collapsing farm prices, not to mention additional privations during the Great Depression and World War II.

At the drugstore, she'd smoothed her cotton skirt under the table and imagined how Charles must view her, in her starched, high-necked dress, her brown hair pulled back in a bun. She guessed Charles had probably known a lot of women. What different lives the two led. She wouldn't tell him about her other activities, like playing in piano recitals and arranging luncheons with her friends—frivolous goings-on, while he was supporting himself with farm-labor jobs and sporting matches. No need to tell him about her mother, since she'd never see him again.

The telephone rang, jerking Mildred out of her reverie. Four rings on their party line. It was the farm-machinery dealer in Lake Park. Dale hadn't picked up some planter shovels. They were used and the price was good. This was his second phone call; he couldn't hold them much longer. Charles would be upset that Dale hadn't picked them up. She would have to remind him.

During their four days in Yuma, Mildred spent mornings with her father and Harold, exploring the town, and afternoons with Charles.

"You haven't mentioned your mother," Charles said one afternoon as they sat in the café. "Isn't she with you?"

Mildred blushed, and her hands trembled as she clutched her can of soda.

"Mama's sick a lot," she said, avoiding his gaze. "She had pneumonia and got out of the hospital just before we left to come here. She wasn't strong enough to travel, so she's staying with my Aunt Grace on her farm. She told us to go without her, so Papa didn't cancel our trip."

Lightning should strike her dead. Her first big lie. Or evasion. Whatever she called the betrayal of her mother, it was so wrong.

Charles placed his hand over hers. "It's too bad about your mother," he said. How kind of him to say that, she thought.

Over the days they spent together, she noticed his flirtatious manner.

"You're lookin' mighty good there, Agnes," he said to the waitress at the drugstore. "Bet your husband—or your boyfriend—can't keep his hands off you." Agnes's face would turn red, and she'd walk away, smiling. Mildred was embarrassed by these comments but also a little charmed by them. What was wrong with making someone feel special?

"What'd you do for fun?" she asked Charles one afternoon, wanting to learn more about his life.

"When we were young, Mother turned us outdoors most of the year. Said to stay there until supper. Lots for kids to do outside on a farm. We were rascals, climbin' up trees and on roofs and fightin' with each other, but we lived through it all. Then, when we were teenagers, there were dances at the local community hall. Did a bit too much drinkin', I'm sad to say." He looked out the window of the café. "I'm tryin' to watch that."

"You said your dad was hard on you."

"Yeah, pretty strict. Whipped us with a belt if we got out of line, but I learned how to work hard." He grimaced. "He'd hire us out to work on other farms, to make a little extra money. It's true, farming's not for sissies. There's always stuff to do, and I liked most of it, especially raisin' animals." He smiled. "It's great to watch calves and pigs grow up. But when I was in my late teens, I left, because my brothers were old enough to help my dad out. And I wanted to see the rest of the country. And look who I met on my travels." He grinned at her. "I'm a lucky man." She grinned, too, but couldn't meet his eyes.

"I should be getting back," she said.

Then, on Mildred's last day in Yuma, Charles made a surprising announcement.

"I've been drafted into the Army," he said. "Gotta be at Camp Cody in three weeks." Her heart did a flip-flop. Was she sorry she wouldn't see him again? "Could I write to you?" he'd asked.

Without thinking, she nodded, still taking in the news that this was goodbye. She hadn't been sure how she felt. Weren't they too different for any kind of long-term connection?

When she returned to the boardinghouse, she confessed to her father that she'd been meeting Charles for sodas and walks. Papa had raised his eyebrows but said nothing.

They conducted a courtship by correspondence, mostly from his side, since between the war and his stateside travels, she seldom knew where he was. Now she remembered where she had put the postcards and photographs. She walked through the living room into her bedroom and opened a dresser drawer, pulling out the postcards Charles had sent from France and Germany, as well as some black-and-white pictures. Back at the kitchen table, she slipped off the rubber bands securing the packets of cards and photos.

Next to a picture of troops on parade in Paris, he wrote that he'd won the American Expeditionary Forces wrestling competition. There was a photo of Charles taken after that competition, shirtless and flexing his muscles. The caption read "Private Charles P. Rubel, International Heavyweight Wrestling Champion, April 19, 1919, Paris, France, U.S. Infantry, 42nd Division." Mildred admired the discipline that led to this award. But he was not in any way a cultured man, she thought now, sighing. Yet she'd fallen for him.

She looked at a card he'd sent from a castle on the Rhine and shook her head. "This castle, near Oberwinter, been in it on different occasions many ancient paintings dangle on the walls and 165 Infantry officers reside there." What had she expected from someone who hadn't finished high school? During the year of their correspondence, his signature had gone from "With kindest Regards, Charlie" to "Homesick, heavy hearted, blue, I await yours, as ever, Charlie."

She felt cold air on her legs. Time to stoke the stove again. Opening the door to the basement, she walked down the wobbly wooden steps, hand on the wall for support, past the empty sauerkraut barrel, into the furnace room. She rekindled the fire with newspapers and small sticks of wood, then scooped in some coal from the corner bin. Spotting the pile of potatoes a few feet away, she reminded herself that in a couple of months, Danny would have to cut the potatoes into three parts each, leaving eyes in each triangle, ready for planting in a couple months.

Back upstairs, she opened the *Lake Park Beacon* and glanced over the obituaries. Charles's good friend Oscar Petersen had died. Sad. Charles hadn't even mentioned his death.

Her mind slipped back to 1918. In October, her father had contracted the influenza that swept the country during the last year of the war. Mildred had slept on the floor of his room, kept awake by his harsh, raspy breathing and experiencing her first migraine, worrying about his high temperatures, hacking coughs, and severe nosebleeds. The hospitals were overcrowded, so aside from an occasional visit from a public health nurse, the family was on its own. Sitting on his bed in her gauze mask, Mildred had spoon-fed her father hot soup, cough medicine, whiskey, and aspirin, remedies she had learned in a Red Cross first-aid course.

Three months later, when Papa was able to leave his bed, Mildred sobbed in relief. How had her father survived when so many thousands had died? But with schools and church services closed, even public funerals banned, to prevent the epidemic's spread, she delayed college.

One day, her father showed her an article in a Richmond newspaper about a push to train more nurses. Indiana had just passed a law to encourage it.

"You helped me get well," he told her. "You should think about nursing."

"I'm not sure." She remembered how frightened she'd been when her father was ill. "I want to think about teaching. At school I was good in English and Latin."

"Yes, you're a bookworm," he agreed. "But nursing is more practical." He pointed to the newspaper story. "Some nursing programs offer stipends, but I'm not sure teaching does."

One day in May 1919, Charles appeared on their doorstep in his army fatigues and black boots, holding his green cap. He'd been discharged and had interrupted the train trip from Fort Dix to his hometown of Audubon, Iowa, to see her. In the living room, he sat on the edge of the couch across the room from her father, fingering his cap. Mildred bustled about with rhubarb pie and coffee. Unable to meet the gaze of either man, she took a small bite of pie, barely able to swallow, and set the plate down. What did Papa think of this man?

"Mr. Rubel," her father said, "how was your war experience, and what's next for you?"

"I got shot in the leg in Germany and was in the hospital for a few weeks," Charles replied. "The war was peterin' out, and our soldiers were mostly done fightin'." He wiped his mouth with a napkin and smiled. "I want to rent a farm in Iowa near where I grew up and save money to buy my own land there. You know, Iowa's got some of the best farmland in the world," he added. "My father's one of the most prosperous farmers in Audubon County, in central Iowa. When he came over from Germany in the 1860s, he started out rentin' eighty acres. Now he has three hundred and twenty. He raises mostly corn, wheat, cattle, and hogs. And the government's still givin' out farm supports, even though the war is over."

Charles glanced at Mildred.

"I'm a hard worker, so I'm hopin' I'll be at least half as successful as he is." He drained his coffee cup, then stabbed the pie, finishing it off in several bites.

After Charles left, her father turned to her. "That man is looking for a wife. Farming's risky, in spite of what he said about his father. Want to live the rest of your life on a farm?"

"I don't know, Papa," she'd murmured.

"He's pretty rough around the edges," her father said. "I think Rainey would be better for you. He's going to college; you said he's going to study industrial engineering. These days that's a solid career choice for a boy. Not as precarious as farming. You know, farming's not just playing tag in the cornfields, like you do at Aunt Grace's. Imagine living there year-round, cleaning out the barn or chicken house, planting crops, and likely no indoor plumbing." His eyes narrowed as he looked at her.

Whatever doubts she'd had, she'd ignored them. Would Rainey have been a better choice? But it had been her own decision—no use rethinking the whole thing at this late date. Charles hadn't asked about her mother on that visit, so she hadn't had to lie to him again. What a despicable person she was, keeping such an enormous secret from him. She had to tell him now.

She tried to focus on dinner. Meatloaf. The kids liked that. She walked out to the porch, grabbed a pound of hamburger from the freezer, put it on the kitchen counter to defrost, perched on her metal stool, and began chopping onions. Tearing from the onions, she thought again about her father.

In June, a month and a half after Charles's visit, Mildred was three weeks into her first semester at Earlham College in Richmond when her father suffered a cerebral hemorrhage and crashed his Stanley Steamer just blocks from their house. He died there a few hours later. He was forty-six.

After getting the call, a dazed Mildred took the streetcar home, where she found Aunt Mae and Uncle Cleo making funeral arrangements. Over the next two days, they received neighbors, her father's Masonic friends, and his colleagues from the Brotherhood of Locomotive Engineers. At the memorial gathering, people told her how sorry they were, but no one asked after Ida, not even her years-long women friends from the neighborhood. Was Ida's illness that shameful? But Mildred herself treated it as mortifying, so how could she criticize others?

Harold surprised them by getting twenty-four-hour com-passionate leave from the Navy, even though he'd joined just a month earlier, right out of high school. Mildred remembered how handsome he had looked in his dark-blue jacket and trou-sers, knee-high black-leather boots, and white cap with black brim and bill.

"How's Mama?" he asked in a hoarse voice. "I can't stop think-ing about her in that horrible place. I want to see her before I go back to Illinois tomorrow."

"She's sad when I visit each week," Mildred told him. "She misses us. She especially likes hearing from you." After Harold left, Mildred felt like an orphan, though her mother was still alive. Days later, Uncle Cleo sat her down at her father's desk to go through his papers.

"There's not much money left," he said. "Your mother's spend-thrift ways, and all that money for the housekeeper." Mildred stiffened. "A lot went to your mother's care," he continued.

What good had the money done if it hadn't made her well? She felt tears coming and pulled out her white handkerchief. Her mother would probably never get better.

"Still," he said, "there's a few hundred dollars for you to continue your education, but you need to be frugal." He looked down at the columns of figures. "At least your brother joined the Navy, so we don't have to worry about him."

Could Charles be the answer to her situation? After his visit, she'd received postcards from him every month or so as he worked farm-labor jobs around Yuma and Casper, Wyoming. He even worked briefly in a small community as a deputy sheriff. Or Rainey? But Mildred wanted to be independent for a while longer. Maybe she should give nursing a chance, as her father had suggested.

Aunt Mae had told Ida about her husband's death; Mildred hadn't had the courage, although she continued to visit her weekly. Ida had streaks of gray in her short brown hair now. Her dresses hung on her, and her stockings sagged around her ankles.

"Mama, sit down," Mildred admonished one day as Ida paced back and forth.

"When does Cleo say I can come home?" Ida sobbed. "Can't Florence take care of me?" She wiped her eyes, then pulled a postcard from her pocket. "Harold wrote this from his Navy training center, in Illinois." She pressed the card to her chest.

"I'm so sorry, Mama," Mildred said, choking up. "The doctor says you're still not well."

Uncle Cleo sold the house, and Mildred decided to pursue nursing, which jolted her out of her previous existence. At first she loved the classroom lectures on anatomy and physiology, the challenge of learning to treat wounds and getting to know her patients. Busy as she was, she couldn't get her mind off Charles. Did she belong with him? Would Papa have approved?

But Papa was dead. If she chose Charles, she'd be abandoning her mother. And she was still seeing Rainey. He called her every two or three weeks, when he came home from Purdue, where he was in his second year studying industrial engineering. They'd get together for coffee, malts, or long walks, discussing his future in engineering and her nurses' training. She still didn't know how they felt about each other.

She took out a picture taken with her closest nursing friends, Shirley, Joan, and Prudence, with whom she still exchanged letters each Christmas. They'd lived in a house with thirteen other young trainees, all chaperoned by Reid Hospital's superintendent of nurses. In the photograph, the four sat on the lawn in their white nursing smocks, grinning at one another, the hospital in the background. Mildred recalled how she and her friends sometimes defied the ten p.m. curfew and sneaked out a ground-floor window to sit on the lawn in the moonlight. In the daytime photo, the sun had brightened their faces, and Joan's head rested on Mildred's shoulder.

Eventually, however, nursing's menial duties had ground her down. Too many hours of cleaning syringes and catheters, washing and patching gloves, bathing difficult patients. After eighteen months, Mildred was exhausted from long days on the hospital wards, plus classes and homework, with only a half-day off on Sundays. A third of her class had already dropped out to get married, including her three friends.

Then, as if sending an answer to what she should do, Charles proposed by postcard: I'm lonesome and blue without you. I want us to spend our lives together. I hope you feel the same.

Would you marry me? Lonely and heartsick, Charles.

What did she risk, marrying Charles and leaving behind everything she'd ever known? She cared for him. She admired the randomness of his life, his seeking the unknown before settling down. And he was settling down, in Iowa looking to rent farmland. She liked being with him, liked his curiosity about her and her life. He'd often smiled at her; was interested in what she had to say. He seemed to care for her. If all that wasn't love, she wasn't sure what love was.

And both were willing to struggle. Charles had always worked hard, and Mildred had experienced grueling labor during her twelve-hour days in nursing. After ruminating for two days, she responded "yes" and mailed her letter to his last address.

But she dreaded telling Rainey. She'd never told him she was writing to Charles.

In late December 1920, they met at the Main Street malt shop. As she sat in the booth across from him, her hands shook so much she couldn't touch the chocolate malt Rainey had ordered for her, knowing that's what she liked. He'd always been so steady, so easy to be around, so diligent in his studies and excited about his future. She knew he'd provide a stable, secure life. But…she'd felt no excitement with him. He was—what was the expression? Like a comfortable old shoe. Did she not know what was good for her?

"I'm thinking about marrying a farmer who wants me to move to Iowa with him," Mildred blurted out. She twisted her hands in her lap, then looked at his face as his eyes widened.

"You never told me." Was that a flash of anger in his eyes? Or just surprise? Either way, she couldn't blame him. "Why not?"

She looked at his thin, gentle face, the slightly smudged lenses of his glasses, his slim, clean fingernails. She thought back to Charles and his bruised knuckles, his broad shoulders, the way he leaned toward her as he asked questions about her life. Why was it all so complicated?

"I don't know," she said. "I was so confused. Am so confused. I wasn't sure about us. Also, I think I need to get away from Richmond. So many things have happened: my dad sick so long with that horrible flu, then dying, my mother's…situation. And I'm disappointed in myself for dropping out of nurses' training. It was so hard."

"But you've always lived in a city. Are you sure?"

"I think it's the right decision for me. I'm so sorry."

He sat for a few minutes, looked at her, then glanced out the window, drumming his fingers on the table. She could see he was trying to decide what to say.

"Hope it all works out for you," he said, standing up suddenly and heading for the door.

Mildred's face had flushed in shame as she walked home. She'd treated him badly. But he'd given her no indication about how he felt. She'd been confused, too, about her feelings for him. What a muddle. Had she made the right decision, to marry Charles? Or did she just want to escape her life and the stigma of a mother in an institution?

A month after she dropped out of nurses' training, in January 1921, she and Charles married in the Richmond City Clerk's office. Aunt Mae and Uncle Cleo attended as witnesses.

"You're moving where?" Aunt Mae had asked, walking back and forth, shooting dagger-looks at Charles. "Wasting all that nurses' training. To godforsaken…Iowa, is it? And leaving your mother." She shook her head, mumbling, "What your father would say…."

Uncle Cleo was more charitable. "I'm sure you'll be fine, my dear," he said, putting his hand gently on her shoulder. "We're sorry you're leaving us. Maybe that training will come in handy where you're going." He frowned. "Too bad Harold couldn't make the ceremony. Probably couldn't get leave."

Mildred had heard nothing from her brother since his last

postcard to their mother, two months earlier. He'd written Ida that he'd decided to make the Navy his career. If he'd served on any of the U.S. Navy ships ferrying men and supplies to France and Germany, they never heard. As far as she knew, he was still at the Naval Air Base in Key West, Florida, where he'd gone after Illinois. Mildred sent him her married name and future mailing address, RFD (Rural Free Delivery), Audubon, Iowa.

Before the ceremony, Mildred had told Charles her mother was sick again with pneumonia and couldn't receive nonfamily visitors. She couldn't meet his eyes.

"It's a shame I won't meet her," he said, "especially if she's as good-lookin' and smart as you are." Charles and his flattery, she thought, but she couldn't help smiling. He put his arm around her shoulder and pulled her to him.

Mildred had groaned inwardly. What a despicable coward she'd been. Such a betrayal of her mother, hiding the truth from her new husband. What kind of person was she? Tears filled her eyes, and she'd buried her face against Charles's shoulder.

On their last visit, when Mildred told her mother she was getting married, Ida lay curled up facing the wall. Mildred put her hand on her mother's back, almost recoiling from the sharpness of her shoulder blade.

"Mama, his name is Charles, like Papa." She tried not to cry. "I'm moving to Iowa with him, to live on a farm."

Ida had turned over and looked at her daughter. "When will I see you again?"

"I'm not sure, Mama." Mildred had burst into tears and rested her head on her mother's chest. Ida stroked her daughter's long brown hair, not secured in a bun today. Mildred could think of no more words to soften the blow. The nurse had already been in with her tray of medications. After what seemed like hours, Ida's eyes closed, and Mildred slipped out the door.

MILDRED STRUGGLED TO RECALL her arrival by train in Iowa, as a new bride, thirty-five years ago. In the middle of winter. Four months before her twenty-first birthday. Still numb from saying goodbye to her mother. She recalled looking out the window at the expanse of barren fields, withered cornstalks sticking up out of the snow and, in the distance, the scattered, desolate-looking farm buildings.

"It's gloomy now, in January," Charles had said, holding her hand, "but it's mostly pretty the rest of the year. Just a little muddy in the spring when the snow melts."

What had she done, leaving her whole life behind her? And the worst thing: abandoning her mother and lying to Charles. She'd told him that when Ida was out of the hospital, she'd live with Aunt Grace on her farm.

Approaching Charles's family farm in a rented horse and cart, Mildred saw a two-story white-frame house with green shutters and freshly painted outbuildings. A big tractor, a wooden wagon, and a piece of machinery she couldn't identify were lined up in a neat row next to a large red barn. She had been surprised to see such a well-kept place.

"Charley says you're a proper young woman," his dad, Peter, had said with a heavy German accent and a handshake. "Such a city girl, how do you think you'll do, living on a farm?" Had he smirked when she said she'd spent summers on a farm?

Peter was seventy-seven at the time, and Charles's mom, Amelia, was in her mid-forties. Albert, the next-oldest brother, and their sister Mary were both recently married, but seven boys and one girl remained at home. The youngest, Glen, was twelve. Minnie, sixteen, helped her mother manage the household. Had Mildred imagined it, or did Amelia, very thin and her hair already white, appear frazzled after bearing eleven babies?

As Mildred observed her, she determined not to exhaust her own body with so many births. Had Amelia really wanted so many children? Was birth control even an option? The strict Lutheran church Charles had told her the family attended probably forbade it.

During nurses' training, Mildred had learned about puerperal fever, a dangerous uterine infection that afflicted many women after giving birth. It was often fatal, and Amelia was fortunate to have avoided or survived it. Beyond preventive measures, such as constant handwashing and copious use of disinfectant, and dispensing aspirin to keep the high fever down, Mildred knew there was little to be done about the infection. There was still no cure.

So, birth control: Though it was illegal for doctors to prescribe contraceptives except to "protect a woman's health," Mildred had heard chatter among the nursing students about men using condoms and women, pessaries (later called diaphragms). And she knew the government had legalized condom use, because too many soldiers had returned from the war with venereal diseases.

She'd discuss family size with Charles at some point but decided then and there she'd have no more than three children, possibly five, maximum. It would be awkward to discuss birth control with her new husband, but they'd have time to work it out.

The couple settled on a hundred-acre rental farm an hour and a half north of Audubon, near the small town of Webb. She'd agreed it was good for Charles to get away from his successful father and make it on his own. The house was much humbler than his parents' residence. The living room and kitchen were a decent size, but the three upstairs bedrooms were very small. She stood in the middle of the living room and felt a pang of longing for her cozy room at the hospital. And she ached for her long-ago family home.

Charles had bought a few pieces of furniture, but much had to be done to make it comfortable.

"You'll make it nice," Charles said, putting his arms around her and pulling her into a hug. "Buy whatever things you want."

Looking back now, that first year of becoming a farm wife seemed like a trial by fire. In the beginning, she'd found the winter cold and the many sunless days sad. But she made the house cozy by sewing curtains—thank goodness for home economics class—and buying rugs and a few more pieces of furniture. Charles fashioned a bookcase of boards and bricks for her small collection of books. She learned to stoke the kitchen's cooking stove and basement furnace with corncobs and wood and, years later, coal.

She also learned to use—and steeled herself to scrub—the outhouse, something she hadn't expected. They had regular electricity but no running water until the 1940s, so she lugged buckets of water from the outside pump for cooking and baths. A couple times a week, she walked the mile into town to the one-room library and the tiny grocery store. She'd considered joining the Presbyterian church, the only other local church being Methodist. It would be years, though, before she'd be able to attend any church on a Sunday.

But Charles had had her mother's upright piano and sheet music shipped to the farm, and sitting at the piano reminded her of home. He liked listening to her play, especially "There Is a Tavern in the Town." He'd lean back in his chair and close his eyes as she struggled to remember how to read base clef—most difficult in "The Holy City" and "The Old Cathedral Chimes," two of her favorites from long ago.

Because Charles thought every farm wife needed "egg money," he ordered a hundred baby chicks and a brooder to warm them in the little chicken coop he built. Then she experienced her first disaster: Almost twenty died, from the heat lamp turned too high or from dehydration, even though she'd kept them fed and watered and had monitored the chicks closely. For weeks after, she pictured the limp bodies of the tiny yellow creatures where she'd left them, on a dirt pile behind the barn. But she learned to care for the hens and roosters the remaining chicks became.

She'd even overcome her revulsion at wielding an axe to chop the head off a rooster for supper, though she never got used to the headless bodies jerking around the stained tree stump, gushing blood, before collapsing. She once looked down at the stained axe blade and her soiled, unlined hands, marveling that, just three years earlier, these fingers had played "Nola" and "Westminster Chimes" in a recital at Richmond's Second Presbyterian Church. Now she looked down at hands crisscrossed with bluish veins, with sharp ridges and a few age spots, along with an impossible-to-remove gold wedding band.

In that first year of married life, Charles's parents and Minnie had driven over once a month, and Mildred worked hard to ingratiate herself. Under her sister-in-law's tutelage, she refined her cooking skills, moving on from frying pork chops and eggs to making casseroles and baking her own bread. (In the 1950s, Minnie opened her own café, Minnie's, in Audubon.) Amelia, with whom she became close over the years, taught her the complicated skill of preparing sauerkraut, a favorite of Charles's. Mastering the tricky balance of salt and brine level, Mildred had "nursed" a half-barrel in the basement of every house they lived in.

That first spring, Mary and Minnie helped her plant her vegetable garden, with beans, melons, lettuce, tomatoes, and other vegetables that she harvested over the summer and learned to can, along with apples from their four apple trees, for the winter. Charles had purchased milk cows as well as beef cattle, and she learned to churn butter from their milk.

In September 1921, nine months after their arrival in Iowa, Dale was born. He had Mildred's rounded chin and sculpted cheekbones and his father's dark hair. Charles had winked at Mildred, "We need a few more of these to help me with farm chores." Enchanted by his first son, he held Dale often, stroking the mass of thick black hair like his own. Most evenings, Charles would fall asleep with Dale on his lap, his large hand resting on the baby's head.

Every day, Mildred had wished she could show her baby son to Ida. How often did Ida think about her daughter's abandonment? Did she even remember Mildred?

And Harold. He'd written that the Navy was sending him to college, so he would stay in Pensacola. When would she see either of them again?

Vern arrived in May 1923, Marguerite in February 1925, Norman in September 1926. Mildred was often exhausted from the care of four children under seven, plus keeping the household and garden going.

After Marguerite's birth, she had asked Charles to wear a condom. He would, sometimes. She'd asked her doctor, a man in his sixties, about birth control: Frowning at her, he said she had a duty to bear as many children as God sent her. She talked to her farm-wife friends about contraception: They sometimes used douches, injecting chemicals like Lysol, which could damage their insides and horrified Mildred. She tried diaphragms and finally found a female doctor in Spencer who fitted her diaphragm properly, to use with spermicidal jelly.

But her efforts failed spectacularly. After Evelyn's birth, in January 1928, she banished Charles some nights to the boys' room, insisting they couldn't afford more children. She refused to dwell on how she had tried to balance her fear of pregnancy, Charles's reluctance to wear a condom, and the obligation to be a "dutiful" wife.

She'd done her best to become a passable farm wife and mother. Tired as she always was, she tried to enjoy her children, reading them library books and telling them stories. She'd been fortunate that in those first years, during summers and school vacations, Minnie had stayed with them. And she'd been heartened by how the local farmers helped one another during tough times. Several families would gather to pick one family's corn or harvest their alfalfa, and the noontime dinners they shared created an almost festive atmosphere.

Farming had been profitable during the war, when it was considered patriotic to raise crops such as corn, alfalfa, wheat, and sorghum to supply Europe and help with the war effort. But Mildred never forgot her father's warning from not that many years earlier: "Farming's risky. Are you sure this is what you want?"

And soon enough, in the early 1920s, the markets crashed due to overproduction. The radio and newspapers were filled with reports on the falling prices of farm products and land losing its value. Like other farmers, Charles applied for government price supports for his crops, but those had ended. In the next couple of years, to stabilize prices, the government bought struggling farmers' crops to feed those in the U.S. who were hungry. And Charles took the payment offered to slaughter his thirty hogs for food. Grumbling, he accepted what he called the government "giveaways."

"I don't want the goddamned government in my business," he complained. "But we gotta eat."

When half of Iowa's farmers sold their land, however, he refused to give up. Some rented smaller plots to avoid mortgage payments. Some of their neighbors took jobs in town as carpenters, post office clerks, or department store salespeople. Charles continued to raise basic crops: corn, wheat, and alfalfa. People and animals still needed farm-raised products, he said, including residents of nearby towns who could afford fresh produce.

The family survived on their garden vegetables, the apples

from their trees, the beef they butchered from the few steers they'd held onto, as well as Mildred's canned produce, eggs, and the milk, cream, and churned butter from their milk cows, which she sold to the local creamery. She sewed diapers and, later, the children's clothing from flour and chicken-feed sacks.

Charles was sure prices would go back up if he held on long enough. But in 1925, when he couldn't get a bank loan at a decent rate to pay the rent on the farm, he told Mildred he had to resume his boxing career, and they rented a forty-acre plot of land near Spencer. In the northwest corner of the state, it was a half-hour farther away from Charles's family, and she saw less of them. Amelia couldn't drive, Peter suffered from heart disease, and Minnie, now married, was busy with her own family. Mildred had never realized just how much they had helped her begin her farming life.

Charles borrowed money from his father to hire a coach, a local retired boxer, and began training with him. Every day, he punched a canvas bag of oats hanging from a tree and ran on dirt roads for hours. Over six months of fighting "lesser" opponents, Charles worked up to earning one thousand to three thousand dollars a fight, competing every few weeks all over northern Iowa.

Mildred hadn't liked Charles's boxing—an odious sport, she felt, watching men batter each other. But hadn't this sport been part of her attraction to him? His confidence, his pride in his body's strength and brawn?

The local newspaper wrote up Charles's competitions in great detail. He was variously referred to as "the heavyweight king of Clay County boxers," "farmer, pugilist and wrestler," and "Champion of Northern Iowa."

He even stoked the news by calling out potential rivals and marketing his attributes in the *Spencer Tribune*'s sports column. Mildred shook her head as she remembered one of his comments in an article, something like "I feel like a kid again. In fact, just the other day I took a left jab at a brick wall near my place, and much to my surprise, it crumpled up." She had to smile at his sense of humor.

And his fights attracted crowds: fourteen hundred people at the Grand Opera House in Spencer, two thousand at the fairground in Spirit Lake. Those bouts had supported them, she had to admit. The family could have been poverty-stricken without the proceeds from his boxing matches.

His winnings brought enough to pay a young girl to help with the children most days after school. They even bought their first car, a Ford Model T. Mildred desperately wanted to visit her mother during those financially secure years, but the idea of traveling with small children—five by 1928—was too daunting to contemplate. And she'd had no one to leave them with.

She wondered if Charles's boxing had made him more aggressive outside the ring. He'd knocked down the vet in Spencer who treated one of their milk cows for mastitis. Why he punched the landlord of the farm they'd been renting, she couldn't remember. He'd been fined or jailed for a few days for each offense. She'd tried to push those unpleasant details aside.

She was sure he would never hit her or the children, but when he drank, she remained watchful and tense. On those occasions, she'd even considered leaving, but where would she go? If she returned to Richmond, she'd have to acknowledge she'd made the wrong choice. And how could she start over in a new place, with no money and a troop of young children in her wake? And she knew no one locally who was divorced, if it came to that. So she'd stuck it out.

And there were bright spots to farm life. Springtime, with the apple trees swathed in white blossoms, the sweet fragrance of lilac blooms outside the front door; in summer, the crisp bites of freshly harvested carrots, beans, tomatoes, and other vegetables from her garden. She loved watching the children bottle-feed four orphan lambs the year they had sheep and Dale tenderly caring for an orphan pig in a cardboard box on the back porch.

When the children got older, they trapped fur-bearing animals for money. She smiled recalling the time Vern was sent home from school for reeking of skunk. They swam in the river near one of their homesteads, were usually able to walk the mile or two to school or ride there on horseback. In bitterly cold weather, Charles would hitch up the horses and take the children in a wagon outfitted with ski runners. Sometimes the boys would tie a rope to the back and get pulled to school on a sled.

Their land was near a golf and country club, and the boys earned money returning golf balls. Her gentlest of sons, Norman, often dashed around on their pony with Charles's 30-30 rifle, trying to shoot whatever he could, mostly birds. Mildred almost smacked the little scamp after he confessed he'd hung the rifle on a hook by its trigger, and a bullet discharged inches from his foot. She should have kept a better eye on him, but it was hard to keep track of any of the boys when they were outdoors.

She'd nursed each baby as long as possible, hoping she wouldn't get pregnant again, though she knew of no other mother who nursed. Bottle feeding was the trend. The diaphragm worked for a while, and she allowed Charles back in their bedroom on a regular basis. Then, in spite of her precautions, she became pregnant and gave birth to Bob in May 1932.

Disconsolate, she suffered from migraine headaches, trouble sleeping, sadness, and irritability. No wonder, with six children under eleven. The other children were excited about their baby sibling, however, and helped as much as they could, even Evelyn, age four. And Charles was thrilled when she had a fourth boy.

But 1932 was also the year Charles's sports career collapsed. People had no more money for entertainment, and they began renting farms again. Charles raised corn for his cattle and pigs while also supplying grain to other farmers for cash. And Mildred turned to what got them through hard times ten years earlier: raising vegetables; harvesting apples for applesauce and apple butter, which she sold in Spencer; canning produce; even making soap from lard.

She recalled only miscellaneous details of the six or seven farms they'd rented until purchasing the final homestead, in the mid-1940s. The giant boulder in the front yard of one, which a drunk driver crashed into in the middle of the night. The house that caught fire one night, Charles dousing it with buckets of water before severe damage occurred. The place near Okoboji that had a windmill, enabling them to pump water and run a generator for electric lights in the outbuildings, previously lit by kerosene lamps.

It was clearer now how she and Charles had grown so far apart. And so hostile. Worries about money. Always another pregnancy. Children born too close together. She had been at fault sometimes, expelling him from their bedroom or punishing Charles with the silent treatment until he stormed out of the house, often not returning until late after drinking with friends at a local bar. He drank more heavily when farm prices fell.

After Bob's birth, she'd slowly regained her good spirits. She couldn't find a doctor who'd tie her tubes, but she had another diaphragm fitted and insisted Charles wear a condom.

Nine years later, she went into another bout of depression. She was forty-one years old and pregnant with Sandy. Eighteen months after that, she had Danny. She'd been certain she was too old for childbearing. She decided she and Charles would no longer share a bedroom, and she moved to the living room couch. He was angry, but it was the right decision. She couldn't chance another pregnancy.

But she never saw her mother again. There'd been too many

children and never enough money or any childcare to enable a trip to Indiana. Now Mildred rocked back and forth in her chair, trying not to imagine Ida languishing in the institution. She'd died there in 1944, just before her sixtieth birthday. Mildred hadn't seen Harold since her father's memorial service, but he sent a letter every Christmas—he'd married a woman named Helen; they had no children—and he wrote with the news about their mother. Harold hadn't mentioned a service for Ida, and Aunt Mae and Uncle Cleo hadn't kept in touch. Mildred desperately wanted to travel to Indiana, but with no one to leave her baby and toddler with, and, at forty-four, with no extra energy, she felt unable to cope with small children on a train. So she hadn't gone.

Mildred bent over the kitchen table, tears coursing down her cheeks. How she had missed her mother and Harold. She wiped her eyes, then stamped her foot. Enough reminiscing about the past. Time to focus on the present. She was grateful that she and Charles had grown closer. Hardly "close," but at least they had normal conversations. And now they needed to talk about Dale. Perhaps if they'd talked more when they were younger, instead of his lashing out and her long silences, their life might have gone more smoothly. But she'd been so tired.

She heard a clumping noise and choked back a sob. Dale was coming downstairs. Her hand shook as she dried her face with a tissue. How would he be? Dale opened the door at the bottom of the stairs. He'd been so neat and clean-cut; now his wrinkled denim shirt hung outside his jeans. His hair looked unwashed and uncombed, and a two-day growth of whiskers darkened his jaw. He wouldn't look at her as he plodded past.

"Are you okay?" she asked, barely able to get the words out. "Can I get you some breakfast?" She stood up. "You've got to eat something. Want coffee?"

"No," he growled, waving his arm as if to push her away. "Leave me alone." He grabbed his flannel-lined corduroy jacket from the porch and went outside. She dropped her head in her hands again. She'd forgotten to tell him about the planter shovels.

———

THE MARCH SKY LOOMED with threatening clouds as Mildred returned from her late-afternoon walk to the pasture beyond the barn. Trudging over ground muddy from melting snow, she passed the machine shed, where Charles and Dale were installing shovels on the corn planter. As spring planting approached, Dale had resumed his work tasks. He was quieter, but some of his agreeable personality had returned. At least for now. He had stopped ignoring Danny and Sandy and took Danny on some of his errands. Dropped both kids off to see a cowboy movie in Lake Park the previous Saturday.

"Mom," Danny had said, grinning, after Dale brought them home. "Dale gave us money for popcorn and candy." How long would this "change for the better" last?

Up at the house, Gladys Nelson was dropping Sandy off after basketball practice. Mildred saw Sandy run into the house as she walked up to the car. Gladys got out to chat while her daughter, Nancy, bent over a book in the back seat.

"Did you hear the Larsons took their daughter to Cherokee?" Gladys asked, leaning against the car door and looking eager to pass on some gossip.

"Cherokee?" Mildred repeated. "What happened?" She shuddered, remembering she'd read that Cherokee State Hospital, fifty miles away in Storm Lake, had originally been named Cherokee Lunatic Asylum.

"I heard from the Larsons' neighbor," her friend said, "that Kathleen had a nervous breakdown. Been actin' strange for a while. Wouldn't get out of bed for days, then she'd start jobs and not finish them. She used to be the most good-natured person, but she'd start terrible arguments with her parents." Gladys shook her head. "They never had any trouble with her before now. Only in her early twenties. Sad." She turned toward her car. "Gotta go." She got in and drove off, waving goodbye.

Charles walked up from the machine shed, a long wrench dangling from his hand. "Who was that?" he asked, eager for any neighborhood news. "I'm not surprised," he said after hearing about Kathleen. "They're a nutty bunch. Old man Larson's tribe won't work; just look at their farm—junky machinery parts everywhere, corn leakin' out of the corn crib. They don't look like they own property, or they'd keep up their place."

Mildred wondered what the state of the Larsons' farm had to do with Kathleen's mental state.

"Don't you think we should get Dale checked over by a doctor?" Mildred asked. They looked over at their son, crouched down by the corn planter.

"You're nuts," Charles snarled, gesturing with the wrench. "He was just going through a bad patch. Off his feed. Look at him. I couldn't work out how to put the new shovels on the planter. And he figured it out right away."

Charles didn't want to admit Dale had a problem, Mildred realized. He looked at her and frowned.

"We couldn't run the farm without him. Leave him alone." Charles walked away, the tool swinging by his side.

"Charles, wait," Mildred stammered, her thoughts jumbled in her head. "I need to tell you something."

He turned around, shifting the wrench from hand to hand. "Hurry up. I haven't got all day."

"It was a long time ago, about my mother, I never told you. It's my fault Dale's…different…." She stopped. She couldn't face his reaction. He'd probably be furious, and she wouldn't blame him. She'd live with her guilt. And with whatever happened with Dale.

"What're you jabberin' about, woman? I need to help Dale finish up."

Dale stood by the planter, stretching his back, watching his parents.

If Your Wish Is Granted…

I N EARLY MARCH 1956, six miles south of a small town in northwestern Iowa, in a four-bedroom farmhouse off a gravel road, a woman and her teenage daughter waited in their living room for the start of the popular television show *Queen for a Day.*

"Mom, this is so exciting," Sandy gushed, fidgeting in the recliner in front of the seventeen-inch black-and-white television set they'd had for a year now. "I can't wait to see who wins Marguerite's coat." A burst of snow swirled across the screen, obscuring the picture, but it reappeared after a few seconds.

Mildred's oldest daughter, Marguerite, had called a few days earlier to tell them to watch the show. One of her raincoats, which she'd designed and manufactured in San Francisco, was going to be a prize. But she couldn't tell them which day the garment would be featured.

Mildred watched this afternoon show once every couple of weeks. Since just one contestant with a tragic story won, she thought the piling on of fancy clothes, jewelry, and household appliances was disgusting. Better to share all that stuff with the other needy women. Today, though, she was eager to see which of the deserving contestants the studio audience would choose as the queen. Mildred had told a few of her friends Marguerite's coat would be one of the prizes this week. Not that she wanted to brag, but….

The show's host, Jack Bailey, strode onto the stage to music that Mildred recognized as *Pomp and Circumstance.* In his dark tailored suit, with his jet-black hair combed flat and his thin mustache, he looked like a banker, Mildred thought, albeit a little sleazy. Clutching a microphone, he called out his usual greeting.

"Would *you* like to be Queen for a Day?" The hundreds of women and the few men in the audience yelled, "Yes," as they cheered and applauded.

Between glances at the television, Mildred slid her crochet hook back and forth through the half-finished red-and-black-wool afghan in her lap.

As usual, the show began with five young women wearing crowns parading across the stage. Each held a cardboard box that covered her torso while exposing her nylon-stocking-clad legs. Each box displayed a sponsor's name and its logo: Ex-Lax, Pepsodent, Hartz Mountain.

"In a few minutes, we'll meet contestant number one," Bailey said, "but first, a commercial." An advertisement for Hartz Animal Treats appeared: "…nourishing, good for your pet… includes vitamins and minerals for a happier animal…. Make your cat more playful…."

The camera turned to the four contestants, sitting in a row at a long table. When the first of the women, in a long-sleeve polka-dot dress, stood up and approached Bailey, her shoulders slumped forward as if she carried a heavy burden.

"So, Vera, where are you from?" Bailey asked after glancing at her name tag.

"Hoboken, New Jersey."

"New Jersey. That state has some beautiful areas. What do you do there?"

"Well, I take care of my children. I got five kids under eight years old."

"My goodness, you do have your hands full. What does your hubby do for work?"

"He's a carpenter and maintenance person for a school district. But he's between jobs now. It's been a long…." She pulled out a hanky and wiped her eyes.

"It looks like you're having a rough time, Vera. If you're voted our queen, what would you like?"

"I need a new washing machine," Vera said. "Mine's broken, and I can't afford a new one." She tried to smile but couldn't quite manage it. Mildred thought she saw her lips quiver. Was she really going to cry?

"Mom, Mom, hear that?" Sandy said. "She wants a washing machine. We need one of those fancy ones."

"Well, Vera," Bailey said, "if your wish is granted, you'll get that washing machine and much, much more. You take care of yourself now."

Mildred knew she wasn't as poor as Vera and even felt a little ashamed for comparing herself to this unfortunate woman. But she could dream, couldn't she? She desperately wanted a newfangled washer with a spin-drying cycle. If she were ever voted queen, she'd put the new appliance in the kitchen next to the refrigerator. Then there'd be no more trudging down the ten rickety steps to the basement, lugging dirty laundry to her old ringer washing machine. Once a week she stood for hours on the dirt floor, feeding wet clothing, sheets, and towels through the two rubber rollers. Then, her back and arms aching, she hauled the damp laundry up those same precarious steps outdoors to the clothesline.

"I'm always scared I'm gonna get my hand caught in those rollers like Danny," Sandy said, one hand massaging the other.

Mildred also feared getting her hand caught and smashed, as her youngest had done when he was ten. Danny had insisted on helping feed the wet items through the rollers and snagged his thumb and forefinger. She'd pulled the catch release too late and had to rush him to the doctor. He'd fastened the sides of the long cut together with metal clips, then wrapped Danny's hand in a gauze bandage.

While Mildred was dreaming, she'd also like a clothes dryer, especially during summer, when sudden rainstorms soaked the almost-sun-dried clothes. And for wintertime, too, when the wet laundry froze on the line. With the tight quarters in the kitchen, she might have to put the dryer on the closed-in porch.

"…brought to you by Pepsodent, for clean and healthy teeth, to give you a sparkling smile…."

Through the living room window, Mildred saw Dale walking across the lawn, carrying a long board and hammer, probably going to repair one of the slats on the fence next to the gravel road. She sniffed. Her oldest son's moods were all over the place these days, mostly gloomy. And he seemed to have lost his focus and incentive to work, leading to more and more arguments with his dad. This was such a contrast with his enthusiastic return from college years earlier, when he was eager to apply the new farming techniques he'd learned. His father hadn't listened then, and at sixty-five, when he could be slowing down, he was even less inclined to do anything but boss Dale around. Charles probably hoped his son would get past his unhappiness and just get back to work. Mildred so wished Dale could be off on his own—away from his dad's domineering presence.

"Hello there, Theresa," Bailey said to contestant number two. "Tell our audience about yourself, where you're from and what you do."

"Well, I'm from Kansas City, Kansas. We have three kids I take care of. My husband manages a lumber yard."

"How old are your kids?"

"Twelve, eight, and five."

"And they're not enough to keep you busy, I understand. You're doing something else that's extra special, from the goodness of your heart."

"Yeah, we take in foster children. Right now we have a boy and a girl. Denny is eleven, and Margaret seven. We love them to pieces."

"So, Theresa, what is it you want if you're voted our queen

today? Anything to do with those lucky kids?"

"Well, we're doing okay, generally. But we'd like to take all five children to Disneyland. Denny and Margaret have never been out of Kansas City, and they deserve some fun. They had a rough life before they came to us. It would be a special treat for my own kids, too."

"Well, Theresa, you're a very special mother, and you'll definitely get your wish if you're the lucky one today."

"And here is some of the queen's royal wardrobe," proclaimed the television announcer. Young models paraded across the screen as the voice described each outfit: "…a white satin dress with baby-doll sleeves and a lace inset…a floating skirt, the wide belt featuring a red bow…a black wool suit with subtle white stripes…all for Her Majesty."

"Where's Marguerite's coat?" Sandy asked, tapping her foot on the floor.

"Don't be so impatient," Mildred said, yanking out one of the stitches in her afghan. "This is only the first day. Could be a lot more, maybe even a week before her coat's on."

"I can't wait that long." Sandy stood up restlessly, then plopped back down in her chair, the Naugahyde squeaking. "How'd Marguerite do it? Sewing such complicated things."

"She started small," Mildred said, looking up from her crocheting. "When your sisters were both younger than you, they sewed dresses and skirts out of animal-feed sacks. At home and in their Home Ec classes. Those sacks came in pretty prints. The Sears Roebuck catalogue even had dresses and skirts in some feed-sack designs. Both Marguerite and Evelyn thought it was fun to find a pattern and then decide which dress would look good in a certain feed-sack print. We couldn't afford to buy real fabric, and especially not store-bought clothes."

Sandy looked down at her jeans and wrinkled her nose. "You mean sacks like our chicken feed comes in? Yuck."

"Yup," Mildred said. "Bags for crop fertilizer and flour, too. I remember it took two feed sacks to make a blouse or skirt, and three to make a dress. And I sewed diapers out of them, too."

Suddenly the front door opened, and Mildred was shocked back to the present when Dale walked into the room. He wore a clean plaid flannel shirt and blue jeans; his wavy coal-black hair was combed straight back, and his face showed barely a trace of a five o'clock shadow. He looked pretty good, Mildred thought, and a little more upbeat than usual. Thank goodness he was back doing most of his chores, though sometimes he still paced during the night, then slept much of the following day.

"What're you watching?" Dale asked. The family was late in owning a television set compared to most of their neighbors. A silly expense, Charles had said. Dale had paid for it, curious about how the new "gadget" operated, the same reason he used to take car engines apart in the shop. But once he figured it out, he wasn't eager to watch many programs.

"One of Marguerite's coats is supposed to be on *Queen for a Day*," Sandy said, bouncing in her chair. "Stay and watch with us. Today might be the day."

"You gotta move the bags of chicken feed to the henhouse," Dale barked.

"I will," Sandy said, staring at the television. "At four o'clock. After the program's over."

Dale left, and Mildred heard him open and close the icebox, then slam the kitchen door as he went back outside. She was so tired of focusing on Dale's discontent and moods.

"Corbet perfume, out of Paris, a luxury fragrance…the ultimate sensual bouquet…promise her the world but give her Arpège…exotic…delicate…the essence of roses…."

Hearing Jack Bailey's voice again, Mildred turned to the television as the next contestant approached him and his microphone.

"You look very serious, Eileen," Bailey said. Eileen's dark hair was pulled back in a ponytail, and she wore a sleeveless white blouse with a red bow at her neck. "Where are you from, young lady?"

"San Bernardino, California."

"Not a great distance from here. What does your husband do?"

"He manages loans for a bank," she said. "But he's not making many loans these days. Interest rates are too high."

"I'm sorry to hear that. But I think your wish has something to do with one of your kiddos. What can we do for you?"

"I have two boys, thirteen and fifteen," Eileen said. "My oldest boy is crippled with polio and has to stay home. I'd like a wheelchair for him. Also, a special bicycle so he can exercise." She hesitated for a moment. "I can't work right now. I was a restaurant hostess and had to have an operation on my leg."

"Of course, standing on your feet all day. What bad luck you've had. Can we do something for you once your boy is taken care of?"

"Well, for me, if it's okay, I'd like a record player. It relaxes me to listen to music. I sang in the glee club in high school. But…." Mildred noticed Eileen couldn't meet Bailey's eyes. "Mostly I need stuff for my boy."

"You sound like a loving mother. At least you have one healthy son. Is he doing okay?"

"Yes, he's great. Helps me with his brother."

"Well, if you're chosen, we'll get you what you want."

Poor woman, thought Mildred. But a record player. How she would love a new phonograph. The needle on her machine skipped and scratched up her 78s.

Her mind drifted to Marguerite's musical boyfriend. Mildred had squirreled away egg money and been able to coax extra cash out of Charles for an occasional trip to San Francisco to see her children there. On her last visit, Mildred had been smitten with

Bill, a good-looking lawyer who had opened doors for her and Sandy and asked them about life on a farm. Mildred liked Bill even more when she learned he loved opera and classical music.

"Sandy, do you remember Bill?" Mildred asked.

"Yeah, he was really nice. And kinda handsome."

"Sandy's taking piano and accordion lessons," Mildred had told him one afternoon in Marguerite's charming one-room apartment, with its brightly colored sofa pillows and the ruffled floral-print bedcover Marguerite had sewn herself. "And she plays in an accordion band."

"Mom, please, this is so embarrassing," Sandy had said under her breath. Had she been ashamed, Mildred wondered, at her mother's lack of sophistication? Or was it just a young girl's general mortification with her mother's comments?

"Mom," Sandy said now, laughing, "I think you had a little crush on Bill. Because he liked music so much."

"Hush, that's stupid," stammered Mildred. "Don't be silly." Why was she so irritated at this ridiculous comment?

Mildred thought back to that visit, when she'd continued to ingratiate herself with Bill, only slightly self-conscious about it.

"And I belong to a classical-record club," she told him. "Every month, I get a new record in the mail from Columbia Records. I especially love Strauss and Mozart." Mildred had pictured Bill attending glitzy live performances in the city's concert halls, while she listened to music on her records or on the radio.

"Since you're so busy bragging," Sandy had furiously whispered in Mildred's ear, "why don't you tell Bill about your singing in the *Messiah* last Christmas?"

Mildred was almost humiliated herself, the way she went on and on. Why did she need to curry favor with her daughter's boyfriend?

"Good for both of you," he said, the skin around his eyes crinkling as he smiled.

What a cultured man he is, Mildred thought, someone who probably reads books. Unlike Marguerite, who Mildred couldn't recall ever having read anything but magazines. And who preferred country-and-western music. Was their relationship something like hers and Charles's had been, the uneducated versus the educated? Mildred suddenly had a disloyal thought: Bill was too good for her daughter. What a snob I am, she thought.

———

"Was Evelyn as good at sewing as Marguerite?" Sandy asked Mildred the next day, as they sat in the living room waiting for contestant number three. No sign yet of Marguerite's coat.

"Probably better, especially at detail work," Mildred responded, looking up from her classical-record catalogue, trying to recall her two older daughters as teenagers. "Marguerite was impatient. She'd bribe Evelyn, offer to dry the dishes, or gather the eggs for her, if she'd finish her buttonholes or baste the hem of a skirt. Marguerite was more creative at choosing fabric a dress or blouse would look best in."

"I'll never be that good at sewing," Sandy said, scowling. "Or even as good as you. I can't get excited about it. The skirt I'm making in Home Ec. Can't get the dumb zipper in straight."

"Neither could Marguerite," Mildred said, laughing. "She'd have Evelyn do it for her. Marguerite spent hours looking at catalogues and pattern books, then sketched clothing she liked. Both girls learned how to make patterns in Home Ec class."

"Didn't other kids laugh at their homemade clothes?" Sandy asked. "Like Penny makes fun of the skirt and blouse you sewed for me." Mildred saw her daughter's cheeks reddening as Sandy looked away and wriggled in her recliner. "Sorry, Mom."

"You're so spoiled," Mildred admonished her gently, somewhat exasperated but smiling. "When Evelyn and Marguerite were young, everybody made their own clothes. Nobody had money to buy store clothes."

"…the Hoover Floor Polisher works on all kinds of floors, linoleum or wood, low and high speeds, quiet while operating… fast, reliable results…a choice of brushes, dual-speed buffers…."

Sandy turned to her mother. "Why'd Marguerite and Evelyn leave home so young? I still don't understand. Evelyn was just fifteen." Sandy shook her head vigorously. "I'd have to leave home in just a year to do that. I couldn't."

"Marguerite was eighteen," Mildred said. "She'd finished high school, and her waitress job in Spirit Lake didn't pay well. I think she was bored here. And Evelyn didn't want to be left behind, said she could finish high school anywhere."

"I was just a baby when they went. They both just took off, didn't they?" Sandy stared at her mother, as if waiting to hear a good reason for her sisters' leaving.

"There was a war on, Sandy," Mildred said, laying her catalogue down in her lap. "Airplane factories needed workers. A lot of men were at war, so they were hiring women. Paid much better than waitressing. Why stay in Iowa when exciting stuff was happening someplace else? They spent a year in Omaha; I think they lived in a boardinghouse."

"Airplanes, really?" Sandy said, sitting upright, eyes fixed on her mother.

"Marguerite learned how to rivet sheet metal onto the wings of airplanes, I think. Pretty easy, she said, once she got the hang of it. Evelyn was too young for most things, but she lied about her age—said she was seventeen—and got work using her sewing skills."

Mildred chuckled. "Isn't that funny? Evelyn said they were desperate for people to cut out fabric parts and stitch covers for airplane bodies and wings. And parachutes and pilot seats. Guess not enough men could do that. Fingers too big or didn't want to. And Evelyn had to show she could use a sewing machine."

How amazing it was that the girls' sewing expertise could help them get jobs and Marguerite to start a business. Too bad Sandy didn't like sewing.

"Why didn't they stay in Omaha?"

"One of their roommates got hurt from some flying metal. And they got tired of working long hours, so they decided to go to San Francisco, hitchhiking again. They'd heard it was an exciting place. No aircraft factories there, but they found waitress jobs."

In fact, in addition to waitressing in several Italian restaurants, Marguerite had modeled hats, dresses, and coats for department-store buyers and fashion-magazine editors, until she saved enough to buy a small grocery store in Chinatown. When Sandy and Danny were seven and five, Bob, then sixteen, had driven the four of them to California in their old Chevrolet. Marguerite had pressed Bob into helping her unpack and stock the shelves with canned goods and boxes of cereal, crackers, and other nonperishable items. Several years later, when she sold the store, she was able to set up the small factory where she manufactured her coats.

Mildred admired the fierce determination that had led to Marguerite's design and manufacturing career. And she pondered the quiet life of her middle daughter. Evelyn, who worked as a bookkeeper, was married to a nice bakery-truck driver and lived in the suburbs. A good life, but less stimulating than Marguerite's.

Pleased as Mildred was about her oldest daughter's success, she found herself on tenterhooks whenever she and Sandy visited. Staying with Evelyn or Norman, who had followed his sisters to California a few years later, was like being in a different world. They were as kind as Marguerite was hurtful.

"Shut up, Mom," Marguerite had admonished her once, when Mildred had ventured an opinion during a conversation with two of her daughter's employees. The next day, when they were at a restaurant and a group of Marguerite's friends came by, her daughter had left with them, not even waiting for Mildred to catch up.

Each time, Mildred had been near tears; but now she recalled a nice gesture by her daughter. Marguerite had bought her an elegant purple suit and hat in a fancy San Francisco department store. The first time she'd worn it, Mildred attracted the attention of an older man who whistled at her. And Marguerite sometimes invited her to lunch with her friends, who asked many questions about farm life. But was that enough to excuse her daughter's small cruelties?

Perhaps Marguerite was worried about money. She often joked that each month she had to decide whether to pay her rent or buy fabric. To avoid her scolding, Mildred learned not to agitate her, to venture few opinions, to try to stay on her "good" side. She was proud of her daughter's success but ashamed of her behavior. Marguerite was turning out like her father, often disrespectful and downright rude, interested in no one's feelings but her own. How was she supposed to feel about a daughter so difficult to love?

"Weren't you sad, Mom?" Sandy asked. "About my sisters leaving?"

"Of course I was sad," Mildred said. She had told herself that children were meant to leave home, if not so young; and that her children had made successful lives. But had success for Dale meant leaving college to return to the farm?

She touched her chest, aware of her rapid heartbeat. How she wished she could stop worrying about Dale. She hoped her son's good mood would last, that he and his dad could end their arguing and make their partnership work. Oh, how she wished for that.

The sound of the television brought Mildred out of her reverie.

"Own your very own Adler Sewing Machine, for the finest sewing projects…choice of cabinet, oak or pine." One thing she didn't need. Mildred's pedal-driven Singer machine would last her awhile yet. If she could just keep her fingers out of the way of the needle, which had pierced her thumb twice over the years.

A FEW DAYS LATER, contestant number three walked up to Jack Bailey.

"Okay, Mom," Sandy said, slamming her book shut. "We've been watching almost a week. When's Marguerite's coat gonna be on?"

"Jewel. What a pretty name," Bailey said. "But you and I were talking a little before the program. Your brother had some darn bad luck. Want to tell us about it?"

"My brother was shot in a hunting accident," Jewel said, a fist on her chest, as if, Mildred thought, she was holding her heart in. "I live in Michigan, and he's in Tennessee. I go there to help his family out as often as I can. But I have my own kids to take care of."

Bailey frowned as he listened to Jewel's story. "Does he have any other family?"

"His wife, but she's busy taking care of their two little kids." Jewel started sobbing, and Bailey pulled a handkerchief out of his pocket and handed it to her.

"What a rough road you all have," Bailey said. "So, what can we do for you, if you're voted our queen?"

"He needs a special bed, 'cause he has to lie on his back for the rest of his life."

"We'll see what we can do for you," Bailey said. "You take care, now." Jewel wiped her tears away and returned to the table.

"Jewel gets my vote, Mom," Sandy said, nodding her head vigorously. "Her poor brother. What do you think?"

"I'm going to wait and see. Hard to believe, but there might be a sadder story."

"For softer skin, treat your face with Pond's Skin Cream…for a silkier feeling…when your face is feeling taut and dry…. For nighttime skin care…for a beauty routine…your face will never be softer…. This is not your mother's cold cream…gentle and relaxing, too…."

Mildred's mind wandered again. During that last visit to California, Sandy had been entranced by Marguerite. One day at the factory, Mildred saw Sandy's eyes open wide as she watched her sister, within just a few minutes, discuss a delivery of coats on the telephone, direct her seamstresses at their sewing machines, and demonstrate to the newly hired cutter how to place a pattern on the rolled-out fabric and wield the enormous shears.

Mildred pondered her youngest daughter against the murmur of commercials. "Enhance your personality with Maybelline products…make your eyes even more beautiful, more eye-catching…. Buy Ship'n Shore blouses…save hours of your valuable time…these lovely garments that need no ironing…." Nothing to offer Sandy around here, except farming and waitressing. Her last daughter, who'd surely feel the pull of her sister's very public success.

Hearing Jack Bailey's voice, Mildred and Sandy turned their attention to the television as he began interviewing the fourth and final contestant. He glanced at her name tag and asked how to pronounce and spell her name.

"Marguerite," said the woman, spelling it out. Sandy and Mildred looked at each other, amazed.

"I don't believe it," Sandy said, giggling. "Nobody names their kid Marguerite. Except you, Mom." Mildred rolled her eyes. "Kidding, Mom. Maybe a little old-fashioned. But it's kind of a pretty name." Sandy laughed, and Mildred smiled back.

"The person who did your tag spelled your name wrong," said

Bailey, then he got to the business at hand. "Marguerite, we were talking before the program. Sounds like you're going through a terrible time. Tell us about your situation."

"I lost the two disabled kids I took care of for years, then looked after another disabled young man. Then my husband and both my parents died."

Bailey frowned. "Such bad luck. So, what do you wish for, Marguerite?"

"I want a vacation. I'm so tired. I just want to get away."

"You're a brave woman, Marguerite. If anybody needs a vacation, you do. Where would you like to go?"

"I don't care where," Marguerite said, wringing her hands. "Maybe a nice motel with a swimming pool."

"If you become queen, we'll see you get your wish."

Sandy stood up and paced back and forth in front of the television. "Mom, what a nightmare that woman's life has been. But I'm still choosing Jewel. I can't stop thinking about her brother spending his life on his back. Who you gonna vote for?"

"I'd vote for Marguerite, I think. Losing kids she took care of for so long, then her own family, too. All so sad. But she and Jewel are both tragic cases."

After an advertisement for a chocolate-flavored laxative— "Constipation can be a problem for anyone.... Ex-Lax is used by millions.... Don't let your normal regularity be interrupted... can be used overnight and with confidence...effective, gentle, natural"—Bailey announced it was time to choose today's queen.

As the studio audience clapped in turn for each contestant, the arrow on the applause meter moved slowly to the right. Mildred could see her daughter holding her breath. Why did she care who won? Some of these contestants had tragic lives, but so did lots of women. As the clapping grew louder, the applause meter extended further and further, for Marguerite. Marguerite, who'd lost so many loved ones and now wished for her first vacation ever.

"Mom, you chose the winner!" Sandy yelled.

Attendants draped a dazed and teary-eyed Marguerite in a red velvet, fur-trimmed robe, placed a bejeweled crown on her head, led her to a velveteen throne, and handed her four dozen long-stemmed red roses. Bailey promised her a two-week paid vacation at the Jamaica Inn in Corona del Mar, California, lunch at the famous Brown Derby restaurant, along with a record player, a hundred dollars' worth of records, and—Mildred gasped—a washing machine, refrigerator, and many other gifts.

Then came the queen's wardrobe. As they had all week, Mildred and Sandy's eyes fastened on the television screen as the models paraded across the stage. One wore a knee-length dark-gray wool suit, the jacket narrowed at the waist, with a full skirt; another, a long-sleeve lavender silk dress with a princess collar, set off by a string of pearls. Finally, a woman flounced onto the stage in a black-and-white-checked raincoat, buttoned to the neck, collar turned up, the model turning right, then left, then twirling around, the flared skirt swinging.

"This lovely garment," the announcer said, "is an all-purpose coat that can be worn in any kind of weather, designed and manufactured by Marguerite Rubel Manufacturing of San Francisco, California."

Sandy squealed and hopped out of her chair. "There it is, there it is. I can't believe it."

Mildred clapped her hands along with the television audience. Then she grinned and thought, goodness, I think I saw that coat at her factory last time we were there.

"This is a first," Bailey said. "The winning contestant and the designer of the prize coat have the same name." Then his voice was drowned out by audience applause.

The back door slammed, and Dale trudged into the room.

"Marguerite's coat was just on the show," Sandy babbled, her eyes still glued to the television screen.

"Congratulations to you and best wishes," Bailey said to Marguerite, patting her on the shoulder.

Above the studio audience's shouting and applause, Bailey delivered his signoff. "This is Jack Bailey, wishing we could make every woman a queen for every single day!"

Sandy walked over and switched off the television. "It was so exciting, Dale. You should have seen it. Marguerite's raincoat was a prize."

He stood a moment, looking at the blank screen, his brow furrowed. Then he turned away and walked through the kitchen, clomping up the stairs to his room. What had he thought, Mildred wondered, as Sandy jabbered on about Marguerite's triumph? That his sister was out in California leading an exciting life, while he was stuck at home, under his father's thumb, unable to break away?

Mildred didn't need a new record player. Or even a modern washing machine. Her only wish was one that Jack Bailey could never grant: that Dale would be happy and healthy again, leading the life he wanted.

Abandoned

W HAT WAS THAT POUNDING noise? Danny looked out the window of his bedroom. Dale's olive-green 1953 Dodge was parked in front of the workshop, not in its usual spot near the diesel-gas tank. He checked his watch: three-thirty, time to do chores, but he was curious about what his oldest brother was working on. Did Danny dare offer to help him? His brother would probably bite his head off.

He'd become a different person in the last few months, so grouchy, not his usual good-natured self. He was no longer the guy who'd bought Danny a used bike, fixed it up, and surprised him with it almost a year ago, on his twelfth birthday. He never took him and Sandy for ice cream in Spirit Lake, four dips for a dime, anymore.

Danny's curiosity finally got the better of him. He left his half-finished balsam model airplane on the desk, clumped down the stairs and out the front door. His brother's feet were sticking out from underneath the car, his open toolbox nearby.

"What're you doing?" Danny asked, looking at Dale's leather shoes. "Can I help?"

"Get away from here," Dale shouted. Danny jumped, then heard a tool clatter to the ground. "Haven't you got chores to do?"

Danny's chin trembled. His thirty-four-year-old brother used to show him any project he was working on and make a lesson out of it. Instead of crawling under the car to help, Danny walked toward the barn, sniffing. He'd only asked a simple question. He milked the cows and fed oats and corn to the pigs. An hour later, he found Dale filling his car with gas from the diesel tank.

"Where're you going?" Danny asked, his shoulders rigid. "Can

I come, too?"

"No," Dale said in an irritated voice, hanging up the hose. How come Dale was so cranky? "Hey, Danny," he called a minute later, as Danny was headed toward the house. He turned around, hopeful. "A steer's loose around the house," Dale said. "Get it in before it gets dark."

"Okay," Danny said quietly, still stung by his brother's scolding. He found the steer grazing on the front lawn, chased it toward the barn and into the pasture. By the time he turned back toward the house, Dale's car was gone.

That evening, at an Easter supper of ham and stuffed baked potatoes with Mom and his older sister, Dale's chair was empty. Other families made a bigger deal of Easter Sunday. The three had attended Sunday school that morning, but that was the extent of any celebration.

Danny didn't mind his brother's not being there. He'd been so crabby earlier, working under his car. Since Dale had missed meals before, neither Mom nor Sandy seemed to think anything was amiss.

Around seven the next morning, Dad came in after driving out from his house in Spirit Lake. Sandy and Danny were gobbling up cereal, Danny turning the pages of a *Batman* comic book and Sandy those of a history textbook.

"So, Dale not up yet?" Dad asked Mom, looking around the kitchen. "Still trouble sleeping?"

"He never came home last night," Mom said, pouring Dad a cup of coffee.

"What?" Dad sat down hard in a kitchen chair. "That's strange. S'pose he stayed at Fruichi's place? His friend from the Masons. Or at Alice's?"

"No," Mom said. "Not Alice's. I'm not sure they're together anymore. She called a couple times last week, and he wouldn't talk to her." She stirred milk into her coffee. "I didn't know what to say to her."

Danny looked up from his comic. Why were his parents worried about Dale? He was a grown-up. Maybe Dale just needed time away. There'd been so many arguments between him and Dad lately. He could be spending a night with a friend, like he and Sandy did sometimes.

At school, Danny occasionally wondered where Dale could be, but he knew that wherever he was, he'd be back on Thursday to take him to the craft store in Spirit Lake. His brother had said he'd buy Danny a little motor for his latest model airplane. Danny smiled as he thought about how Dale would help him fit the engine into the model and maybe get it to fly. That is, he remembered, if he'd gotten over his bad temper.

At dinner, no one talked about Dale, just nibbled at their slices of leftover ham, boiled green beans, and mashed potatoes. Mom frowned a lot, didn't ask them about school or what homework they had. After dinner, Sandy went up to her room, probably to read. Danny stayed at the table to focus on his eighth-grade algebra homework, trying to keep decimal equivalents and integers straight.

Tuesday morning, as the three sat at the table, Dad came in, slamming the door.

"Home yet?" he asked.

"Nope," Mom said. Danny tried to tune out his parents' conversation, taking in only snippets. Dad: Damn, where could he be, he's never gone away before without letting us know. Mom: Maybe he just needed a break. I always told him he should leave home and be on his own. Dad: What? I need him here. I can't run this place by myself. Mom: You guys argue so much. Maybe he got fed up. Dad, slamming his cup down: Shit! I do my best with him. He's been so gloomy. I don't know how to handle him. Then Dad stopped his ranting and stared at the floor.

At school, Danny tried to concentrate in English class,

watching Mrs. Brandenburg diagram sentences on the board. In P.E., the last class of the day, he told Coach Martin, who was also the school principal, he was feeling sick, too tired to practice basketball.

"Are you okay?" Mr. Martin asked. "Should I call your mother?"

"No, no," Danny said. "I'll be okay. Just a stomachache."

That evening, after another quiet supper, Danny went upstairs and stared at the door of Dale's room, a few steps from his own. Danny had often heard his brother pacing back and forth for hours, unable to sleep. Did he dare go in?

His hand shook as he twisted the doorknob and opened the door. Moonlight streamed into the room through the open window. After Danny reached up and pulled the chain dangling from the ceiling light socket, a faint light from the bare bulb illuminated the room. He sat in the wooden chair by Dale's roll-top desk, next to the window that looked out to the lawn and the gravel road beyond. A framed photo of Dale sat on the shelf above the desktop, his brother in Navy dress whites, his dark hair slicked back—the same photograph Mom displayed on the piano. Dale had tucked a small picture of Alice in the corner of the frame.

Then Danny perched on the edge of Dale's unmade bed, where a couple magazines lay open, including *Popular Mechanics* and, strangely, *True Confessions*. A woman with thick, dark, curly hair and heavily rouged cheeks and lips posed on the cover. Danny looked up at the photo of Alice. She resembled the glamorous picture on the magazine cover, minus the makeup. He glanced at the open door, ears tuned for any noise on the stairs, in case Dale came home suddenly. He'd been in such a bad mood, he'd probably scold Danny, or even smack him for snooping.

Danny looked at the wall-mounted bookshelf, with its pile of *Popular Mechanics* magazines and the books on agriculture, physics, and math from Dale's college years. Dale had studied growing crops and what he called animal husbandry, which, he'd explained to Danny, was about raising farm animals. Dale said he wanted to be a farmer who owned lots of land.

"That's how you make money," Dale had said. "Buy more land for more corn crops, cattle, and hogs. And improve your breeding stock."

Danny remembered how Dale would sleep on a Navy fold-up cot in the hog house each year after the birth of new piglets, to make sure the mothers wouldn't roll over on the babies. Danny smiled, recalling the trip he and Dale took in the pickup truck last fall to pick up a breeding boar they'd bought in Minnesota. They'd left at three a.m. on a Sunday morning and, on the way back home, they stopped for breakfast in a small town. While they were eating, the animal escaped into a crowd of churchgoers. Laughing their heads off, he and Dale had finally lassoed the hog and got him back in the truck.

Books entitled *How to Improve Your Memory* and *Toastmasters* were also on the bookshelf. Dale had said public speaking helped him get over his shyness. Danny had laughed at the stories and jokes Dale memorized from *10,000 Jokes, Toasts & Stories* to use in talks to groups like his school's Parent-Teacher Association and at his Masonic lodge.

Danny grabbed an old cigar box off the shelf and flipped through photos that he guessed were from his brother's college years. He stopped at a picture of Dale leaning against his car alongside two attractive girls. Then another of him reclining in a rowboat, again with good-looking girls. So this was what Dale looked like in college. He looked so happy. What a shame he couldn't be that cheerful now.

Wednesday morning, Mom had stood at the sink and looked out the window. Dad sat drinking his coffee.

"Whaddya think, Mom?" Sandy asked as she buttered two slices of toast. "Is Dale in North Carolina with Vern? Or with

Marguerite, Evelyn, or Norman in California?"

Danny tried to remember what each of them did. Norman was some kind of engineer. Marguerite had a coat factory, and Evelyn was married and worked as a bookkeeper. They'd all moved out long ago, almost before he was even born.

"I don't know," she said, turning around. "But he would have let us know if he was going anywhere. He's never just disappeared."

"I called the Masons and got Fruichi's number," Dad said. "The guy hasn't seen Dale." He took off his engineer's cap and ran his hands through his wavy and thinning gray hair. "It's gettin' curiouser and curiouser. That he'd just take off."

Now, three days since they'd last seen Dale, Danny sat alone at the kitchen table after school, having given up on doing his math homework. A neighbor's phone call a few minutes earlier had made his mom anxious, and she'd gone to the barn to fetch Dad. Danny folded one end of the sheet of math problems into an airplane tail, then the two sides into wings. What were his parents doing? The airplane sailed across the room, landing in the sink.

Just then, the kitchen door swung open with a loud creak.

"Come on, Danny," Dad said, his lips pressed tightly together.

Danny followed him out and got into the passenger seat of the mud-spattered white pickup truck. He rolled down the window to dilute the manure smell from his dad's boots. Gravel crunched under the pickup's wheels as they turned from the driveway onto the road. His dad's jaw clenched under the gray stubble. He chomped down on his chewing tobacco, then spit a dark-brown stream out the window. Glancing in the side mirror, Danny saw Mrs. Hensley pulling in their driveway to drop Sandy off after basketball practice.

The pickup truck bumped along for three miles, past fields of leveled black soil where corn hadn't been planted or hadn't yet sprouted. They passed a red tractor pulling a two-bottom plow in a field. As they made a left turn a quarter-mile past Danny's school, his dad's hands held tight to the steering wheel, unlike his usual casual driving style.

"I'm afraid of what we're gonna find," Dad said in a hoarse voice, staring straight ahead. "I shouldn't have brought you."

"What do you mean?" Danny asked.

His father shifted into first gear, turned through an open gate, and rumbled over a metal culvert and into their alfalfa field. Danny heard plants brushing the underside of the truck. Then Dale's car appeared just below the top of a rise, facing the road.

"Why's Dale's car here?" Danny asked as they bounced over the field. "Maybe he ran out of gas. But I saw him fill up the tank last Sunday."

Stopping several yards from Dale's car, Dad shut off the ignition, closed his eyes, and gripped the steering wheel. Then he opened the door.

"You stay here," Dad ordered. Danny waited a minute, then followed his father. Where could Dale be?

Danny would never forget the sight of the body collapsed against the passenger door, left foot on the gas pedal. It reminded Danny of a bloated steer killed by lightning he'd once seen in the pasture. Danny stared at the engorged face, at the stained and torn denim work shirt and jeans. Averting his eyes, he watched a tractor trundling down the gravel road outside the field. No way could this be his brother. It didn't even look like him. No, it wasn't him. He looked over at Dad, who was leaning over a front fender of Dale's car, his body shaking with quiet sobs. He'd never seen his dad cry.

"Why?" Dad sobbed, staring into the car, tears trailing down his face. "Why did you do it?"

Danny paced among the alfalfa plants, away from the body in the car, away from his father. He crossed his arms across his chest in a tight hug.

"Let's go," his dad finally said. They drove home in silence,

Dad barely keeping the truck on the road, while Danny leaned against the passenger door, as far from his father as he could get.

At home, he stood outside the kitchen, peering through the screen door. He couldn't face Mom and Sandy right away.

"We found Dale's car." Dad wiped away tears with his fist. "And his body." As he paced back and forth, shaking his head, Sandy began sobbing, and Mom collapsed in a kitchen chair. "Carbon monoxide poisoning. He killed himself."

"How could he do this?" asked Mom, holding her head in her hands. "I told him he should just leave if he was so miserable here." She stood up and leaned against the sink, her back to them, and blew her nose on a tissue.

"Mom, can't you be a little sorry he's gone?" Sandy asked, wiping her eyes with her shirt. "It doesn't matter that you told him to go."

Danny finally opened the screen door and joined the family. He blinked to contain his tears. Maybe Mom was relieved Dale was gone. They had all been fighting for so long, and Dale had gotten so mean. First, Mom and Dad had argued about the divorce. Nobody else he knew had parents who'd gotten divorced. Nobody he knew killed themselves, either. He thought back to Sunday, trying to recall the moments of the last time he'd seen Dale, how his brother had been busy under his car. Then a thought struck him.

"Dad," he said. His father looked up, his face tear-stained. "Sunday afternoon, awhile before Dale left. He was…he was…" Danny shuddered, "pounding something under his car. I wanted to help, but he told me to get away." Dad didn't respond but cradled his face in his hands.

A few minutes later, Dad went into the living room to the telephone table, and Danny heard pages rustling in the telephone book.

"Sheriff Anderson, this is Charlie Rubel," Dad said, then

paused. "Yeah, that's the one…five miles south, on the Everly Road. But not there.… My boy.…"

Danny flattened his hands over his ears. He didn't need to hear all that. He went into the living room, passed his dad returning to the kitchen, and turned on the television. It was his favorite show, *Captain Video and His Video Rangers*. A silver spaceship and a comet hurtled toward each other, a city skyline at the bottom of the screen. But he found it difficult to take in the familiar images. It felt like there was no air in the room. Suddenly chilled, he folded his arms over his chest again.

He turned away and looked out the window at the short green grass in the waning afternoon light. He and Dale had always taken turns mowing the lawn. A couple years ago, when Danny was eleven, his brother had patiently showed him how to pull the mower's starter rope and set the choke to start the machine. Dale had nodded in approval when Danny could finally maneuver the heavy machine over the two acres of lawn by himself.

And Danny could picture the board swing around the corner of the house, which Dale had hung from a branch at least twenty feet off the ground for his younger siblings. How could Danny ever look at the grass or the swing again without thinking of Dale? But then, the body in the car hadn't even looked like his brother, so Danny could hope that Dale wasn't really gone. Maybe he'd joined a brother or sister in North Carolina or California, and they weren't telling.

"How can you watch television at a time like this?" Sandy shouted in his ear. She stomped out of the living room, and he heard her going upstairs. Her bedroom door slammed.

Dad came in the room again, saying he was going to call Bob, Danny's nearest brother, away at college. Danny turned up the television to block out the sound of his father's voice.

After a few minutes, he looked out the window and saw Dad's

car turn from their driveway onto the gravel road. He wished Dad had said goodbye when he left. He would have liked to go with him to see Ella, his stepmother. She would serve him ice cream and blueberry trifle, his favorite dessert, which might help get his mind off the horrible scene in the car.

"Dinner's ready," Mom called from the kitchen.

"I'm not hungry," Danny mumbled to himself. Then Mom was on the phone, probably calling his other brothers and sisters. And Alice. Danny stuffed his fingers in his ears to block out Mom's voice. The spaceship and comet on television zoomed closer to a collision. Would Captain Video and the Rangers save the day? He took his fingers from his ears. He'd see what happened and then maybe eat. A few minutes later, Danny heard his mother running water in the sink and opening and closing the icebox.

"I'm going to lie down," Mom said, walking into the living room. She had pinned her hair up in a bun and wore her reading glasses low on her nose. She glanced at him but quickly averted her eyes. A few minutes later, he heard her crying in her bedroom, just off the living room. He'd heard Mom cry before, but remembering his dad's tears—the idea of both his parents bawling—it was too much. Danny held his eyes tightly closed. He would not cry.

He wiped his eyes and switched off the television. The spaceship and comet had sped past each other. Captain Video had come to the rescue. In the kitchen, he saw two plates of hamburger patties and green beans on the table. Sandy hadn't eaten, and he had no appetite, either.

The next morning, Dad's heavy footsteps trudging up the stairs woke Danny. He sat up, groggy from too little sleep. From Dale's room, he heard the sound of drawers opening and closing. Then Dad knocked on his door.

"Get up," he yelled.

Downstairs in the kitchen, Danny slouched at the table, where Mom, Dad, and Sandy just sat, no one eating breakfast. Mom wore a rumpled housedress, and messy wisps of gray hair had escaped her bun. Her white-knuckled fingers clutched a coffee cup. Dad was staring at a couple of papers on the table while turning a tiny box over and over in his hands.

"I went through Dale's desk and found these wedding and engagement rings Dale bought for Alice." He brushed away tears. "And a note." He hesitated, then, his voice cracking, "'I'm fed up and tired of being yelled and sworn at,'" he read from the paper in his hand. "'I leave everything to Danny. Dale.'"

Mom stood up, wiping her eyes with a dishtowel. Sandy cradled her face in her hands. Danny gripped the edge of the table and felt the room sway around him.

It was Dad's fault. Danny couldn't stand to look at him.

"Dale left this paper next to his note, something he must have copied from somewhere," Dad said. "'It is most appalling to note that ninety percent of people drift aimlessly through life, without the slightest conception of the work for which they are best fitted.'"

Dad's hand trembled as he dropped the paper and it fluttered to the floor.

"He went to college," Dad said, looking at Danny. "He could have left home anytime. Did I keep Dale from doin' what he wanted?"

"You never gave him any money," Danny shouted. "You were supposed to be partners."

Storming out of the house, Danny stopped near the barn to draw cold water from the pump to splash on his face. When he entered the barn, the milk cows looked at him from their stalls. Danny grabbed the halter rope of his 4-H calf, Nitro, who stood in the stall Dale had helped him build, and tried to lead the calf to the outside water trough. But the animal balked.

"Move," Danny yelled. He yanked the rope and kicked the calf in the belly. Nitro pulled back, refusing to budge.

"Jerks, worthless numbskulls, both you and Dad."

He dropped the rope, sat down on an overturned bucket, and studied the stubborn calf, who was nibbling corn and silage in the half-finished feed trough. The animal was almost big enough to auction off at this summer's county fair in Spirit Lake. Danny would sell Nitro and use the money for a Greyhound bus ticket to California, where he'd find his favorite cowboy hero, Roy Rogers, and the whole happy Roy Rogers family.

WEEKS LATER, DANNY WAS still hoping against hope he could prove everyone wrong, that the body inside the car had not been Dale. Every day, he rode his bike the half-mile to the mailbox, looking for a letter from his brother.

"What are you expecting in the mail?" his mom asked once. He felt himself blush and rushed outside. Maybe it was time to accept that Dale was gone for good.

Now Danny stood in the kitchen and squirmed as he thought about the "day of the car." What had Dad been thinking?

He was used to Dad's being tight. In fact, his father often joked that he "squeezed a nickel so tight, the Indian was ridin' the buffalo." Prying school lunch money out of him was always an ordeal. He'd dole it out in pennies and nickels, complaining to Danny and Sandy each time, "What, you two back again?"

But to make money from Dale's car? You had to hold your nose if you just opened a door. Think about Dale for a change, he wanted to yell at Dad, not just about money.

The "day of the car," Danny had gotten off the school bus and plodded up the long gravel driveway. He ran his hand along the white pickets on top of the fence around the house and lawn that Danny had helped Dale paint. They'd built a trellis at the end of the sidewalk that led to the front of the house, now draped with the lilacs Mom had planted. The two brothers had been proud of their work.

At the top of the driveway, Dad was leaning against Dale's Dodge, trimming his fingernails with his pocketknife. The buttons of his red-flannel shirt strained over his beer belly, and his shirttail hung halfway out of his jeans. Seeing him, Danny wanted to be anywhere but home. But it was too late to turn around.

"Get in," Dad said. "We're goin' to Lake Park to sell the car."

"What?" Danny backed away. "I'm not gettin' in that thing."

He'd opened the wooden gate under the trellis to walk to the house. Dad was crazy, always thinking about money.

"Get in, goddamn it," Dad growled. He opened the passenger door and held it open. "Nobody here wants to drive it. And we can use the cash."

Danny felt his shoulders droop. Why not sell the car? Don't waste things, Dad always said. The aluminum tube Dale had used to kill himself? Dad put it back on the water wagon that Dale had built to water the cattle more efficiently.

But wait a minute. Maybe Dad wanted to get rid of something that reminded him of his dead son. And so it wasn't just about money. Maybe it was okay, then. But who'd want to buy a car with such a putrid smell?

Danny climbed in the car but wouldn't sit in the front, where Dale had spent his last hours. Dried stains remained on the passenger seat. Dad had placed a mat over the hole in the floor where the tube had run from the exhaust pipe. He'd sprayed lemon aerosol freshener to camouflage the smell of death, but the stink still clung to the upholstery. The stench reminded Danny of the squirrel that got stuck in the blades of the manure spreader. It took several days to get close enough to dislodge the small carcass with a stick.

On the blacktop road to Lake Park, they passed the Johnsons' rundown farm, with its machine shed's rusting metal roof and the barn's flaking white paint. A mile further on, the Lunds' farm appeared orderly, with new siding on the house and tiny green corn plants in their nearby field.

All six miles to town, Danny hung his head out the car window. The wind blew the reek of death from his nostrils and the tears from his eyes. He wondered what Dale had thought about in his final moments. Alice? Danny? How Dad would be sorry he was gone?

When they arrived at the used-car lot, Danny jumped out and took a deep breath of fresh air. The dealer walked around the vehicle, then opened the hood and studied the engine. When he got in the car, he jumped out immediately.

"I'm not buyin' this stinkin' heap," he said, holding his nose.

"Ain't nothin' wrong with this car," Dad replied, "'cept my boy killed himself in it."

At these words, Danny turned and rushed away, his cheeks flaming. How could Dad talk about Dale with a complete stranger? He headed down Main Street past McGuin's Barber Shop to the bowling alley. Inside, he took in the rumble and banging of balls and pins, familiar and even comforting sounds, because bowling sometimes counted as school physical education. Now and then, Danny stayed after class to help the P.E. teacher set pins for the next group.

A half-hour later, back at the dealership, Dad was leaning against Dale's car, drinking a bottle of beer.

"Where the hell were you?" he said, throwing the bottle into a nearby trash can.

Danny slowly got back to his old life of farm chores and, with school over, seeing friends. He didn't talk to his father much, but one day he suggested to Dad that they buy a grease gun: You'd fill it with cartridges and lubricate the farm machinery that way. More efficient and less messy, Danny told him.

But his father scoffed. "If that was such a good idea, Dale would have done it," he said.

What a small and stupid thing to reject, Danny thought, when they had so many machine surfaces to grease. Frustrated, he stomped into the shady oak grove behind the workshop, where rusty pieces of unused farm equipment sat. He liked to pretend to drive the ancient tractor, whose steel wheels had sunk into the soil. He climbed onto the metal seat, jerked the tractor wheel right and left for a few minutes, then got down and walked to Dale's car. They'd left it near the old wooden playhouse.

He touched the dusty hood of the car that Dale had kept so clean and polished. Opening the trunk, he saw the inner tubes he and Sandy used whenever Dale took them swimming at Pike's Point. He quickly slammed it shut again.

Danny hadn't been in the car since Dad tried to sell it. Opening the driver's door, he smelled the still-ripe odor, hesitated, then got in and rested both hands on the steering wheel. He rolled down the window and slid the ashtray open. Cigarette butts stained with Alice's lipstick filled the small metal drawer. Nobody had emptied it.

After a few minutes, he got out and slammed the door. Dad had offered to buy Danny a car when he turned fifteen and a half, but it would be awhile before he could leave home. He would request a two-door Ford hardtop, V8 automatic transmission, in white. Dad had also told Sandy he'd get her a new saddle for her horse. Hard as he tried, Danny could not forget what Dale had written in the note he left behind that explained how bad Dad had made him feel. Now, though, Danny realized that Dad's promises to buy those items for his youngest two were giant steps, given his stinginess. He was trying to make it up to his children still at home the only way he knew how.

On one of his weekly visits to Dad and Ella's house, Danny saw that his dad had posted mementos of Dale on the wall by his desk: his Navy photo and his high school graduation picture. Danny trembled the first time he saw Dale's baby picture next to the obituary from the *Lake Park Beacon*. Dad often sat, bent over in his chair, staring at those reminders. Also, sometimes during the day, his father would suddenly stop working and peer into the distance, a tear working its way down his craggy face. The man was hurting.

Through the trees, he saw Dad walking from the barn to the workshop. Danny accepted that Dad had treated Dale badly. He treated other people badly, too. That was just his way. But Danny knew something must have been wrong with Dale—he'd become so mean and unhappy, a totally different person, one Danny didn't recognize. The changes in Dale couldn't have been all Dad's fault, because he was the same person he'd always been. It was Dale who had changed.

Dad would always blame himself for Dale's death. Maybe it was time for Danny to stop doing that.

He could remember his brother and forgive Dad.

Dilemma

HE WORDS STILL RANG in his ears. His dad had telephoned the tragic news. With no details, other than telling Bob he had to drop out of college.

Dale was dead. He couldn't believe it. How could Dad just hang up without telling him what had happened to his oldest brother? Bob shuddered as his thoughts roamed over the many gruesome ways Dale could have died: a tractor or car accident, mangled to death by a corn picker or combine—some of which had happened to their neighbors.

Batting away those grim scenarios, Bob closed his calculus book. Forget the test tomorrow. He glanced at his watch. Six o'clock, and he desperately needed a drink. And food. Fortunately, his roommate was out; Bob would be terrible company. But if he was going to leave early tomorrow, he'd have to go easy on the beer. And he had to stop by the Iowa State admin office on his way out. They'd let each of his professors know that he'd miss classes for at least a week.

In the kitchen, he grabbed a beer from the icebox and a bag of chips from a cupboard. God, Dale gone. How could that be? Eleven years older, his brother had taught him so much about farming. How to drive a tractor, sitting behind him to guide his steering. How to milk a cow, squeezing and pulling at the same time, a tricky skill to master. How to shape boards on the lathe in the workshop for all their different kinds of fences.

Bob finished the beer and the chips, then packed his bag. He'd still have to study, so he added one textbook for each of his classes: Crop Development, Animal Nutrition, Management of Livestock, and Calculus.

Next morning, he drove off in the 1954 Ford Dad had

bought him before he left for college, providing he promised to return to the farm once he graduated. Leaving Ames that early April, Bob drove past acres of newly plowed fields, ready for spring planting. Trying to get his mind off Dale, he contrasted his "book learning" with the way most farmers his dad's age did things. Like the field he'd just passed, where corn—Bob's family's main crop—would likely be planted. After harvest in October, would they chop up the shrunken, wilted cornstalks, spread manure for fertilizer, and plow it all under? Or would they just burn the stalks and then plow them under? That saved time and effort, but it also caused clouds of smoke and bad air, and it didn't nourish the soil. It wouldn't restore the potash and potassium that was important for corn.

Another dilemma: They used manure, but was it time to move to more efficient chemical fertilizer on their crops of corn, oats, and soybeans? Should they continue to plow out the weeds, as his father did, or spray them with chemical fertilizer? He and Dale had often discussed updated farming methods, but now he couldn't think of any specific conversations they'd had.

Bob wondered what he would find at home. How were his parents doing? And his younger brother and sister?

Six hours later, exhausted from a restless sleep and the long drive, Bob stood in the kitchen. Mom, Sandy, and Danny had met him at the door and ushered him into the house. Bob had wanted to ask about Dale, but no one would look him in the eye. He was eager to change out of his wrinkled khaki pants and sweat-stained blue cotton shirt, but he waited for an explanation.

"You must be tired," Mom said. "Want some water or pop?"

He craved a beer, but Mom hadn't allowed alcohol in her house since Dad moved out, though he still came every day to work the farm.

"Your dad's feeding the cattle," Mom said, handing him an orange drink. "He'll be here in a little while. Go in the living room and sit down." There the three of them sat, Bob collapsed on the maroon-and-gray-leather hassock he'd brought home after leaving the Navy, almost three years ago. Sandy, his four-teen-year-old sister, stood gazing out the window overlooking the lawn, wiping away tears. Her curly blond hair hung in an unwashed tangle. Danny, thirteen, sat cross-legged on the floor, leaning against the wall. He was clutching a tube of glue, and pieces of a balsam model airplane were scattered around him. Staring into the distance, he looked unreachable.

Mom was on the couch, her forehead creased as she bent over the half-finished wool afghan she was crocheting, the red, blue, and green squares a bright contrast to the faded black sectional couch. A bit of upholstery bulged from the corner of one of the couch's three lumpy sections, and a spider web draped across a corner of the ceiling.

Bob's eyes fixed on the top shelf of the bookcase, sagging under a pile of Mom's magazines and books. There sat the shiny gold clock with a flywheel and pendulum, which he'd brought back on leave. The clock stood out against the shabby surround-ings, its polished exterior almost gleaming.

Are we going to sit here all day not saying anything? he won-dered. He forced his eyes back to Mom. Had he not noticed, or was her hair this gray, her face this lined and packed with weariness, when he'd been home at Christmas?

"I gotta know what happened to Dale," he said, desperate to break the silence. Desperate for answers. He held his breath, preparing himself for the gory description of a farm-machinery accident.

Mom put down the afghan, took a tissue out of the pocket of her blue print housedress, and blew her nose. Her eyes glistened with tears as she looked at him.

Just then, Dad clomped in from the kitchen, dragging a wooden chair in one hand and holding a Folgers coffee can in the other. Bob winced at the screech of wood over linoleum.

"He killed himself," Dad said in a hoarse voice.

"What?" Bob said, clutching the sides of the hassock, suddenly feeling dizzy. Not Dale, his strong, smart older brother. Not him. Impossible.

Dad set his chair down backwards and slumped onto the seat. At sixty-five, his dad looked like a shrunken old man, a shell of the professional boxer he'd been into his late thirties. Was this the guy who still started his chores at five a.m.? Who sat for hours riding a tractor in the sun? His lined, gray-stubbled jaw worked a wad of chewing tobacco, a long-held habit that had stained his teeth with streaks of brown. He placed the coffee can on the floor, then leaned forward against the chair's solid back, folded his arms, and hid his face in them.

"How?" Bob asked, barely able to get the word out.

Dad lifted his head. "Gassed himself."

Sandy collapsed into the recliner and sobbed. Jaw clenched, eyes locked on his dad, Bob waited for the grim details. Slowly, Dad described how he and Danny had found Dale in his car in their alfalfa field. The sheriff told them he had rigged up a hose that led from the exhaust pipe to the passenger seat, the car running until it was out of gas.

"Buried him this morning. He was in bad shape after going missing for three days," Dad said. "Couldn't wait for you. We told the other kids it was no use coming back."

"Jesus Christ," Bob whispered. He rubbed his sweaty palms on his knees. It had taken a lot of guts to do what Dale had done. God almighty. What was going on in this place?

"Dale changed so much in the last few months," Dad said, gripping the back of his chair. "Wouldn't talk much, seemed real sad. Couldn't sleep at night. Some days he just laid on the couch for a long time and wouldn't work. Doctor Pell in Lake Park called this morning. We didn't know he was even goin' to the doctor. Said Dale wanted medicine to sleep." Dad shook his head and looked down at the cracked green linoleum.

"What else did the doctor say?" Bob asked.

"He was useless," Dad said. "Said he gave Dale sleeping pills. Don't know if he took 'em, 'cause he still had trouble sleeping. The doc probably couldn't figure out what was wrong. Just like we couldn't." He looked at Bob through red-rimmed eyes. "Maybe I was too hard on him."

Sadness and not working, that wasn't Dale. Always up at the crack of dawn, feeding the animals or building something from scratch. He'd spent weeks creating the vertical board fence around the small pasture opposite the barn where Sandy's horse grazed. He'd doubled the size of the new corncrib, then created a tractor-and-wagon drive-through in the crib's middle section, so they could unload grain more easily.

Bob thought back to the last time he and Dale had talked, in the workshop when Bob was home over Christmas break. Leaning over two transmissions on the workbench, Dale said he was remodeling them to produce more and different speeds, ultimately to fit one in an old junk truck he'd found somewhere. Bob watched as Dale adjusted engine parts, explaining what each did. All of a sudden, his brother had gone quiet and still. He'd held a socket wrench in mid-air and stared into the distance. It was like a cloud of gloom had settled over him. But it soon passed, and Dale continued his work.

Everyone was sad sometimes, Bob thought, then you got over it.

He'd seen his brother tense up whenever Dad yelled at him. But Dad had always yelled at his sons. They all lived with it. Perhaps he and Alice were having problems. Mom and Dad had never been models of a happy couple. Or maybe they wanted to marry, and he was nervous about such a gigantic step. Was he worried about his financial future, and how to get along with

Dad if he left and had a family? Or maybe Dale had wanted to leave the farm but couldn't figure out how.

Mom suddenly spoke up, looking up from her crocheting. "I called Alice to tell her about Dale, and she was real broken up. Didn't say if they were still together."

"Put your stuff away and change your clothes," Dad told Bob.

He picked up the coffee can, spit in a gob of tobacco, then, with an effort, stood up. He stumbled to the wall and sagged against it.

"I need you here now, Bob. College can wait. We gotta feed the hogs and get the milkin' done. And later fix the pasture fence and get the crops planted." He tucked his shirttail into his jeans. "You, too, Danny," he said, glancing at his youngest son. Danny put down a model-airplane wing, resealed the tube of glue, and stood up.

Mom shoved her afghan into a plastic bag and trailed after Dad and Danny. Bob heard the back door slam. Why in hell should he drop out of Iowa State now? Dale had quit after two years of college and look what happened to him. Bob would stay home maybe a week at most to help Dad get on his feet. Then he'd get back to school.

"I'm really glad you're home, Bob," Sandy said, startling him. He'd forgotten she was in the room. "It's all so sad." Rising from the recliner, Sandy pulled a red kerchief from her jeans pocket and blew her nose. "You should have seen Dad after he found Dale. I never saw him cry before. I wanna be mad at Dad, 'cause he yelled at Dale so much. But he feels so awful." She wiped her eyes. "Do you think it's Dad's fault?"

Bob had no answer for her. "I better get to work," he said in a husky voice. Dad crying? Must have been tough to see.

In the kitchen, his mother sat on her white metal stepstool at the sink, clutching a bunch of carrots. As she scraped, slender strips of orange fell away. When she wiped the back of her hand over her red, puffy eyes, Bob saw her wedding band buried in the flesh of her ring finger. He assumed that after the divorce, she hadn't been able to remove it.

The family hadn't known Dad was remarried until a year ago, when he moved into his new wife's house, in Spirit Lake. Bob had gotten to know her a little. What that gentle, considerate woman saw in his gruff, quick-to-anger father, he couldn't imagine. And nobody talked about the divorce or remarriage—the usual silence about family stuff. Except his dad had just now talked openly about Dale. And he'd been crying. Maybe things were changing around here.

"The Delaneys brought over scalloped potatoes with cheese," Mom said. She pointed to a covered dish on the table. "Your favorite. And Sandy got you some books from the library. But now you better go out and help with chores or your dad'll have a fit."

Bob bent over, feeling sick to his stomach. Dale had only been in the ground a few hours, and Mom was talking about food and books.

He grabbed his duffel bag, opened the door to the stairway, and went up to his room. Seeing Dale's closed bedroom door, he closed his eyes. Whenever he was home from college, Dale had told him to "make sure you crack the books." He'd also lecture Bob on his fondness for beer and his too-often late-into-the-evening drinking sessions with his high school buddies.

"I've dragged Dad out of too many bars," Dale said. "Don't make me do that for you." Bob had ignored him. The fact that Dale didn't like alcohol had nothing to do with him. Bob had been boozing since high school—too much sometimes, same as his friends, but that was his business. He could manage his own life. He'd succeeded so far.

Opening the door to his room, Bob wondered again what had driven Dale to kill himself. Dad and Mom both saw something was wrong, but evidently couldn't figure out what it was or how to get help for him. Were there answers anywhere? His brain felt dizzy.

On the desk lay the library books Sandy must have gotten this morning when they were in town for the burial. His younger sister liked finding novels for him and always read them after he finished. Choosing books must have helped her get her mind off Dale. He scanned the hardcovers by Zane Grey and Louis L'Amour, two of his favorites, then changed into a work shirt and jeans and went back downstairs.

Mom was still perched on her stool, snapping fresh beans into a bowl in the sink. He gripped the doorknob to go outdoors but hesitated.

"Why do you think Dale did it?" he asked.

Mom looked at him, then turned to glance out the window. "There's something I should tell you…." Her voice trailed off, and her hands hovered over the bowl of vegetables.

"What?" Bob asked. "Did you see something Dad missed?" He followed her gaze to the red and purple pansies and petunias she'd planted, a kaleidoscope of color next to the whitewashed garage attached to the workshop. She and Dale had worked hard to make the place look good. Bob remembered as a young teenager helping Dad and Dale create the angled sidewalk over the dirt path from the front door to the garage. Under Dale's eagle eye, Bob had smoothed out the cement with a trowel and helped frame the new walkway with vertical boards, the three of them working against the roar of the cement mixer. He'd felt so grown-up, allowed to help on such a big project.

"I don't know what went wrong. With Dale," his mother finally said. "He was just so unhappy. Your dad got Dale to drop out of college, but you have to finish. Don't get trapped here like Dale did. Just stay here 'til things get settled."

"I want to finish college," Bob said. "I'm old as it is to be a junior—twenty-four next month. I only have a year and a half to go. Dad'll have to learn to manage on his own."

———

THE NEXT MORNING, BOB and Danny walked toward the machine shed, where Bob would help Dad mount the plow on the tractor for plowing their clover field.

"So, those model airplanes you build?" Bob asked Danny. He still struggled to make conversation with his younger brother. "Can you make the little motors go all by yourself?"

"Dale used to help me get 'em goin'," Danny said, pulling his cap further down over his forehead. "Now I'll have to ask the guy at the craft store to help me." He turned away, his shoulders quaking. "Dale bought me that little Ford tractor." He pointed to the small gray machine in front of the corncrib. "Dale said I needed a tractor. Showed me how to drive it. And he let me drive the pick-up truck. Dad never does anything like that." Danny wiped his snotty nose with a fist.

"Yeah," Bob said, unable to meet Danny's eyes. Bob remembered a morning years ago, he'd been about the same age Danny was now. Bob had gone to school excited to tell his best friend, Verle, about his new baby brother. Guess he hadn't been as happy about the baby sister born a year and a half earlier.

Danny turned toward the barn before Bob could think of anything to say. "I have to feed and water Nitro."

Sighing, Bob joined his dad in the machine shed, where the two lifted the heavy iron frame of the plow with attached blade to the back of the tractor. Bob held it in place while his dad fastened the attachment bolts.

"Dad, we're having a discussion in my Crop Development class at school. Should farmers do away with cover crops and just buy nitrogen, another kind of fertilizer?"

"Nope," Dad said as he turned the last bolt, then stood up

and threw the wrench on the ground. "Dale said we should stick with cover crops and use manure for fertilizer."

Okay, Bob thought, climbing onto the tractor and driving slowly down the dirt road behind the barn to the field. But it wouldn't hurt just to consider a new idea.

He decided he had to go slow with Dad, cut him some slack. An old-school farmer, he mostly relied on the practices he'd learned growing up on a farm himself. He was reluctant to try anything his neighbors hadn't attempted. Dale had brought home from university notions about contour planting and how to raise leaner hogs. Ideas that Dad had called useless, mere "book smarts." But Dad had eventually accepted some of Dale's ideas, so maybe in time he'd hear Bob out. Now, though, Dad was having a tough time, clearly taking a lot of the fault for Dale's death. Did Bob need to heap more blame on him?

Turning into the field with its limp, dried-out clover, he recalled how he always admired the white blossoms that appeared not long after they planted the crop in the fall. Some of their neighbors didn't plant cover crops, though Bob knew that their roots grow deep in the soil and provide for good water retention and lessen erosion. And the soil got valuable nutrients when the plants decompose. Even though Dale might not have agreed with him about moving onto fertilizer, at least they'd have had the discussion.

As Bob guided the tractor through the field, the plow dug into the earth, turned the plant residue under, and broke up large clods of soil. At the end of each row, he turned around and tackled the next one, back and forth. He didn't mind plowing, a routine chore, perhaps because once the job was done, it gave him the satisfaction of finishing something. In a couple of weeks, they'd make another pass-through, this time with the circular discs hooked behind the tractor, to level out the ground for planting corn, oats, or soybeans.

Bob had always planned to come back to the farm after college. He wouldn't be the mechanical genius Dale was. He'd be the guy who was good at math, the numbers guy who'd handle the business end. But that was when Dale was alive.

Three days later, Bob and Dad were repairing the barbed-wire fence around the feedlot. In a few days, Bob would have to tell him he'd be going back to school. He dreaded that conversation. As Dad held the wire taut with pliers, Bob hammered U-nails into the posts to hold the wire in place. But how could the old man do all the work by himself? Danny was too young to take over. And hired men never stayed long, since Dad made them work long, exhausting hours for low wages. Over the years, they'd sometimes employed a "displaced" person or family from Russia or Hungary, but even those workers soon moved on to better-paying situations.

After a couple hours of work, Dad sat down on the toolbox, pulled a handkerchief from his overalls, and wiped his sweaty face. From his can of chewing tobacco, he scooped out a portion of snuff with his pocketknife and tipped it into his mouth. Bob sat on the ground and sipped cool water from a thermos.

"If you forget about college, I'll give you a forty percent partnership in the farm instead of paying you wages," Dad mumbled, his cheek fat with tobacco. "You're a pretty good worker."

"The same deal you gave Dale?" Bob's hands shook as he clutched the thermos. If he accepted the arrangement, would Dad treat him any better? Could the old man change his behavior at his age? This was Bob's future they were talking about, his life.

"Dale was such a talented boy," Dad said, rocking back and forth. "Once he took an old wagon, worked night and day to make a thousand-gallon tank out of it to water the cattle." Dad smiled with lips chapped and cracked by the sun. He stood up and walked to where the fence turned a corner, then back to where Bob sat. "I was too hard on him, cussed him and hollered at him for no reason. I never appreciated your brother, I was just a slave driver, a moron, a bully."

Jesus. He was suffering, that was clear. Bob felt bad for him. He guessed his dad would always feel guilty about Dale. But was this what he'd be signing up for? Always in Dale's shadow and under Dad's thumb?

A few nights later, Dad joined the family at dinner.

"Gotta head out tomorrow, back to college," Bob said, his shoulders tense. He sliced into a pork chop. "It's only six weeks until end of the semester. Can't miss final exams." He held his breath, waiting for Dad's response.

"It's important you finish," Mom said, addressing Bob but glaring at Dad.

"No, no," Dad said, his knife clattering to his plate. "Goddamn it, I can't do all the work by myself."

"How about a hired man?" Bob put his fork down. "You've had 'em before."

"That's a joke." Dad struck a match on the table and lit his cigar. "I can't find one worth shit. One guy we hired stole my car and checks from my checkbook and drove the car to Sioux Falls. Dale had to take the bus seventy miles to pick it up. Another asshole sat in the garage and smoked Pall Mall cigarettes. When the neighbor boy stole them, he quit. And there was a guy named Mohawk...."

"Okay, okay," Bob said, his shoulders sagging. "If you hired somebody reliable, you wouldn't have these problems. Dale said you pick up guys in bars or on the street. What do you expect? Try the Farm Bureau, talk to your neighbors. You have to pay decent to get someone good."

"You can't leave," Dad begged. "How about just until fall? By then, we should have things worked out, and I'll find somebody."

Couldn't Dad wait six weeks, until he finished this semester?

"Gotta get the ground ready to plant corn and beans. Dale

and I didn't finish adjustin' the cultivator shovels and the planter discs. Fences fallin' down everywhere. Barn needs cleanin' out."

The next day, Bob called the college and requested an incomplete in his classes. He said he'd definitely be back in September.

———

"Get dressed, goddamn it," Dad yelled, bursting into Bob's room. "Your mother said you didn't get home until after midnight. Livestock and crops don't take days off." He stomped out and slammed the door.

It was now well into May, and over the month he'd been home, Bob hadn't been able to stop getting plastered most weekends. It was worse than in high school or college. Maybe Dale had been right. He should be more sensible about drinking. But could he?

When Bob stood up, the room seemed to swirl around him. He leaned against his dresser. No quick movements, or the ball of pain in his head might thud against his skull.

Shuddering, he remembered last night's close call. On the way home from Red's Café in Hartley, Stan was driving his '54 Pontiac down Highway 18 at over a hundred miles an hour. He lost control on a left turn, and the car rolled. Verle cut his hand in the accident, but no one else was injured. A stranger had stopped and driven them back to Hartley to pick up Verle's car.

Bob sat back down on his bed and rubbed his forehead. What if he himself had been driving? They could've all been killed. A damn close call. His hands shook as he pulled on his jeans and denim shirt. Drinking and socializing with his friends helped him relax after days of hard physical labor. And coping with Dad. But drinking and driving? So dangerous and stupid.

Did he belong here? What made him want to stay? He tried to recall what he'd liked about this place the family had moved to when he was thirteen. What he still liked. The cool early mornings. Sitting on the tractor with mounted cultivator, lumbering down a row of corn, plowing out weeds—an ongoing battle but seeing the stalks higher at each pass-through—the reward of planting seeds. Resting his forehead against the warm, soft flank of a milk cow, hearing the streams of milk pinging against the sides of the metal bucket, the barn cozy from the warmth of the animals and the scent of alfalfa hay in the loft.

And what about Sandy and Danny? He couldn't fill the void left by Dale or form the bond he'd had with them, almost like a surrogate parent, especially with Danny. Dad had never taken much interest in their activities and only drove the kids somewhere when he needed help on a farm errand. And Bob hadn't the energy or desire to spend time taking them places like Dale had. Bob had liked playing gin rummy with them over the years; he'd even taught Danny the card game of cribbage. He'd learned quickly and won a couple games. Sandy always wanted to talk about the books both were reading: Were the characters believable, was the plot ridiculous, until Bob grew impatient. He just wanted to know how the story ended.

He had to trust that his younger siblings would be okay, because he had to get back to school. Spring semester would end in a few weeks, and he'd definitely be back to school in the fall.

Bob stood up, took a few minutes to feel steady on his feet, then crept downstairs. Danny sat at the kitchen table eating shredded wheat, his head of curly brown hair bent over a *Superman* comic book. Mom stood at the stove frying eggs, bacon, and sliced potatoes.

At the back door, Sandy held an egg basket, her forehead furrowed with concern. "Are you okay?" she asked as Mom poured him a cup of coffee. "You look kinda sick."

Bob didn't answer. He took his coffee into the bathroom off the porch and downed two aspirin from the medicine cabinet. Then he splashed water on his face and slicked back his straight brown hair. Bloodshot eyes stared at him from the mirror. Back in the kitchen, he refused the plate of eggs and bacon Mom offered. He drank two more cups of coffee, then slipped on Dale's rubber boots on the porch and headed to the barn.

What was on tap for today? Mucking out the cow barn. He didn't look forward to leaning over a pitchfork, inhaling the reek of manure and shoveling it in the manure spreader, later pulling it behind the tractor and scattering it on newly planted crops. Though a nasty chore, it did lead to healthy crop growth.

———

THE SUMMER MONTHS TICKED past. He helped Dad feed the cattle and repair more fences; after planting corn and soybeans in May, he cultivated weeds out of the crops with the tractor once every two weeks until July 4th and sprayed them once for weeds. He milked their four cows and replaced their straw bedding every few days; fed the hogs corn and oats twice a day, along with so many of the other chores life on a farm entailed.

Most weekend evenings, he'd go out with Stan and Verle to play pool or sit in Roscoe's Bar, in Lake Park, or at the Green Door in Milford, drinking and talking until the wee hours. Sometimes on Saturdays, he'd drop Sandy and Danny off at a cowboy movie in Lake Park or take Danny to Spirit Lake to look at model-airplane kits.

In mid-September, it was haying time, and Danny stayed home from school to help. The brothers walked out past the barn, the hogs in the adjoining outdoor pen squealing over the corn and kitchen scraps Dad had fed them. Dad hitched the flat-bed wagon behind the tractor, and Bob and Danny hopped on, their legs dangling from the bouncing wagon as they passed the barn, then moved along the dirt road past the elm grove where Bob used to play hide-and-seek with his friends. Shafts of light sliced through the trees, glinting on the gold and light-brown leaves dotting the trees.

He loved these late-summer mornings when the sun was just coming up, his favorite time of day. When he hadn't had a rough night, that is. He breathed in the musty aroma of black soil and looked at the shoulder-high corn plants standing like sentries. With corn thriving, hay bales soon to be stacked high, the cattle and hogs gaining weight, farming still looked good to him—the only thing he'd ever wanted to do.

Dad stopped the tractor near the hay baler, at the edge of the alfalfa field. He attached the baler to the tractor, hooked the wagon behind the baler, then pulled both into the nearest row. As they moved along each row, the baler scooped up long rows of dried greenish-yellow alfalfa hay, then spit solid blocks tied with two strands of twine onto the wagon, where Bob and Danny grabbed and stacked the rectangles of hay.

After three hours, the roar of the machinery reverberated in Bob's head. Dust clogged his throat and nostrils, the sun burned the back of his neck, and he struggled to keep his balance on the rolling hay wagon. With his denim sleeve, he wiped away the grit on his sweaty face as the bales piled up around him. Exhausted, his back aching, he knew that tonight he'd feel a satisfied tiredness, the sense of accomplishment that came from physical labor. It was a little like the good feeling he got at college after acing a calculus test. But did these experiences outweigh the conflicts with Dad? A dilemma. He needed to do some hard thinking.

Later today, he, Danny, and Dad would pack most of the bales in the barn's haymow. The rest they'd stack in a pile in the feedlot, where they'd cover it with canvas, leaving a few bales out for the cattle to nibble. But right now, he needed a break.

After dropping Dad and Danny off at the barn, Bob drove the tractor back to the machine shed. His 1954 Ford was parked in the shade of the oak grove near the workshop. He thought again about Dad having bought Dale a car, too, to get him to drop out of college. Dale had died in that car.

Bob trembled and braced himself against the Ford for support. College, then farming? Was that still his plan? He hadn't opened any of his textbooks all summer. The fall semester had started, and he hadn't registered for classes. Was it simple inertia; inability to make a serious decision? Or maybe, away for so many months, he'd lost interest?

He opened the car trunk and reached a grimy, callused hand in to open the cooler and grab a beer from under the melting ice. Leaning back against the fender, he flipped off the cap and took a long swallow.

"Jesus Christ," Dad yelled.

Bob jumped. Foaming beer gushed from the bottle.

"Drinkin' on the damn job." Dad pounded a fist on the fender. "I don't pay you to guzzle beer. At least Dale wasn't a drinker." The old man stomped off toward his car.

Asshole. That hypocrite put away plenty of alcohol. Maybe if Dale had been a drinker, he'd still be alive. Bob finished his beer and pitched the bottle among the oak trees behind the workshop. The hell with him, Bob thought. I kill myself working, and he still yells at me. Bob had been drinking less, not staying out past midnight on weekends, getting up early to get his work done. No wonder Dale didn't want to stick around.

Breathing hard, Bob stomped into the dimness of the workshop to cool off. To hell with the rest of the afternoon. To hell with Dad. He'd always be a slave driver. He hadn't even hired the extra help he'd promised if Bob stayed through the summer.

With its cement floor, the space felt almost cold after the baking heat outside. The smell of grease, dirt, and gasoline hung in the air. A single light bulb drooped from the ceiling.

Light from the door fell on the back wall, where four guns hung on hooks: a 30-30 rifle, a 22 rifle, a 12-gauge shotgun, and a pistol and holster belt. He caressed the shotgun's smooth, cool barrel, then moved to the 22. Best gun for pheasants. The last time he'd hunted them was in October, home for a long weekend to help harvest the corn. He'd taken a book with him to the cornfield to fill the time while he hunkered down and waited for birds to come feast on the spilled corn kernels. He'd been so absorbed in reading he hadn't shot a single bird.

There might be some pheasants in the pasture now. He hadn't practiced his draw in a while, so he slipped the pistol in its holster and buckled the belt around his waist. Then, clutching the gun, he widened his stance and bent his knees. He drew back the hammer and fingered the trigger.

The shot startled him. He fell backward onto the concrete floor, dropping the gun. He lay flat, his foot throbbing, then braced himself on his elbows and sat up. Blood oozed through a hole in his leather boot. He pushed down on the instep to hold back the pain. He staggered up, unbuckled the belt, and threw it in a corner.

God, what a moron he was. He knew guns. Why hadn't he checked to see if it was loaded? Shit, it hurt. He limped out of the shop, dragging his foot.

"What in hell happened?" Dad yelled, running to him from the barn. "I heard a shot. What'd you do?" Dad's white face shocked Bob.

Almost unable to speak, he finally stuttered, "I shot myself in the foot." Sweat poured down his temples. "It was an accident."

"Are you hurt bad? Let me look." Dad knelt down to inspect the wound, his hands trembling as he pulled off Bob's boot. "You idiot, you're damn lucky it's just your foot. The bullet could have ricocheted and killed you. Let's get you to the doctor."

He put his arm around Bob's shoulders and supported him as Bob hopped to the pickup truck on his uninjured foot. Dad opened the passenger door and helped him onto the seat. Then his dad gently lifted his wounded foot and placed it on the floor.

Dad sped down the driveway, onto the half-mile of gravel road to the blacktop highway leading to Lake Park. Bob squirmed in pain.

"Hang on," Dad said. "We'll get there pretty quick." Bob swallowed hard, amazed by his father's concern. Yet a cold fear knotted his stomach. Was the shooting some kind of sign? That was crazy thinking. But maybe he should give up his dream of farming. Was it time to get the hell out?

THE SECOND WEEK AFTER his accident, Bob assisted in farm tasks the best he could. Sitting on a stool in the workshop, he used the lathe to shape wooden slats to replace those broken on the corncrib and fences; organized their tools in the shop—they could never find anything after Dale died; helped Dad nail the storm windows on the house; read numerous library books; and played countless games of cribbage with Danny. Most of those projects were unfulfilling but passed the time until his foot healed.

A couple of weeks later, at the beginning of October, his dad dropped Bob off at Roscoe's. Inside, Bob hobbled on his crutches toward a wooden table. He nodded to Joe Erickson, who sat hunched over at the bar, a fixture here, he'd heard. The two had played basketball and baseball together in high school. Bob had heard that Joe was drunk most weekends but still managed to keep the family farm going. Bob was sure not going to end up like that guy. And one way to ensure that would be figuring out if he could keep working without conflict with his dad.

Bob laid his crutches under a chair and sat down while Stan brought over two beers. A few days after the accident, Verle and Stan had stopped by the farm on their way out for an evening of drinking. Bob had had no desire to join them. After the near-fatal car rollover, he was determined to cut back on alcohol.

"Bet your dad was mad when you shot yourself," Stan said as they sipped their drinks.

"Yeah, one less worker for a few weeks," Bob said over the clack of balls from the backroom pool tables. But as he studied the beer's foamy white peaks, he thought about how caring Dad had been when he shot himself. He'd never seen that kind of gentleness from him. Had he ever shown that softness with Dale? Bob shook his head, to get his mind back to the present. "But, good news. He found a part-time hired man, a good worker. The guy still does some work for the Groffs, across from the school. So Danny won't have to do so much."

"I'm thinking about going to California," Stan said out of the blue. He took a long drink of beer and stretched out his legs. "My brother just got out there and says there's jobs in the oil fields near Anaheim, about thirty miles south of Los Angeles. You should come with me. And guess what? Verle might, too. But a little later. His dad's thinking about selling their farm, and he wants his parents settled before he goes."

"Really?" Bob said. He licked foam from his upper lip. Should he pack it in? "Maybe I will, if you can wait. Need to think about it. Can't leave until my foot heals, anyway. Probably another two to three weeks."

"Sure. I can wait. Just want to head out before the snow falls. But what about college?"

"Maybe I'll finish in California, study something besides agriculture. Farming's all I ever wanted to do. But Dad can't get over Dale. He'll always compare me to him. I don't think we can get along over the long haul." Since Bob had declined Dad's offer to become "partners" in the farm, he'd saved most of his wages, enough to make a move. If he chose to.

"And your old man?" Stan said. "He'll disown you."

"Yeah, not sure how to tell him. It won't be pretty." He pondered: First the accident, then the unexpected offer from one

of his best friends. And Verle, too. But was he ready to aban-
don farming? He'd thought a lot since his accident, that maybe
his heart was no longer in agriculture. Probably not resuming
college to continue his studies and his conflicts with Dad had
both dampened his desire to farm. Almost six months since he'd
left school, and he hadn't once looked at his college textbooks
or *Farm Journal*, the magazine Dale had regularly consulted,
unread issues of which lay piled up on Mom's bookcase.

———

HE PACKED HIS DUFFEL bag, then looked around his room.
The ratty brown chenille bedspread. The photo of his sophomore
basketball team on the wall. His discolored baseball glove from
the high school summer league. On the bookshelf alongside his
dusty textbooks were the *Popular Mechanics* magazines Dale
had given him and two overdue library books. A pile of Danny's
Superman and *Batman* comics lay on the desk with several of his
model airplanes.

Danny won't miss me, he thought. Lots more space for his
stuff. He wondered if Dale's room would stay empty.

Down in the kitchen, Mom served up scrambled eggs and
ham slices. And cinnamon rolls, her specialty. Bob loved these
rolls. She seldom went to the trouble. Sandy and Danny were
already at the table, eating buns and drinking milk.

"Your dad's really angry," Mom said as she poured him a cup
of coffee.

Tough shit, Bob thought, scooping up a forkful of eggs. A
week ago, he'd finally worked up the courage to tell Dad he
was leaving. That Dad could sell Bob's car and keep the money,
allowing Bob to feel a tad less guilty about leaving. He could
buy a crappy car in California just to get by until he saved
some money.

"Goddamn you," Dad had said and stalked off to the barn.

"I hate that you're going," Sandy said in a quavering voice. "Be sure to write and tell me what you're reading."

"You guys'll be okay," Bob said, wanting to believe it. His brother and sister were doing all right in school, weren't they? Mom went to Sandy's basketball games and piano recitals and drove her to spend nights with her girlfriends. Danny had become a decent football player and baseball pitcher.

Bob wasn't sure he was doing the right thing, abandoning the only kind of work he knew. Leaving his dad on his own. But he hoped the oil fields would give him a fresh start.

"Some fried egg sandwiches for the trip," Mom said, handing him a paper sack. She slumped on her stool and turned away from him, her shoulders shaking.

"Thanks, Mom." He didn't know what else to say to her. A car horn honked, and he gulped the last of his coffee.

"That's Stan," Bob said. He tousled Danny's hair, then touched Sandy's shoulder. He looked at his mother, still turned away. Tough to leave, but….

He grabbed his duffel bag and opened the kitchen door.

"I'll call after I get to California," he called over his shoulder. If he looked back, he might change his mind.

He noticed the white fence looked weathered and the paint blistered. Dale would have repainted it right away. On this gray, early November day, the farm's outbuildings looked drab and worn. The barn could also use a paint job. Dim sunlight shone on the bare branches of the lilac bush. In summer, he loved the color and fragrance of lilacs. Did they grow them in California?

Near the henhouse, a few chickens poked at the ground. In the machine shed, the Farmall tractor sat idle. He suddenly recalled how, when he and Verle were kids, they argued over whose dad's tractor was best. Verle always defended his father's John Deere machine, and Bob argued that nothing could beat a Farmall.

Shaking his head, Bob tried to clear his mind. He'd made a decision and was heading into his future, whatever it was. Sad that Dad was losing another son, but maybe Danny would eventually take Bob's place. Poor kid, the youngest of the five boys, left on the farm. Would he fare any better under Dad's bossiness and hard-nosed attitudes than he and Dale had?

Waving to Stan, he opened the trunk of the car and threw in his bag. Climbing into the car, he grinned as Stan said, "Hi."

A new challenge in California. He was ready. He'd served four years in the U.S. Navy, studied in college for almost three years, toiled on his family's farm. He could handle whatever the future threw at him. Couldn't he?

God's Plan

N ORMAN GAZED AT DALE'S headstone in the Lake Park cemetery, a simple marble slab carved with Dale's date of birth, in September 1921, his death, in April 1956, and his four years of service in the U.S. Navy. Norman made the sign of the cross, silently begging his brother to forgive him for not returning to Iowa until three months after his death. Norman had been unable to leave his wife, Jean, who had just given birth to twins, and their three older children, all under the age of seven. But he was here now.

He grieved for his brother, but Dale had taken his own life, a grave sin, even if that person was not a member of the faith. Could Norman forgive Dale? Was it even his place to forgive him? It didn't seem right to judge his brother, even if his act was a terrible offense in the eyes of Norman's Catholic Church.

Long ago, his and Dale's lives had diverged. Like Norman, Dale had experienced the outside world, both in the Navy and at college, but then he'd heeded Dad's call to quit school and return home. After that, for whatever reason, Dale had been unable to leave again.

How was Norman able to flee the farm and make a new life when Dale hadn't? And now this: Dale's death by his own hand. As impossible as it was to understand, Norman had to believe that how Dale died and Norman managed to find his own way elsewhere had all been part of God's plan.

NORMAN'S FLIGHT FROM THE family farm began in 1941, when he was just fourteen, after his failed run to town with a wagonload of corn. With his older brothers off doing military service, the burden of helping Dad with farm work had fallen on him. His father had promised him money from the sale of some corn if he worked hard that summer. It was now early August, and Dad hadn't kept that promise. Norman was determined to make up for that.

So one afternoon, right after Dad had left to take two hogs to the butcher shop in Spencer—an hour round trip in the old pickup, and his dad would probably stop for a nip at the local bar—Norman got out the wooden wagon, with its foot-high sideboards and clunky wooden wheels. He planned to sell a load of corn and keep the money he deserved for all his years of slave labor. Tired of going to school in ragged and patched overalls, he would use the cash to buy blue jeans without holes in the knees and patches coming unsewn; a plaid shirt unfaded from numerous washings; and a pair of shoes to replace his single pair, dirty, worn, and lined with newspaper to make them last.

He backed the wagon up to the corncrib, a square wooden structure with a peaked roof, elevated on posts to keep the rats out, its walls of narrow slats fastened with wire and a couple inches apart so the air could keep moving and keep the corn dry and mold-free. It was half filled with last October's harvest. Wielding a one-gallon scoop, Norman shoveled the corn flowing from the crib's opened chute into the wagon, scooping furiously. Every few minutes, he stopped to catch his breath and look out for his dad.

When the wagon was half full, he backed up the old Ford, grabbed the wagon's wooden tongue, and hooked it to the car hitch. Too young to drive to town, he had convinced his mom to tow the wagon. She always tried to make life easier when she could, sympathetic that he'd taken on so much of his brothers' farm work now that Dale had joined the Navy and Vern the Air Force. Mom recognized his frustration when his dad forced him to miss school and never gave him any money.

Just recently, he'd studied hard for an algebra test that he'd told his dad was important. But Dad kept him home that day, saying Norman needed to help repair the crates in which the sows would soon give birth. Norman's teacher said he could take the test another day, but that didn't lessen his irritation.

Halfway to Lake Park's grain elevator, six miles away, the Ford died trying to tow the heavy wagon up a hill. Mom got it started again, but twice more, the car stalled. As they sat, slumped in their seats, a neighbor came by in his pickup truck. By the time Mr. Groff backed his truck up to their car, got the cables in place, and jumpstarted the engine, they'd run out of time.

"Let's go home, Mom," said Norman, his voice breaking. "I give up."

Not wanting to risk the car stalling again, he unhooked the wagon and left it by the side of the road. His small act of rebellion had gotten him nowhere.

As Mom reached the farm and pulled into the driveway, Norman held his breath. No pickup truck. Dad hadn't gotten back yet. Norman broke into a sweat, realizing his close call. As he drove the tractor back to fetch the wagon, he wondered if he should go on to Lake Park. But he was exhausted, ashamed of his failure, and wrestling with a smidgeon of guilt for trying to make off with some of the family's income. Even if Dad had promised it to him. By the time he reached the wagon, he had decided to tow the load back home. So what if his father caught him? He couldn't punish him by working him any harder than he already did.

Back in the farmyard and racing against time, Norman shoveled the corn back into the crib. From now on, he'd count the days until he could leave the farm like his brothers had.

The chores on the farm were endless: milking the cows at five a.m.; digging out manure from their stalls; feeding oats and hay to the cows, pigs, and cattle being fattened for market; lugging buckets of water to the animals from the pump. In the fall, they burned cornstalks from last year's crop, spread manure to fertilize the soil, and plowed it all under to prepare the soil for spring planting. He had to finish some of the work before heading off to school—that is, if his dad didn't keep him home. Nine-year-old Bob was too young to be of much use with heavier outdoor chores. And Norman's older sisters, Marguerite and Evelyn, did women's work: feeding the chickens, gathering eggs, and tending the garden with Mom. The two also helped care for their infant sister and sewed their own clothes.

But Norman's frustrations kept piling up. One sweltering afternoon, Dad was pitching forkfuls of hay from the wagon up into the hayloft, where Norman tugged it to the back of the loft with a pitchfork. After half an hour, his parched throat demanded water, but he had to keep up with Dad's pace. He rested every few minutes, leaning on his pitchfork.

Suddenly feeling dizzy, he clutched the fork to stay on his feet. The next thing he knew, Dad was pulling him out from deep in the hay. He was slapping Norman's cheeks and calling, "Wake up, wake up, are you all right?"

Norman took several seconds to focus, then saw his dad's face furrowed with concern.

"Yeah, I'm fine," he whispered. He tried to sit up, struggling to remember where he was. "Guess the heat got to me."

Dad pulled him to his feet. "Get some water," he ordered as Norman bent over, still dizzy and feeling nauseous. "Hurry up. We gotta get the rest of the hay in. It's supposed to rain tomorrow."

***

BUT THERE WERE TENDER moments, Norman remembered, staring at Dale's headstone. Like the time Dad taught him to swim in the narrow river that ran through their pasture. He probably wasn't even ten when Dad put him in the water face-down, placed one hand under his stomach to hold him up, and told him to paddle his hands and feet. Then he'd drop his hand slightly to see if Norman could stay afloat. He did that over and over until Norman learned to swim.

Had he ever felt sorry for his dad as he tried to keep the homestead going with little money? Probably not. He was just a kid focused on an education that would free him from back-breaking farm work for the rest of his life.

His escape from the farm had been part of God's plan, of course. Otherwise, why had his mother started attending the local Methodist church on Sunday mornings? Mom told him she liked singing gospel songs with the congregation and had happy childhood memories of her Presbyterian church in Richmond, Indiana. She said she'd been in a girls' group there, which mended donated clothing for the poor through the Red Cross, and sometimes performed in piano recitals.

On that first visit, he didn't think about whether or not he believed in God, or in religion at all. He just liked the peaceful hour away from early-morning chores. Filling the wooden benches were farmers in blue jeans or overalls, or an occasional suit, and women in flowered dresses. Behind the minister, preaching from a wooden pulpit on an upraised dais, hung a picture of Jesus in a flowing white robe, with shoulder-length brown wavy hair and a slight smile.

His siblings had no interest in attending church. But each week, upon entering the pew and touching its smooth, dark wood, Norman savored the quiet of the building and the rustle of hymnal pages before the congregation sang. His favorite psalms were "Blessed Assurance" and "Just a Closer Walk with Thee." He always closed his eyes and delighted in the mellow notes from the piano before the lifting up of voices.

He usually napped during sermons, especially those about

accepting Christ as your savior. No reason for that, in his view, nor for following the commandment to obey your parents. None of it helped him cope with life at home. His father was hard on him, and harder on his mother when he drank too much beer at dinner and yelled at her, Norman powerless to stop him.

After the sermon, while Mom sat in on adult bible study, he went to Sunday school in the church basement. Norman liked some of the bible stories, especially the one about the prodigal son. But that parable didn't apply to him. Dad would never give him an inheritance he might blow on wild living.

All the kids in Sunday school, Norman included, made a heroic effort to wear their cleanest and best clothes to church, patched as they might be. One boy, Henry, looked particularly cared for, with dirt-free overalls, ironed checkered shirts, scrubbed fingernails, and cropped hair. Norman was always begging his mom to cut his long, unruly curls, but she rarely got around to it. Sometimes he got one of his sisters to hack off a few.

Norman wasn't sure why he and Henry Johnson became friends. Probably because he was the only boy Henry's age. He lived on a nearby farm but attended school in Spirit Lake, a town twice the size of Lake Park. People said the high school there was much better than the all-ages school Norman and his siblings attended.

One day, Henry asked Norman what it was like at Norman's school. Which classes did he like?

"Math," Norman said. "I'm pretty good at math, so my class is really easy. Excelsior doesn't have anything above Algebra I. You're so lucky you go to school in Spirit Lake." He looked out the small window to a soybean field and a tractor moving down the rows. "Probably more math classes there, since it's so big."

"Yeah, there's geometry and calculus at Spirit Lake, too," Henry said.

Henry played baseball, too. Norman told his friend he wanted to do sports, but his chores after school and on weekends interfered with practices and games.

"I can't wait to get away from farming," Norman said, sighing. "I want to go to college like my brothers plan to, after they get out of the service."

"I'm not sure about college," Henry told him. He said he liked to ride the tractor and help his dad plow up weeds, harvest crops, and take care of their cattle and hogs. "Maybe I'll take over our farm when I'm older."

In mid-August, Henry invited Norman home for mid-day dinner. "We can drive you back," he promised.

"We're happy to have any friend of Henry's," Mrs. Johnson said, greeting him in a house bathed in delicious aromas of roasting meat and fresh bread. She wore a print housedress with a frilly white starched apron, her short brown hair neatly combed. Mom's appearance always seemed a bit disheveled. Mrs. Johnson put a gentle hand on his shoulder and guided him to the dining room table, laid out with four place settings—no chipped plates here. With no dining room, Norman's family ate in the kitchen.

Henry handed Norman serving plates with sliced pot roast, mashed potatoes, and sliced carrots that, at first delicious taste, he could tell had been cooked in butter. Norman had never had a meal like this. Seemed like Mom served the same food every day, mostly cooked in lard: fried eggs, pork chops, ground beef. Then he felt a jolt of guilt. Besides him, Mom had four kids at home, one a baby, and the household to run. And a vegetable garden to maintain.

"So, Henry says you're thinking about college," Mr. Johnson said. Dressed in clean striped overalls, he had a gentle, soft-spoken way of speaking. "Hope you consider coming back afterwards. Iowa can use smart farmers."

"Not sure what I want to do yet. Probably something using

math, since it's fun and easy for me, but I'd like harder classes. I'd probably like college."

As he passed food across the table, Norman glanced down at his much-mended overalls and patched-together shoes. He hoped the family wouldn't notice his dirty fingernails. Mom tried to manage a bath a week for each of her children. She spent hours feeding the stove with wood and coal, then heating enough water to fill the galvanized tub she dragged into the kitchen.

Since the Johnsons seemed interested, Norman described his two hours of early-morning chores and how he had to miss school when his dad needed help.

"You poor thing," Mrs. Johnson said. "Sounds like your father is pretty hard on you."

"Yeah, I guess he is. But I'm the oldest boy still at home, 'cause my brothers are in the service. And Dad says he can't afford a hired man."

Soon Norman was often joining the Johnsons for Sunday dinner. He could relax there, where the conversation was quieter, more respectful, each person speaking only when the other was finished. Lots of talk about what the boys were doing in school as well as what farm chores needed finishing.

Toward the end of September, the couple proposed he come to live with them.

"We've got an extra room. You could help us with chores," Mr. Johnson said. "After school and just for your keep. And you can go to school in Spirit Lake."

Norman's forkful of chuck roast hovered halfway to his mouth. Leave home? Impossible. Crazy, in fact. If your parents weren't beating you, what kind of kid leaves his family? Sure, Dad came home drunk sometimes and threw dishes at his mom. Norman worried he would hit her, but he never did.

Lots of kids got pushed hard. That was farm work. But if he

left, that would mean one less mouth to feed and less laundry for Mom.

Norman lowered his fork to his plate. "I don't think so," he mumbled, suddenly finding it difficult to breathe. "No, I couldn't. I'd be leaving my dad in a jam. He can't do all the work by himself." And his mother…he dreaded thinking about Mom's reaction, how sad she'd be.

But the idea of going to high school in Spirit Lake tantalized him. Harder classes and more subjects would help him get into college. No more exhausting five a.m. chores. A less-crowded household, amazing meals.

"Well, think about it," Mr. Johnson told him. "Come next week to talk about it."

The following Sunday, Norman accepted the Johnsons' offer, then agonized for days about how to tell his parents. A chance to go to a great high school was an opportunity too good to pass up. He could still go home to visit, once he made peace with Dad.

When Mom heard the news, her eyes widened in surprise. Dad might deserve his leaving, but Mom didn't. His sisters and younger brother sat stunned and silent. Maybe leaving his family farm wasn't the right move. He used to think he had a perfectly decent family. So why was he abandoning them?

"Damn you," Dad yelled at Norman. "Leaving me in the lurch to do all the work by myself." He pounded the table.

Norman gripped his chair with shaking hands. Despite feeling guilty, he refused to give in.

"If you leave, don't bother coming back," Dad shouted.

He moved in with the Johnsons in early October, not long after his fifteenth birthday.

Soon after Norman left home, Mom switched congregations. She told him that Bethel Non-Denominational Church, contrary to its name, had Southern Baptist leanings. The assembly's focus was less on a loving God and doing good, she said, and

more on each person's innate sinfulness and risk of eternal dam-
nation. Mom didn't necessarily support that emphasis, she said,
but she had a couple of friends there, and the worshippers, about
thirty strong, also sang gospel songs and had bible-study sessions.
It was about the same distance from the farm but in the opposite
direction. Norman guessed she'd made the change because she
didn't want to run into the family that "stole" her son.

"How's that pansy friend of yours?" Dad asked whenever
Norman hitchhiked home, every two weeks or so. "It's damn
strange he wants you to stay at his house." Norman didn't bother
reminding him that it was Henry's parents who'd asked him to
move in.

One Saturday afternoon when Henry drove Norman back
to the farm, Dad was just emerging from the barn, carrying two
pails of water.

"What're you doin' here?" he yelled at Henry. "Get off my
property."

"Sorry, sorry," Henry said, backing away. "I'm just dropping
Norman off. Mr. Rubel, you should be proud of him. He's doing
really well at Spirit Lake."

Dad set the buckets down, stomped over to Henry, and
punched him in the jaw. Henry stumbled backward and fell to
the ground.

"Dad, stop!"

Henry cradled his jaw as Norman helped him up. He put
him in his car and climbed in after him.

"I'm so sorry," Norman said later to Mrs. Johnson, gazing at
Henry's swollen jaw. "I'll get a place in town."

"No, you won't." She placed a hand on his shoulder. "Henry's
all right. His jaw's probably just bruised. We'll get him to the
doctor if need be. Anyway, you're not responsible for your dad's
behavior. You stay with us as long as you like."

That was the last time Norman went home. After that, he

called Mom and arranged to meet her and his siblings at a park or café in Spirit Lake.

Norman did well in Spirit Lake High's tougher courses. Within a couple months, teachers often asked him to teach the geometry and calculus classes.

However, at the end of March 1942, after six months in the Johnson household, he left their house. Norman had wearied of feeling indebted, even though he earned his room and board by helping with farm chores. The family never made him feel he was imposing, but he worried about eating too much and hated depending on others for rides to after-school activities or anywhere else. He wanted to be on his own, spending money he had earned. He found lodging and a job in Spirit Lake.

"You've been so good to me," he said to Mrs. Johnson, blinking back tears.

She hugged him tight. "I'm so sorry you're leaving. We'll miss you. But stay with us on weekends. We can always use extra hands around here. And you probably wouldn't mind a good home-cooked meal."

He moved into a room in the home of a nice old couple named Hill. Every evening, Mrs. Hill left a plate of dinner outside his door at no extra charge. And some weekends, Norman stayed with Henry's family.

Now, at the cemetery, he tried to remember how many jobs he'd worked in Spirit Lake to support himself until graduation: pumping gas at Donovan's Gas Station, washing dishes at the Busy Bee, the diner where his sister Marguerite worked after school, plucking chickens at the hatchery, stocking shelves in a grocery store.

Norman traced Dale's name in the chiseled marble slab, then paced among the gravestones. Fingering the crucifix around his neck, he thought about how his conversion to Catholicism involved forgiveness, the Sacrament of Penance. Norman had asked God to forgive him for abandoning his family, for leaving his dad to do all the work. He'd long ago forgiven Dad for being so hard on him. Norman had seen during this three-day visit how Dad was suffering over Dale's death, feeling such terrible guilt, even wondering aloud if he'd kept Dale trapped on the farm and treated him badly.

Bob, home from college for the summer, told Norman that Dad had done something surprising. He'd bought Sandy a new saddle for her horse, driving her all the way to Sioux City, a hundred miles each way, to find a nice one. While they were there, he bought Danny a bunch of model-airplane kits, with motors. All expensive.

"I didn't expect him to follow through. You know how Dad hates to spend money. And he promised Danny a car when he turns sixteen." Bob shook his head. "We'll see."

"Dad's usually so stingy," Danny added. "The school principal rolls his eyes when he sees us coming, with our lunch money in nickels and pennies."

Of course, most of his farming life, his dad had had to worry about money. Norman pondered his new attitude. Dad did seem to have become a more attentive father. Talked more softly, asked after Jean and the kids. This attempt with his two youngest children must be a way to atone for Dale's death, which—a wild guess here—might have helped him become aware of possibly neglecting Sandy and Danny. On some level, Norman thought, shuddering, Dad wanted to prevent them from doing what Dale had done. God help us, he thought, and crossed himself again.

OVER THE NEXT COUPLE of years, Norman moved further and further from his family, the farm, and Iowa. After he graduated from high school, in 1944, he joined the Army Air Force.

His mom had objected to his leaving—"Two of my sons are already in the service," she said, starting to cry—but he wanted to become a pilot, like Vern, who was training in Florida at Pensacola's Naval Air Station.

He called home every couple of months. Mom said Bob had started playing baseball. Evelyn and Marguerite had left the farm and were working in Omaha, Nebraska. Little Sandy and Danny were doing well. Dad sometimes asked about him, she said. By then, Norman realized how bad his timing had been in leaving home. Finding good workers then was hard, Mom told him, and money was scarce. To take Norman's place on the farm, his dad had hired a laborer who was 4-F.

Six months or so after he left Spirit Lake, Norman called home and Dad answered the phone.

"Hi, Dad, how's everything going?" Norman asked, panicked.

There were a few seconds of silence.

"Goin' okay," his dad said. "The hired man's not as good a worker as you, but he'll do. Where are you? Fightin' in the war?"

"I'm thinking about the Air Force, but not sure yet." Norman hesitated, then said, "I'm sorry, Dad, that I left you with so much work to do."

"Yeah, well, I guess I was a son-of-a-gun. Just get back here for a visit sometime."

Dad hung up, and Norman took several deep breaths. At least he and Dad were finally talking.

He stayed in touch with Henry. After being declared 4-F, as some farmers were, Henry wrote that he'd decided to forgo college and was farming with his dad. Norman was glad his friend was doing what he wanted to do and could work peacefully with his father.

The Air Force sent Norman to Coe College, a small liberal arts school in Cedar Rapids, Iowa. For one semester, he took general education courses, math, and physics. Basic training in

Texas came next, then cadet training for future pilots at Lowry Field, in Denver.

In 1945, at war's end, he dropped out of the cadet program and requested a discharge. Having decided against becoming a pilot—his heart wasn't in additional training—he enrolled in Iowa State College and majored in engineering. After two semesters, he decided to join his two sisters, now in San Francisco. He'd been accepted to the topnotch engineering program at the University of California at Berkeley, just across San Francisco Bay, to begin in fall 1946. Norman lived with Marguerite in her tiny apartment on Pine Street for a month, until he found his own place a few blocks away. Both his sisters were working as waitresses, and through Marguerite's union connections, Norman found work in Polo's restaurant, on Market Street. After a year, the union sent him to Valentino's, a nightclub in Vallejo, twenty miles north of Berkeley.

There he became friends with Jimmy Pearson, a waiter about fifteen years older, who introduced Norman to golf and pool. Perhaps suspecting that Norman missed his family, Jimmy invited him on his next visit to his brother's family, who lived in a small, uncluttered white-frame house on a quiet street in Vallejo. Mrs. Pearson's warm smile immediately made Norman feel welcome. In a white shirt and dress pants, Mr. Pearson was rather formal but friendly. He told Norman he had a white-collar job with the state government.

Before the evening meal, the family bowed in prayer, a new experience for Norman. As Mr. Pearson gave thanks, Norman closed his eyes, appreciating a quiet moment to reflect on his good fortune: attending an excellent university, working a good-paying job, his sisters living nearby, and in contact with the rest of his family.

Over several visits, Norman became smitten with the Pearsons' daughter, Jean, a high school junior. She had long dark hair that curled over her shoulders, fair skin, and intense blue eyes. Kind and thoughtful, she was at once curious about his military service and his farm life, experiences so unlike hers. He liked hearing her singing softly as she helped her mother prepare meals. Her lovely voice reminded him of the pleasure he'd felt humming along with the gospel songs at the Methodist church. He'd never sing aloud himself. As for a serious girlfriend? He'd never had time. Or maybe been too shy.

Eventually, Jean agreed to meet him for a walk. Soon, whenever Norman wasn't working or in class, he would walk her home from St. Vincent's Catholic School or from her part-time job as a salesgirl at the Broadway department store. He occasionally picked her up in his first car, a 1934 Plymouth coupe. Jean loved sitting in the fold-down rumble seat, in the rear above the trunk, while they talked.

Jean told him she liked school, particularly reading, grammar, and choral music, and was decent at math. She enjoyed the discussions they had in her religion classes.

"I went to a Methodist church for a while when I was young," Norman told her. "Didn't take it seriously. So far, I've been okay without religion."

Jean frowned at that statement.

"My faith helps me decide how I should live," she said. "I pray a lot about what God has in store for me. So right now I'm not sure about college. I'm thinking I'll probably just get a job after graduation."

Norman thought about how he hadn't needed God, since he'd largely relied on himself since he'd turned fifteen. But Jean did, and he'd try to understand that.

"Why did you choose engineering?" she asked him one day.

"Well, I'm good at math and geometry," Norman said, "which is what you need for civil engineering. I like the idea of using something I'm good at to design and create structures like buildings and bridges, and to figure out which materials to use. When I was a kid, I was always curious about the shapes and angles of our farm buildings. Like why silos are tall, narrow, and circular. And when you should use wood or metal."

Walking Jean, now a senior, home one sunlit April day, he observed how impossibly young she looked in her school uniform: white blouse, pleated blue-and-white-plaid skirt, and knee-high white socks. Though he would be only twenty in September, he felt like an old man next to her. He clasped her hand and squeezed it. They'd been talking about the future.

"You know, my parents aren't going to let us get married unless you convert to Catholicism," Jean told him, gently withdrawing her hand.

"I know," he said, taking her hand again. "I'm thinking about it, but conversion's a big deal."

He remembered how his country church had at first meant only a break from farm chores. And how quickly he'd been soothed by the hush upon entering the building, the rich tones of the piano before singing the hymns began. If all he had to do to win Jean was to go to church each week, he'd start next Sunday. But converting to Catholicism seemed much too momentous a step. He had to be sure, and he wasn't, yet. He was probably being unrealistic, but he had a foolish hope that all would work out. He was certain Jean cared for him, by how she smiled and hurried toward him before each meeting.

"Well, you'd better decide," Jean said, intruding on his thoughts. "I'm trying to figure out what I'll do after graduation, just a couple months away. Whether to get a job, or...." Her voice trailed away. "Or join a convent."

"What?" Norman yelped. He stopped and stared at her. "A convent? That's a pretty radical decision." He suddenly realized how arrogant he'd been, thinking he could ignore the importance of Jean's faith to her, naively hoping their relationship would continue without any action on his part.

"I'm still thinking about it. I've told you how important my faith is. I'm praying for God's guidance, talking to my parents and my religion teacher. I'm just eighteen and need to discover what God wants for me. But you need to make a decision, too."

Norman was speechless. He couldn't imagine a life without Jean.

After graduation, Jean prepared to enter the Dominican convent in San Rafael, about forty miles from Vallejo.

"After a lot of prayer, I feel it's what God is calling me to do," she told Norman on one of their last dates. "This'll give me a chance to make sure. I wouldn't take vows to join the convent permanently for at least a year."

"And your parents?" Norman asked, his body trembling. Was this the end?

"They see it as a blessing for me to become a nun." She looked at him. "I have lots of time to seek God's will, to figure out my future. And, as much as I care about you, I'm not ready to commit myself."

He considered what her devout parents must think of him. They knew little of his background, only that he'd grown up on a farm with no indoor plumbing and had many siblings. He knew they saw Jimmy as a womanizer who used bad language and talked about his sexual encounters. Being the man's friend didn't recommend Norman as a potential son-in-law, nor did working with him in a "shady" nightclub, with boozy patrons that Jean's parents probably didn't consider the best kind of people. The only thing Norman had going for him as a suitor was the prestigious university he attended. And the expectation of a solid future as a civil engineer, he hoped, when he graduated. But Jean wouldn't be in his future if he didn't convert.

He agonized over the next few days. Jean had to decide her future for herself, he realized. He would not pressure her, even at the risk of losing her. And wouldn't it be pressure if he suddenly decided to convert? He'd managed his life pretty well up to now, without any help from God. But he'd support Jean in whatever she decided. He swallowed hard. And live with that decision.

<hr>

AFTER JEAN LEFT, NORMAN took on more hours at the club, and in the fall, he signed up for an additional class. He saw his sisters every couple of weeks. Both were still working as waitresses, and his younger sister was also taking classes toward her high school diploma. Though not the exuberant, ambitious person Marguerite was, Evelyn seemed quietly determined to make her own way. Norman had met her boyfriend, Joe, several times and liked him very much.

One day, Marguerite telephoned Norman and asked him to come by the restaurant. She looked elegant in her light-blue uniform and white apron, a small cap on her shoulder-length hair. He knew that a couple evenings a week, she modeled women's coats and dresses for clothing manufacturers hoping to sell their designs to local department stores. She'd once shown Norman a smiling photo of herself in a leopard-skin coat and hat. But today, her pretty face lacked the usual bright-red lipstick and was creased in a frown.

Moving among the tables arranging silverware and napkins, Marguerite wouldn't meet his eyes.

"Norman," she said abruptly, "you have to pray for me."

"What?" Of all the people he knew, Marguerite would be the last one to request a prayer. He summoned the courage to respond. "What's wrong?" he asked, fearing her answer.

"I'm in big trouble," she said, facing him. "Can't say why, just need you to light a candle and pray for me. You went to church when we were kids. You can help me."

As she put down a tray of glasses, Marguerite's hands shook.

"Can't tell you why," she repeated, "but my boyfriend says that praying and lighting a candle works for him. Pray, okay? You promise?"

She wouldn't say any more. What kind of trouble was she in? All Norman knew was that his sister was going out with a guy in the Teamsters union. Was he abusive? Was she pregnant? Was it a health issue? Money troubles? Having sewn her own clothes for years, she'd described to Norman her plan to set up a factory in which she'd manufacture her own designs. She was saving money to pursue that dream. Had her ambition met some headwinds?

When he got no more information, he left, still shaky. What could he offer that was more realistic and practical than prayer? He had no answer for that. He owed his sister. She had smoothed the way for his life in the Bay Area, letting him live at her apartment and helping him find work. So he had to find a church, a Catholic church. There was no excuse for not finding one, since there were plenty around Vallejo.

St. Basil's was near Valentino's. As Norman walked through the vestibule into the sanctuary, one evening before work, his mouth dropped open. The soaring wooden arches drew his eyes to the vaulted ceiling, then on to the enormous stained-glass windows depicting bible stories he'd read and heard in Sunday school. What a contrast with the small and confined, cozy country church of his childhood.

His eyes wide, he walked slowly down the gleaming wooden aisle between endless rows of cushioned wooden benches. Behind the altar stood a carved wooden figure, Jesus Christ on the cross, body twisted and face contorted in agony. Another contrast with the church of his youth. Its framed image of Jesus, with flowing white robe and gentle smile, had formed his conception of Christ.

Norman recognized the communion rail and knew what

he should do from a few movies he'd seen. But how could an action he'd never performed not feel phony and contrived? He'd try to make it sincere. He knelt down, bowed his head, put his palms together, and closed his eyes, some of the motions he'd performed during obligatory prayers in his childhood church.

"Dear God," he prayed earnestly. "Please help my sister Marguerite with whatever trouble she's in. Please, God."

Within a few seconds, he felt a sudden lightness of heart. A tremendous sense of joy and peace settled over him—an enormous trust in something he couldn't define, a oneness with something outside himself. Though he couldn't understand what it was, the feeling was like a gentle touch on his head. It was as if his heart would expand with love and kindness. He even had a surprising impulse to show compassion and give comfort to others.

In a daze, he stumbled out of St. Basil's. Had he really experienced the presence of God? He'd definitely sensed a connection to something, along with an overwhelming serenity.

He called his sister a couple of days later, not knowing what to expect. Marguerite was so cheerful, it was clear she was beyond her "big trouble." Could it be because of Norman's prayer? He would never know. All he knew was that he felt an urgent desire to become a Catholic—the most important decision of his life, he realized later.

He met with other students at Newman Hall, on the Berkeley campus, to learn about Catholicism, engage in prayer, and participate in community activities. Soon he began making monthly visits to convalescent homes to read and discuss the bible with residents. In later years, he would visit county jails and prisons to spread the word of Christ.

At St. Basil's, having already begun six weeks of instruction, he made a sacramental confession, received conditional baptism, and took Holy Communion at his first mass. From then on, he attended mass and received communion every day.

With all this added to his job, classes, and homework, the months sped by. Almost before he knew it, Jean returned from the convent—he didn't know for how long—and the two met in her parents' living room to talk.

"Before I came home," she told Norman, "I talked a long time with my spiritual advisor at the convent about what God wanted for me. The last two weeks, I secluded myself on a private retreat, in prayer, and…."

Norman's heart was pounding so hard, he was sure she could hear it.

"I decided it wasn't God's will that I become a nun. I can do more in this world if I raise a Catholic family. I want to be a wife and mother."

Norman didn't tell her how desperately he'd prayed she would reach this decision. "I have a lot to tell you," he said.

The two resumed dating, and Jean's parents approved, due to Norman's conversion and his religious work in the community. The couple planned to marry in two years, wanting to save as much money as they could before starting a family. Jean worked as a ticket clerk at the Vallejo Greyhound Bus depot. Later, she joined Norman at Valentino's, earning good tips as a hat-check girl.

In 1949, Norman and Jean married at St. Basil's. Uncle Jimmy was Norman's best man. Marguerite and Evelyn were there, and his mother, who had traveled by train to attend his wedding, leaving his youngest siblings in the care of Dale and seventeen-year-old Bob. Three years later, Norman graduated from UC Berkeley with a degree in engineering. The following month, he started a civil engineering job at a firm in San Leandro, just fifteen miles south of Berkeley.

That day at St. Basil's, he was certain, he'd been in the presence of God. Now he knelt and touched Dale's headstone again, then stood up and looked out over the cemetery, at the differing sizes of headstone, the cornfield beyond. It was July, and the corn was knee high.

He thought about the rest of his family. Mom was so quiet. Maybe she grieved silently. Was something weighing on her? He prayed that her faith, however deep it was, was comforting her. Before he left, he had to help her understand that Dale's death wasn't her fault. Or Dad's, though his dad might never be able to accept that.

But Norman worried about Bob. He made his brother promise he'd return to college. "Whatever you do—stay here or not—you need to finish. It's good you're helping Dad, but you need to get on with your own life."

"I'll finish," Bob said. "I'm just trying to get him settled before I head back in September. Find a decent hired man." He looked away. "Funny, Dale was always nagging me about studying. He would have wanted me to finish, too."

And Danny: Judging by what Dale had taught him, Danny might well grow into a competent man. And a thoughtful brother: He'd shown Norman the saddle rack he was secretly building for Sandy in the workshop. Together, they looked at the V-shaped, sawhorse-like contraption, four legs angling out from the top board.

"See where I welded the metal strips together?" Danny said, grinning. "Dale always made sure I used the welding mask." He had also taught Danny how to use the lathe and to operate a tractor. "And I helped Dale build the corncrib. I'm pretty handy with a hammer."

Dale had taught countless productive skills to all his younger brothers, Norman realized, putting his arm around Danny, for no other reason than being a caring older brother.

As for himself? Norman trusted he was following God's plan through his marriage and creating five new lives for the Church.

Norman took a last look at Dale's headstone. Was he mourning more out of love for his brother or concern for Dale's soul? He paced back and forth on the grassy area between graves. God's plan didn't always lead to good outcomes, or what people considered "good." Norman couldn't claim to understand why Dale had felt trapped and why he himself had had the strength to leave. But he had to believe that both his and his brother's lives had served God's purpose.

Let the guy rest in peace, for God's sake, he told himself, then smiled at his choice of words.

Idolatry

FINALLY! I WAS ON my way to California.

At seventeen and a half, both excited and nervous, I was following the well-worn path taken by my four older brothers and sisters. At the train station in Spencer, twenty miles from our farm, Mom didn't cry, but she blew her nose often. I was her third and last daughter to leave home. When we said goodbye, she hugged me for the first time I could recall. I tried to push away any remorse at abandoning her.

Only Danny, just turned sixteen, still lived at home, the last of the eight of us. Now, on the *City of San Francisco* and my first long-distance train ride, I thought about Danny. He and I had shared a room until I was twelve. Mom and I had been particularly close ever since my dad moved out and I got my own bedroom. More recently, when I went out at night, I'd sit on her bed when I got home, sharing details about my basketball game or how a date went, without mentioning necking or swatting away wandering hands.

But Danny hadn't been close to anyone in our family since Dale died. He and Bob had worked alongside one another doing farm work until Bob left, but they'd never developed the camaraderie he'd had with Dale, who was practically a second father to him. When Mom asked Danny about his football or basketball games or if he'd completed a chore, he gave her one-word answers.

I looked out at the corn stubble poking through the late-January snow as we passed from Iowa into Nebraska. In the distance, farm machinery sat lightly coated with snow near weathered outbuildings; a few cattle ambled in a fenced enclosure. Looking at them, I thought about Dale, as I'd done so often in the two and a half years since his death. He and Bob had been my only siblings who'd hoped to make a life in farming.

Now Danny was the only one left to help Dad.

I pondered my move away from home, family, and friends to move two thousand miles away. But my older brothers and sisters, who'd made the same trek, had thrived.

Bob was working in the Southern California oilfields. In Northern California, my sister Marguerite had a small factory that made coats that she designed. Evelyn was married and employed as a bookkeeper. Norman, married with several children, had an engineering job. Vern, now my oldest brother, lived in Hickory, North Carolina, and sold bookkeeping systems. He was married with three children.

In fact, in the summer before my senior year, Vern and his wife invited me to visit them. I took the Greyhound bus to Hickory, about an hour south of Charlotte. Over those two weeks, Vern and I took long walks and drives, talking for many hours about why Dale had taken his life.

Vern found it difficult to understand how Dale had become a totally different person in the months before his death. His erratic moods had often made him disagreeable and cranky, not his usual good-natured self. He couldn't sleep at night and lay on the couch for hours instead of doing his farm work.

Vern clung to the weird notion that any peculiarities in Dale's behavior stemmed from a fall on his head as a baby. I'd never heard that theory and was skeptical about any effects surfacing decades later. Nevertheless, though only sixteen, I understood that Vern needed to talk out his feelings with a family member. He and Dale were born twenty months apart and had done so much together, including attending college, although Dad got Dale to drop out before he finished. Vern had been to the farm a couple of times since our brother's death, but he and I had not talked then, and I couldn't imagine that Dad, so focused on his own suffering, had been able to talk with his second-oldest son in any depth.

These long conversations with Vern were good for me, too, because at home, none of us had talked about Dale's death at any length. Instead of comforting one another, we tended to stay enveloped in our own pain. Our family had never been much on discussing anything personal. Within a few days of Dale's death, we seldom spoke about him at all.

So Danny hadn't had an experience similar to mine. He'd been on his own. Even I had kind of tuned him out. We were both in our own teenage worlds and went our separate ways. Now I realized how devastating Dale's death must have been for him. I felt more guilt about leaving him than leaving Mom. Would he be okay?

I tried to focus on the adventure ahead. Having no particular plan, I just hoped to absorb some of the magic of Marguerite's achievement as a fashion designer and coat manufacturer.

However, getting to the seat on this train had not been a straight line.

No one at home or at school had ever discussed college with me. Though all four of my older brothers had gone on to higher education, Mom hadn't encouraged me. Even when Mr. Napier, my history teacher, told me I could have done well at Spencer High, three times larger than our school, I didn't consider more education, maybe in part because only two students from our ten-person senior class went on to junior college. Since I typed a hundred words a minute and took shorthand dictation at a hundred and twenty words per minute, I was surely meant to become a secretary.

So, after graduation, in the fall of 1958, I followed my best friend to a commercial school in Des Moines to enhance my secretarial skills. After four tedious months of more shorthand and typing classes, beginning bookkeeping, and "office etiquette,"

I quit. Still confused about a career direction, I was sure I'd discover in California what I was meant to achieve.

My sisters were the first to reach the San Francisco Bay Area. Evelyn was only fifteen when she left home with Marguerite, who was eighteen. It took Evelyn years to get her high school diploma once the two got to San Francisco. But I'd idolized Marguerite, seventeen years my senior, for her flamboyance, glamour, and more visible success.

On my occasional visits to California with Mom, I'd hear Marguerite captivate friends with her funny stories about growing up on a farm, where she was always raising an orphan pig. True or not, she and Evelyn really had sewn dresses and skirts from animal-feed sacks. Marguerite always said her ideas for design came from that early experience and led to starting her business.

I'd seen her behave unkindly to people, even Mom, but I knew she wouldn't treat me that way. She and I would surely become best friends. With her help, I'd find out what I was meant to do.

———

EVELYN AND HER HUSBAND, Joe, met me at the train station. They'd invited me to live with them in Millbrae, a suburb about sixteen miles south of San Francisco. The two made me feel at home. Their snug guest room included a thick duvet on the double bed, an upholstered velveteen chair in the corner, and a tall walnut dresser with many drawers—all a world away from the cheap painted furniture of my girlhood bedroom. Evelyn prepared dishes like lasagna, veal scaloppine, and osso buco, delicious food foreign in every way from Mom's meals of fried meat and potatoes. They even drank wine with dinner. Evelyn said they hoped to adopt a child.

As loving and supportive as Evelyn was, she could be tough. I was late once with my monthly "rent" of forty dollars, and she reminded me that I had to honor financial obligations. She'd worked hard to get where she was, and I could, too. ("Don't be so tough on her," Joe said in the background. "She's just a kid.") Humiliated by her reprimand, I agreed she was right and said I wouldn't be late again.

I soon found full-time secretarial work at a wholesale-furniture business just two long blocks from the more elegant and busier Market Street. Most mornings, a couple of rough-looking winos loitered outside a liquor store I walked by. The job was conveniently located just three blocks from Marguerite Rubel Manufacturing, a ten-thousand-square-foot space in a building at Third and Howard streets, in an industrial neighborhood of unlovely windowless warehouses. I felt lucky to be so close to my sister's factory, so I could visit her on my lunch hour or after work.

Most weekends, my world expanded from the humdrum comfort of Evelyn's house when I took the bus to Marguerite's factory or pretty little apartment. I envied my sister's fashion flair. Department store buyers and other customers often commented on how elegant she looked, in her sleek black dresses, broad-brimmed hats, and smart high heels, her thick brown hair curling over her shoulders.

One of the first things she did was improve my "style." With her brusque but expert advice, I went from a bashful "hick" farm girl, wearing plain cotton blouses and floral skirts Mom had sewn for me, to an up-to-date, urban young woman, in patterned long-sleeve blouses and knee-length A-line skirts or dresses in green, pink, or purple. I had never worn a dress in high school. One day, a coat buyer admired my turquoise stretch pants and asked if my sister chose my clothes.

Marguerite said I was a perfect size twelve—a sample size in coat manufacturing—and tall enough to make a garment look good. Flattered that Marguerite asked me, I modeled her coats when she marketed them to high-end stores or at cloth-ing-manufacturers' shows in luxury hotels like San Francisco's famed Palace. With my twenty-four-inch waist, I felt partic-ularly confident in belted coats. Normally disliking anyone's undivided attention, I relished hearing people tell me how great I looked in my sister's emerald-green, double-breasted belted raincoat or wearing her dark-pink swing coat. I floated in the orbit of my sister's personality and good looks that drew people to her.

I felt Marguerite and I had become close. My dream was fulfilled. Sometimes she even took me with her on marketing trips to Los Angeles and San Diego in her beige 1959 Cadillac. She convinced upscale department stores around California and eventually throughout the U.S. to stock her garments.

When she took me to restaurants and bought me clothes, she made me feel special and grown-up. As Marguerite continued to show me off as her "presentable" younger sister, I grew more sophisticated, yet I continued to crave her approval.

But Marguerite had a gift for wounding with her words. "Can't you hold a knife and fork in a civilized way?" she scolded on one of our weekends.

We were eating lunch with her friend Ellen at the Old Poodle Dog, an old-time French restaurant near Union Square. I was excited to eat Crab Louis for the first time. After I took a couple bites, my sister grabbed my hands and repositioned the utensils.

"And this is how you eat bread," she said impatiently, breaking up a sourdough roll, placing half on my bread plate, then butter-ing the other half. At home on the farm, Mom had only nagged me to keep my elbows off the table.

Ellen put her arm around me and said, "You're doing great, sweetie. Your sister's too hard on you." I tried not to cry. That would make me seem weak, when Marguerite always appeared strong. Thanks to Ellen's kindness, I got through the meal.

Another weekend, at Marguerite's apartment, I did her laundry. I tried to fold the towels correctly, another skill Mom hadn't taught me.

"Get it right or don't even bother," Marguerite yelled, and she refolded the towels.

I tried to let her disapproval wash over me and not allow myself to be hurt by it. In spite of her criticism, I remained enthralled by Marguerite and her world. Keeping my head down, I made a sort of peace with her.

———

IN THE FALL OF 1961, almost nineteen, I enrolled in San Jose State College, an hour south of San Francisco. I was bored with full-time secretarial work. It was time to get a serious education. In high school, I'd gotten my best grades in literature and grammar. In English classes, the rules for constructing sentences fascinated me, but we did very little writing other than short essays. San Jose State had a good English department and offered excellent teacher preparation. Perhaps I'd teach one day.

I majored in English literature and minored in German. Dad's parents had come from Germany; Dad told us that he'd spoken only German until entering first grade. I'd been captivated by simple phrases he'd used in my childhood, such as *du bist schmutzig*, you're dirty; *mach schnell*, hurry up; and *das kleines Mädchen*, the little girl. I would have taken a foreign-language class in high school if my school had offered any.

I moved into a residence hall off campus and found a part-time job with a criminology professor. Some weekends, I took the hour-long bus ride to San Francisco to help Marguerite at her factory and stay at her apartment.

Her criticism continued. "Stand up straight, you're slouching." "You're late." "Come on, get those boxes packed. The post office closes in an hour." I told myself I was too sensitive.

One day, out of the blue, without consulting me, Marguerite said she had arranged for me to play the accordion at a reception for the mayor of San Francisco, whose sister was a friend of hers. I'd made the mistake of telling Marguerite that I'd played the accordion in middle school.

"I can't play anymore," I told her. My hands shook as I swept the factory floor. "It's been five years, and I forget how accordion fingering works. Besides, I'd be scared to death." I looked at her nervously. Would she kick me out of her life if I refused?

"Stop thinking only about yourself," Marguerite said calmly, holding up her compact mirror to freshen her bright-red lipstick. "This party is to honor the mayor."

My sister was so good at making me feel guilty and self-absorbed if I didn't do what she wanted. Not knowing how to say no, I let her push me into it. Renting an instrument at college, I fit practice around classes, homework, and my job for a month.

Katya, the mayor's sister, accompanied me as I lugged the accordion in its case up the steps of City Hall and into the majestic rotunda. Walking among the grand marble columns, I felt small and even more ridiculous in the Swiss-yodeler outfit Marguerite had sewn for me. I'd surely forget the tunes I'd memorized or slip on the marble floor in my new high-heeled boots.

When it was time to perform, I could feel sweat trickling down my chest under my puffy-sleeved blouse. As I strolled among the wine-sipping guests, my right-hand fingers splayed over the white keys while those on the left punched the black buttons. I played "Lady of Spain," "Stormy Weather," and a few polkas. Feeling like an overgrown Heidi, I kept my eyes downturned the whole time.

At the reception, "Hey, you play pretty well," I heard someone say. A cute man in his early twenties was standing nearby with a friend. "Where'd you learn?"

"I was in a middle-school accordion band in Iowa," I mumbled, eyes fixed on the floor. "We performed at county fairs and on the radio. But I haven't really played since then."

"Couldn't tell," the man said. "You sound great."

"Cute outfit," said a woman in a business suit, touching my yellow ruffled skirt.

"My sister made it." The pride in my voice astonished me. Why wasn't I furious at Marguerite for putting me in this terrifying situation?

Then Katya came over and hugged me. "You were wonderful," she whispered.

Though I hated being the center of attention, I was flattered by the praise. Even Marguerite said I'd done well. She had bullied me into performing to make herself look good, and I had let her. But my preparation had paid off. Perhaps facing up to this kind of challenge would help me thrive in the future.

―――――

IN THE SPRING OF 1962, my brother Dan began attending San Jose City College. He hadn't told me he was leaving home.

"Dad's mad I left," Dan said. "But he's over seventy, so he'll probably sell off in the next few years. Now we're all out here except Vern."

We were eating a cheap dinner at the Spaghetti Shack, a few blocks from my apartment. Dan lived with two roommates in an off-campus apartment and was taking general-education courses.

"I don't know what I want to study." He sounded exasperated. "I liked math, though never got above a B in it. But I got As in English. And an A in Latin at Lake Park." Before his senior year, our consolidated country school of grades one through twelve had closed. Dan's class graduated from Lake Park High, where classes were twice as large. "And I was prom king." He blushed.

"Wow," I said. "Brand-new to the school, and you were a hit." He'd gotten good-looking when I hadn't noticed, even with his smashed-looking nose. He'd broken it twice playing high school football but hadn't wanted to go through the pain of getting it cracked again and reset.

"Nobody at home or school talked to me about college," he said. "Isn't that weird?"

"Me, either," I said, "and it took a while to figure out that's what I wanted."

"Norman said I should think about engineering," Dan told me, "that I could master math if I worked hard at it." Norman worked as a civil engineer in San Leandro, thirty miles away, where he lived with his family. I visited them and Evelyn and Joe every few weeks.

"How was Mom?" I asked, changing the subject.

"She's okay, I guess. We never talked much. Not like you and she did. I think she's lonesome, but she sees her friends, and they do things together. I'm not sure what."

As he sat across the table from me, I stared at the bottle of beer he rotated in his hands.

"I won't drink as much as Dad, I promise. Or Bob. I just have a couple beers a week." Avoiding my eyes, he looked out the window at the busy street.

In November, Marguerite married Lowell Kuckenbecker, a wealthy, good-looking widower and farm-machinery dealer in Fresno, three hours from San Francisco. Marguerite had become friends with an assistant buyer of women's clothing for a large department store there, and she introduced them. After high school, Lowell had worked for a farm-machinery dealer until he started his own business, then eventually opened a second dealership twenty-five miles away in the small city of Madera. He was forty-five, eight years older than Marguerite, but he seemed awed by her and her business success in San Francisco.

When Marguerite was with Lowell in Fresno, Dan and I often visited them. He was friendly and generous to us. Lowell loved to cook and treated us to home-cooked meals in his two-bedroom apartment, with its white-shag carpeting, silk-covered couches, and granite kitchen counters. He liked reading history and had several books about World Wars I and II on his bookshelf.

He also liked the grand gesture. Once, I mentioned in passing how much I liked raisins. A week later, a truck pulled up in front of my apartment building and unloaded six cartons. After their marriage, they kept their separate residences in Fresno and San Francisco for a few years, joining each other on alternate weekends, and he bought Marguerite a Lincoln Continental, a twin to his own.

They got married at City Hall in the chambers of a judge, a friend of my sister's. Dan and I stood up for them. Marguerite wore a knee-length white-silk dress, the collar and long sleeves fitted with lace and sewn with pearls. Lowell had on a dark suit, white shirt, and striped tie. Dan and I had scrambled to find suitable clothes. I borrowed a maroon polyester dress from one of my roommates, and Dan wore dark-gray suit pants, a white shirt with a frayed collar, and a navy-blue sport jacket, all from a used-clothing store.

"Doesn't Lowell look handsome, kids?" Marguerite gushed before the ceremony. She couldn't stop smiling. Lowell shook his head as if thinking what silliness this was but wore an embarrassed grin.

"He's marrying glamour and San Francisco, and she's marrying money," Dan said as we left the judge's chambers. "Life in Fresno can't be that exciting."

"Yeah," I agreed. "She used to say she had to choose between paying rent on her apartment or buying fabric." I laughed. "Now she can do both."

———————

About two years later, just before my twenty-third birthday, my stepmother, Ella, called to tell me that my mother had died. "Sweetie, I'm so sorry," she said.

By now, most of the cattle and pigs had been sold, and Dad had rented out much of the pasture and crop land. But there were still milk cows and chickens, and Dad still drove out from Spirit Lake almost every morning to work several hours on the farm. That morning, as usual, Dad came in to have coffee with Mom and found her dead in her bed.

"A heart attack, your dad thinks," Ella said.

I started to cry, realizing I wasn't ready for my mother to be dead at sixty-four. And she'd died alone. I hadn't been considerate enough to her, hadn't asked her enough questions about her life, hadn't visited her often enough.

She had traveled to California a year earlier and met my roommates. I squirmed, thinking how embarrassed I'd felt that my mom was overweight and her hair completely gray. In school, I'd always been self-conscious about Mom being almost twenty years older than my classmates' mothers, even though Mom had supported me all through school, attended my basketball games and music recitals, and so often drove me to friends' houses and shopping. What a terrible daughter I'd been.

Taking incompletes in my classes, I took a Greyhound bus home. I couldn't remember the last time all seven of us children had been there at the same time. Marguerite seemed unusually subdued. The state of the kitchen floor, the green linoleum worn and faded and dirt ground into the corners, made me sad. But a shiny new green-and-yellow-checked oilcloth, still smelling of plastic, brightened the room a bit. We'd eaten so many meals around that table. The ubiquitous coffee pot sat on the Formica counter.

In the living room, with its saggy sectional couch, a couple corners on Mom's wooden record player were chipped and a hinge was loose, so the top no longer fit properly. But she'd increased her vinyl-record collection since I'd been there last. The bookshelf sagged even more with all the books she'd ordered from the Book of the Month Club.

It helped to keep busy. Evelyn and I selected a casket at the funeral home, and I found a light-blue polyester dress embroidered with tiny yellow daisies, one of the few dresses hanging in her closet, for her to wear. A day later, I held back tears as I looked at her for the last time in that casket, though with her artificially made-up face, with excessive powder and rouge, it didn't really look like her.

At the gravesite, we held no formal ceremony; only family members and a number of her women friends gathered there. I held it together until, with the thudding of the dirt shoveled onto her casket as she was lowered into the grave, I felt the finality of her death. My heart broke. Losing my composure, I ran, sobbing, to the car.

That afternoon, all of us wandered through the house and chose items to help us remember Mom. Evelyn and Marguerite argued briefly over her portable sewing machine, but Evelyn gave in, saying she was happy enough with her own machine. I was surprised to see Marguerite so uncharacteristically grateful.

Bob, Dan, and I took some of her books. I grabbed a lovely black, red, and green afghan she'd crocheted; and Vern, long on a health kick, took a pile of *Prevention* magazines, published by J. I. Rodale, an early-fifties pioneer in promoting organic farming and healthy eating. In her final years, Mom had tried to eat more healthfully and took long walks. But genetics probably caught up with her. She'd told me years ago that her father had died of a stroke at age forty-six.

I took several of her classical records, too, while Norman chose those of Enrico Caruso, the famed opera singer. Norman took our family bible as well, with its soft black cover and red-ribbon bookmark. I didn't recall Mom ever reading it, but I knew she liked the bible-study groups at her church. Inside the front cover below Mom's name was one I didn't recognize: Ida Krebehenne Ruble. I assumed it was my grandmother's name. Below that was the name of her father, Charles Ruble (no middle name). I'd known that my parents had similar last names and that's how they'd met. But incurious kid that I was, I never asked for more details.

The next day, we all had dinner at Dad and Ella's house.

"It's so sad about your mom," Ella said, hugging each of us. We siblings had discussed many times how Dad had struck gold when he married Ella. She made him content, as content as he could be. She also received a good income from two farms she'd inherited when her first husband died, after a thirty-year marriage. Dad could finally relax about money.

After my initial dislike because she had replaced my mother, I'd grown to love Ella. In high school, I'd even sneak out to see her and drive her around. Once I fibbed to Mom, saying I was staying with a girlfriend for an unheard-of two nights when I'd agreed to drive Ella a couple hundred miles to see her sister in southern Iowa.

Now, sitting with my dad on the couch, looking at Ella across the room, I thought how she reminded me of Mom. Both wore flowered-print housedresses, thick cotton stockings, and had their short gray hair styled in a tight permanent. Born within a few months of each other, they were nine years younger than Dad. And each needed to keep her hands busy. Mom was always crocheting wool yarn into afghans, while Ella wove rag rugs from cloth scraps.

Ella was a good fifteen pounds thinner than Mom, though, and she was a better housekeeper. Ella kept all the surfaces in her home dusted and uncluttered. Tracks in the beige carpet showed where she had recently run the vacuum cleaner.

Mom hadn't swept and vacuumed the old farmhouse as often as she should have. Looking for a dress to bury her in, I'd found a foot-deep pile of wrinkled clothes on the floor of her closet. Mom was also an indifferent cook, just getting basic meals on the table, while Ella was an amazing one, specializing in desserts. Mom had loved to read, while Ella seldom opened a magazine. And Mom had given birth to eight children, while Ella had none. So Mom, with her large family, got a pass on housekeeping.

As Ella straightened an antimacassar on the arm of the couch and headed into the kitchen, I wondered why I compared the two women when I loved them both.

"Dad, how are you doing?" Norman asked from across the living room.

"I'm still thinkin' about findin' your mother," Dad said, slumped next to me on the couch. "It was rough."

On Mom's last morning, when Dad came into the house, all had been dark, and she didn't answer his call. He shuddered now, and I could see he was still coping with the shock of finding her.

"I'm sorry, Dad," I said, reaching over to squeeze his shoulder. A few minutes passed in silence. I knew we were all thinking the same thing: how he'd discovered Dale dead, too. Would this be another memory that would never leave him?

I pictured Mom in the last few days before her death, rising in the cold house each morning around six to start the fire in the basement furnace, waiting for it to channel its heat through the registers to warm the upper floors. After the blaze got going, she'd climb the rickety stairs into the kitchen to brew the coffee she'd drink with Dad.

Everyone but me had work and some had family to get home to, so I stayed on to pack up Mom's clothes and clean out the house. In truth, I wasn't ready to leave it, knowing it would be for the last time.

Devastating news came a day later when a letter arrived from

Uncle Harold, my mother's only brother, addressed to "The Children of Mildred Rubel." Harold and Mom hadn't seen each other since they were teenagers, and none of us had met him. He'd retired to Florida after years of service in the Navy. In the only picture I'd seen of him, he was probably about eighteen, with slicked-back brown hair, a wide grin, wearing a white sailor shirt, navy-blue trousers, and a narrow tie. He was clutching the railing of a ship, with smokestacks and other metal structures looming behind him.

I was puzzled that Harold said nothing about not attending her funeral. Instead, in six typewritten sentences, Harold wrote that our grandmother, Ida Krebehenne Ruble, had been confined to the Northern Indiana Hospital for the Criminally Insane for more than thirty years. She'd been diagnosed with "acute mania," and died there in the mid-1940s. He said she'd been institution-alized since my mother was sixteen and he was fourteen.

What kind of news was this? I'd had no idea. Perhaps Harold guessed that Mom hadn't told us about our grandmother, and he needed to set us straight. But why, and why now? I had no idea what to think.

Mom never talked about her family—especially her mother, I now realized—and only heard from her brother and his wife at Christmas. Again, being self-absorbed, I hadn't asked Mom any more questions. What was I supposed to do with this upsetting information?

Did my uncle's shocking news suggest that Dale had inherited our grandmother's mental illness, that it had played a role in his suicide? Had Mom wondered that? Thinking back on those years, I recalled seeing her gazing into the distance sometimes, then shaking her head as if to dislodge whatever thoughts had taken her away. One more thing I hadn't stopped to wonder about.

Perhaps Dad hadn't known about his mother-in-law, or he wouldn't have blamed himself so thoroughly for Dale's suicide.

That evening, before dinner with Ella and Dad, I said, "Dad, I'm curious. How well did you know Mom's brother, Harold?"

"I only met him the one time," he said, looking at me with red-rimmed eyes, "when I met your mother, in Colorado. He joined the Navy before we got married. I only met her father once or twice. Her mother was sick a lot and in the hospital. Pneumonia, I think."

It wouldn't do any good to tell him about the note I'd gotten. He was still raw from Dale's death, even after eight years, as well as Mom's, even though they'd been divorced for almost ten.

I tucked Harold's letter away and didn't tell my siblings about it, either. Like my mother, I decided to keep this information secret. Did I feel shame, as my mother must have? No, I did not. But I felt sad that neither Dale nor my grandmother had had the resources to get the help they needed.

THE MORNING OF MY last day, three of Mom's women friends came to the farmhouse, with a tuna casserole, a Jello mold, and a tunnel-of-fudge cake. It felt good to sit with these mothers of my school friends, who'd known my mother for so long.

"Don't know who'll take her place," Mrs. Nelson said, her eyes brimming with tears. "The way she took charge in our Republican Women's Club meetings."

I looked at her, surprised.

"Oh, yes, eight to ten of us. She always had a hand-written agenda and her wooden gavel to get us gabby females down to business. She convinced some of us to go door-to-door getting people to vote in local and national elections. We hadn't done that before. She got ahold of some brochures from Republican headquarters that we handed out."

Mrs. Nelson leaned back and smiled. "And what fun we had at the Republican Convention in Des Moines. A three-and-a-half-hour drive. And staying in a hotel—the first time doing something like that without husbands. The three of us wouldn't have gone if it hadn't been for Mildred."

I stood up to get the coffee and cream I'd forgotten to offer.

"Really," I said, waiting a minute before turning around to pour the coffee. I sat down slowly, looking from one woman to the next. I tried to picture Mom at the head of a table of women, wielding a gavel, projecting authority.

After taking a sip of coffee, Mrs. Delaney said, "When she was the Excelsior Township chairwoman for the Red Cross, she raised two hundred and fifty dollars in a house-to-house canvas. Hard to get farmers' wives to give their hard-earned money."

"Your mom finished courses in standard and advanced first aid," chimed in Mrs. Schroeder. "She got us to do that, too. Said we needed to be prepared for farm accidents. And she raised money for the school band." She smiled at me. "Your mom was so proud you played in the band."

I stood up again, trying to hold back tears. I took the cake from its container, cut several slices, and got small plates from the cupboard.

"Thank you for bringing the cake, one of my favorites," I said as I served the women. Wiping my eyes with a tissue, I sat down again. "Yes, I played piano in the band." I looked around the room, taking in their words, then looked back at Mrs. Schroeder. "I had no idea Mom was so involved. I knew she looked for Soviet airplanes at Spirit Lake Airport. But I didn't really focus on it. Just wrapped up in myself, I guess."

How I wished I could tell Mom how proud I was that she had done all these things; that she was a leader. How self-absorbed I'd been, thinking she'd led a solitary life, pining for her faraway children. Instead, she had continued to do some good in the world. Would I ever emulate her charitable activities? And these dear women. They'd adored my mother. They hadn't cared that she was overweight and years older than they were.

"Yeah, kids can be self-centered," Mrs. Nelson said, wiping her mouth with a napkin. As the three stood up to go, she hugged me. "You've got lots of time to be like your mom."

Back in California, I contacted the professors in whose courses I'd taken incompletes and was able to take a final exam or write a paper. With the aim of graduating after the fall semester, I took two classes in summer school, completed homework in the afternoon, and worked evenings at the *San Jose Mercury News,* typing up copy for their ads. That fall, with a full load and back at my secretarial job with the criminology professor, I got up to the San Francisco area less often. But when I did, I stayed with Evelyn and Joe.

I still worked at Marguerite's factory from time to time. She'd promise me a coat, a dress, or a pantsuit if I'd box garments for shipment, fetch coffee and food, or model coats for potential customers. And I suppose I was still enthralled by her world.

One Saturday morning, I was separating buttons, as well as fabric swatches according to colors, sizes, and types of fabric. My mind was on a paper due in Advanced Shakespeare the following week, and I was trying to recall details of Schiller's *Wilhelm Tell* for a quiz coming up in German class. I must have missorted some items.

"You're so stupid," Marguerite yelled. "Getting a college degree, and you can't even separate fabrics. Can't you tell the difference between corduroy and canvas?"

I should have been used to this, and in some ways I was. But this time, I thought about pitching the buttons and swatches in her face. Instead, I hurled the boxes of buttons to the floor and stalked out. No doubt she was right about the quality of my sorting, but I was tired of her browbeating me.

Outside in the hallway, I leaned against a wall. Despite my thumping heart, I felt an enormous sense of freedom and power.

After graduation in late January, I decided to use the money I'd inherited from my mother and travel to Germany to live for a year or two. I'd always wanted to travel and even live in another country while I was still single and not yet settled into a full-time job.

During the next four years, I seldom saw Marguerite. Again, I'd found a way to make a kind of peace with her.

Taxing Matters

HE VISITING ROOM OF the federal prison in Springfield, Missouri, is empty except for Charles and Ella. The two sit at a long metal table, waiting for a uniformed staff person to summon Vern. Ella busies herself looping cloth strips for the next segment of her rag rug. Her fingers tremble as she handles the colorful pieces of fabric. Every few seconds, she looks toward the door where Vern will likely enter. Charles sees that Ella is extremely nervous about being in a prison. But crap, it was her idea to visit.

Even though he reads true-crime magazines and watches courtroom dramas on television, Charles has never been in a prison, or ever imagined being close to one. So how has his second-born son ended up here? And for more than a year, as they are visiting in the first six months of Vern's two-year term.

Could it somehow be his fault that his son is here? Charles has on a few occasions stayed overnight in small-town jails, the first time around fifty years ago. He punched the landlord of the farm the family was renting near Spencer, Iowa. Around the same time, Charles received a fifteen-day jail sentence for choking the local veterinarian in a dispute about a bill. Neither man was hurt badly, but still…punching the landlord and choking the vet…both serious and idiotic incidents. He'd been five years into his marriage to Mildred.

Charles squirms on the hard plastic chair. Maybe his reckless actions as a young man somehow laid the path for Vern, who was only a small kid at the time. Had Charles's behavior somehow led his son to think it was okay to break the law? Charles can't remember everything from that long ago, but he knows he was quick to use his fists in his younger days.

His last time in jail, just overnight, was sometime in the early 1950s, after a drunk-driving arrest not far from the last farm he'd owned. Now eighty-one, he's dang sure any kind of jail is behind him, let alone a big-time prison like this.

Charles shakes his head. Enough of this pitiful thinking. He can't take on any more guilt. The suicide of his first-born son fills that allotment. After more than fifteen years, his continued suffering around Dale's death—isn't that a form of payment for any offenses?

He studies the tiny grooves in the tan-colored cinder-block walls, then glances up at the windows. Too small and high for escape. And no bars. Vern has written that this is one of those low-security prisons, housing white-collar criminals like himself. So Vern probably won't come out in manacles, dragging chains around his ankles, as Charles has seen on crime shows. His son isn't sharing space with murderers or rapists, just rich bastards.

In fact, Vern hasn't even beaten anybody up. He just refuses to pay his taxes and encourages others to do the same. Charles himself hates paying taxes but never had the gumption to cheat the government that way. It's probably pretty easy to get caught, especially when you talk about your crazy ideas in public. Still, maybe Charles's years-ago railing at the government's telling him what to do on his own farm gave Vern some bad ideas.

"Here he comes," Ella says in a low, quavering voice. She stuffs her rag strips into a small wicker basket and stands up. Charles stays seated. The heavy steel door swings open and Vern appears, alone, with no chains or manacles. The best-looking of his sons, and he had five fine-lookin' boys with Mildred. Vern's short brown hair is shot through with gray, though he looks younger than his forty-nine years. He has hazel eyes, clean-shaven, unblemished skin, and a fine sloping nose. His pris-on-issue uniform, a tan short-sleeve V-neck shirt and matching pants, looks almost like pajamas. After patting Ella's shoulder,

Vern leans over the table to shake hands with his father. Ella resumes her seat, and her arms cradle her basket.

"Thanks for coming." Vern smiles and sits down on an orange plastic chair across from them. "So, you're on your way to Hot Springs?"

"Yes, we both love going there," Ella says, and she smiles at Charles. "We stay at the same boardinghouse, The Happy Hollow, two weeks every year. We especially like sitting in the mineral baths. It helps our rheumatism."

A few seconds pass in an uncomfortable silence, Ella looking to Charles to say something.

"It's a long drive to Arkansas, about thirteen hours, including detouring to visit you," Ella finally adds, stuttering. "When we get halfway, we stay overnight, usually in a motel, like we did last night. Four hours and some to go yet today. When we get too old to drive, we'll take the Greyhound bus." She seems to have run out of breath and presses a hand to her chest.

"So, what's it like here?" Charles asks, rescuing a jumpy Ella by switching topics. Would he have visited his son in the pen if he weren't on the way to Hot Springs? He'd like nothing more than to get up and leave. What's to shoot the breeze about? Charles has paid for his mistakes. Let Vern pay for his. Though he finds it hard to believe his son is a real lawbreaker. Not paying taxes shouldn't land you in prison for two long years. Maybe he should pay some fines, but prison? But Vern did break the law, so he's suffering the consequences, however harsh they may be.

Charles glares at Ella, but her eyes are fixed on Vern. That preachy Lutheran church of hers influences her too much. The congregation probably likes to coddle real criminals. He's relieved Ella doesn't drag him along on Sundays. But now that he and Ella are here, he might as well make the most of the visit. He leans back, pulls a stunted cigar from his shirt pocket, and sticks it in his mouth.

"Can't smoke in here, Dad," Vern mutters as Charles pulls out a match. Vern points to the "No Smoking" sign and then to the staff person at a desk behind an indoor window. "Normally, I'd tell you to ignore the rule, but I've seen them enforce it."

"Shit," Charles says, stowing the cigar stub and match in his shirt pocket. "You're not in a real cell, are you?"

"No, it's a barracks-type setup, like it was in the Navy. Except here they have bunk beds. I'm stuck on the top. The guy below has more seniority."

Vern explains how difficult it is to get enough sleep, since the lights are always on, and the staff wakes "inmates" every few hours for roll call. "The five a.m. check reminds me of when I got up at that ungodly hour to milk cows and feed the pigs. Early hours are easier when you're a kid." Vern offers a weak smile. "It's not bad, the whole situation. I get three square meals a day of okay food. That's something." He looks down at the floor.

"How often do you see your family?" Ella asks.

"Kitty comes to visit every month or so. She brought my two grandkids last time. They're ten and twelve. Talented little buggers. They send me a family newsletter each month. Miles draws pictures of family members, and Maggie writes about them in comic-strip form." He grins and reaches into his shirt pocket. "Darn. Thought I brought one to show you. Must have left it on my bunk."

"That's so sweet," Ella says. "But otherwise, how do you keep busy?"

"There's calisthenics classes. Pretty good inmate instructor. Found somebody to play chess with. The library has the same anti-communist magazines I get at home, like the *National Review* and *The American Conservative*. I made a couple friends who have my political views, so we have some good discussions."

"About how to cheat the government?" Charles asks, his lips curling into a sneer.

"Come on, Dad," Vern says, raising his voice. "You know how corrupt the federal government is and how it's clamping down on our individual rights."

Off on one of his rants, thinks Charles, closing his eyes for a few seconds. Where did his son get this craziness? When he was a student at the University of Minnesota? But Dale was at the same college then, and he didn't come home with such nutty ideas. Yeah, Vern had bitched about government interference in farmers' operations and the free market. Even called Roosevelt a socialist. Hammered the president's New Deal program that paid farmers not to grow certain crops. Yada, yada.

Charles remembers those decades differently, when, unlike Vern, he actually had to make a living. Recalling that time, he reflects that the government was right to interfere in what farmers planted. With a glut of some products, rock-bottom crop prices were causing farmers to go out of business. Charles's family couldn't have survived without the meddling, much as he hated government curtailing his independence.

His son's attitude about farm subsidies must have started his hatred of the government, and then he didn't want to pay taxes to support it. Charles sighs. Who the hell knows how he came to his beliefs? Anyway, he refuses to get in an argument about the past with Vern. Those times were tough enough to live through—the Depression and then World War II.

Ella reaches across the table and puts her hand on Vern's arm. She talks softly to him, probably to calm him down. Vern closes his eyes, and his shoulders slump.

Watching the two, Charles tries to recall what Vern was like as a kid. He studies his son's forehead and fails to find the scar. As a youngster, he was a daredevil and liked to jump into wagonloads of hay. One day, he was knocked senseless after failing to dodge the swing arm of the pulley system used to lift hay into the hayloft.

Then Charles stares at his son's clasped hands. At eight or nine, Vern had caught his pinky in a hand-cranked corn sheller and lost the tip. Shaking his head, he wonders how his kids survived their childhoods.

Vern got into scrapes, like other youngsters did. He was smart and got good grades, if he bothered to do his schoolwork, but was kicked out of school a few times for refusing to go to class or sticking his nose in a book when he should have been paying attention. Vern often said he knew more than the teacher. The young scamp acted out more than his brothers and sisters did. As a senior, he'd refused to show up for picture day, so there was no graduation photo. And when Charles ordered him to stay home from school to help on the farm, he refused, unlike his brothers. Surely none of those small battles started Vern on his path to the pen.

"Dad," Vern said, interrupting Charles's reverie. "I was thinking the other day about how you used to carry me on your shoulders to some of your fights. Remember? I was probably five or six and scared to death of all those people, clapping and yelling."

Is that possible, Charles wonders. This son, so disrespectful and confrontational, was the son he'd take to a fight? He stumbles through the fog of his memory. Funny what he remembers and what he doesn't.

"You'd put me on a chair at the front of the crowd and ask a stranger to watch me. You don't remember?"

"No," Charles admits. "But it's possible, I guess."

What a place to take a kid, he thinks. To those noisy arenas with supporters yelling at two men punching each other. Had Mildred objected to his taking one of their sons to one of his fights? But it hadn't made Vern physically violent.

Aware of a silence in the room, Charles takes the plunge.

"Why'd you think you could get away with not payin' taxes?" He can see Vern taking in deep breaths. Probably getting himself under control. "Aren't you what they call a 'tax preparer' part of the year? Where'd you get such a damn fool idea about cheatin' the government?" Charles shifts in the uncomfortable chair. "You finished law school. Couldn't you at least figure out how to dodge the feds?"

"Charles," Ella says, her tone sharp. She grabs his arm. "Shame on you. He's in jail, learning his lesson, and we hope he's starting on a new path. Don't encourage him to keep breaking the law."

"Ain't none of this my doin', woman," Charles snaps. "He got here on his own, damn it."

Charles sighs. Learning his lesson. Is Vern at all sorry? He sure doesn't sound like it.

For that matter, did Charles ever regret his own behavior? Only once that he can remember, in a boxing ring at the Spirit Lake fairgrounds more than forty years ago, with fourteen hundred people in the audience—at least, that's the number the newspaper printed. He lost an eight-round match against Bernie Hassel. How is it possible he remembers the man's name?

Charles issued a public apology for his behavior during the fight in a letter that ran on the front page of the *Spencer News-Herald*, his hometown newspaper. In it, he'd blamed illness, claiming he was under medical care for a severe cold. He said he shouldn't have committed those fouls, should have canceled the fight, considering how sick he was. Then he had come up with some blather about being a guy who backed good sportsmanship. At the time, he meant those words, seeing as how he wanted to save his reputation as a fair fighter.

Vern suddenly tenses up and points a finger at him.

"You played fast and loose with the government over the years," he says. He stands up and paces back and forth, coming to a stop across from his father. "And you were a mean son-of-a-gun. Remember when you got fined for assault-and-battery after hitting our hired man in downtown Spencer? You were an experienced boxer and hurt him pretty bad. It was even written up in the Spencer paper."

Charles winces. He'd completely forgotten that incident. What had been wrong with him?

"At least I'm not violent," Vern says. "None of us kids were. It's a wonder you didn't spend more time in jail, as often as you got drunk and drove."

What a cocky little shit, Charles thinks. Changing the subject from his bad deeds and jail time to Charles's mistakes, when he'd served his time.

He feels Ella's eyes boring into him. Maybe Vern's right. Charles is partly to blame, considering the shameful things he's done in his life, often after abusing alcohol. All his life he's tried to quit drinking, but it's damn hard. He knows Ella has it rough with him. And Mildred, the mother of his children, had it even worse. In that true Christian spirit of Ella's, she wants to help him be a better person. He puts an arm around her shoulder, then prays silently once again—even though he sure as hell doesn't believe in prayer, like Ella does—that she won't give up on him.

"And the government, Dad," Vern says, sitting down again. "Dale told me you took out a government loan with the oats stored in our crib as collateral. They sealed the oats and told you not to touch it. But as soon as the government guy left, you told Dale to start drawing out the oats to feed the chickens and hogs. That's fraud, Dad. You're lucky nobody found out, or you'd have been in jail for that, too. Or at least paid a fine."

Charles glowers at Vern. "Those loans kept my farm from goin' under. And I always paid them back."

"I guess the apple doesn't fall far from the tree. In the fifties, the feds offered to pay you to leave your land fallow to avoid grain overproduction and the collapsing of commodities prices. You had a chance to say no. But people can't choose not to pay taxes. When I was learning to be a tax preparer, I studied the IRS tax code. Its original purpose wasn't to tax workers' wages and salaries but to tax investments."

"Lots of our neighbors took government money and didn't plant some of their fields," Charles says. "Sometimes I did, and sometimes I didn't. We had cattle, and I needed corn to feed 'em. And I had a family to support."

Why the hell defend himself for things he did years ago? Actions that helped him survive? Charles hadn't wanted the government to interfere with his independence. But he wasn't about to go to jail for that attitude.

"I needed to do what I did with my own fields. But I'm not fool enough to think I could get away with not paying taxes." He folds his arms across his chest, hoping the subject is finished. Hoping that he and Ella can get the hell out of here.

"Yeah, Dad," Vern lashes back. "I never cheated average people, like our neighbors. Danny told me that you set back the counter on the hay baler when neighbors baled for us, to pay for fewer bales. When the gypsies came by the farm to collect old iron, you'd let them pay for the good stuff. Then, when Danny loaded it, you told him to switch it for junk with rust and nails. So don't give me any of that holier-than-thou crap."

"No, you don't," Charles growls. "You can't lay this at my door. You're your own damn person. And you did even worse stuff. This group called the patriots you're part of. You helped people fill out their W-2 forms so they can avoid taxes. You got other people to break the law."

Charles stands up. "Let's go, Ella. I don't need him blamin' me because he's a crook. We made our charity visit, you did your Christian good works. Let's get goin'."

"Sit down," Ella says. She grabs Charles by his flannel shirt-sleeve and yanks him back into his chair. "Stop this bickering." She places her hand on Charles's arm, holding him in place.

"We're family here."

She turns to Vern. "Why did you think what you did was a good idea? What do Kitty and the kids think? You're in prison, for goodness sake."

Vernon nods his head. "Kitty wasn't gung ho about my decision," he says, "but she supported me. I had a good case and a good lawyer. But then a bleeding-heart federal prosecutor came down from New York to try the case. A SWAT team with AK-47s even raided my office, looking for my client files."

Vern pounds a fist on the metal table. "Using guns? To go after small fry like me? It was all on the evening news, embarrassing my family. A lot of people we know saw me and Kitty on television walking into the courthouse." Vern grins. "But I got back at the government. My old tax-prep clients came back. Kitty and our daughter Cathy are keeping the tax business going. And I haven't driven away family with my views. Both Evelyn and Danny visited me in North Carolina before I came here."

Such a talker, and so full of bullshit. Strange to recollect that when Vern first started school, he was so quiet the teacher would give him a penny to coax a single word out of him.

Charles taps his shoe on the cement floor, then pulls his watch out from his shirt pocket. Jesus. They've been here an hour. Perfect guy to be a lawyer, the way he jabbers up a storm. Early on, while in college and to earn money during summers, he used his gift of gab as a salesman, to sell Gold Bond stamps in Iowa. Later he graduated from college somewhere else, but Charles can't remember where. Then, after finishing law school in Atlanta, he moved to North Carolina, where he sold business machines to support his young family. Charles still has no earthly idea why Vern never used his law degree. Maybe he didn't want to bother studying for the bar exam. Or he failed it. No idea if either was the case, and no desire to find out.

Maybe if his son had owned his own farm, he wouldn't have

such crazy ideas. He would've seen how you need to work with the federal government to make a living. But a guy who hated getting his hands dirty wasn't cut out for farm work, even if he grew up on one. Years ago, Vern and his young family would travel to Iowa for occasional visits. Before heading to the barn to help with chores, he never changed out of his khaki pants, short-sleeve dress shirt, and polished leather shoes. He'd even add a canvas hat and cotton gloves. Then he stood back and watched his brothers shovel feed to the animals or scoop manure into the spreader.

Over the years, Vern and Dale had batted around the idea of leasing grassland in Georgia and North Carolina to graze cattle there, then trucking them back to Iowa to fatten on corn before taking them to market. Perhaps the whole enterprise had been too expensive. Charles couldn't remember. Had Dale been discouraged when the idea petered out? Charles had never thought about that before.

He sighs as he remembers how close the two brothers were, just twenty months apart in age, inseparable as youngsters. Together, they trapped muskrats, mink, and rabbits and skinned them to earn money. Charles would spend hours haggling about the prices with a potential buyer. His sons would finally slink away, embarrassed by their dad's behavior. They just wanted their money. The two even attended the same college at the same time for a couple years. How Dale's death must have hurt Vern. But he never talked about it. And he never gave any indication he blamed his dad.

He tunes back into his son's yapping.

"And Ella," Vern is saying, "a friend of mine says the North Carolina constitution gives citizens, especially the workingman, the right to keep the fruits of their labor. That's a right from God. Written in the bible. I'm not a strong believer, though I was a deacon and a Sunday school teacher at my church. I've even gone on several Habitat for Humanity building projects. Anyway, where does the government get the power to take something away when it comes from God?"

"You're wrong," Ella says, shaking a finger at him. "God wants you to obey the law. And you've got four kids. You can't use God and the bible to justify breaking the law. Your dad says you loved being in the Navy during World War II. You used to hitch rides on Navy planes to California to visit Marguerite and Evelyn. Isn't that cheating, since the Navy is part of the government?"

Ella's gentle smile feels soothing to Charles. He puts his hand gently on her shoulder.

"Come on, now," Ella continues. "How can you hate the government and love the Navy? Aren't you being a hypocrite?"

"I guess it's a contradiction," Vern acknowledges, looking away.

Charles sees the slight coloring of his son's fair skin and can't help grinning. My God, Vern is embarrassed that he can hate the government and like it at the same time. Vern walks toward the small windows. After silently looking up for a few minutes, he returns to his chair.

"I was young then. Didn't know any better, and would have been drafted anyway, since we were in the middle of a war that incompetent socialist Roosevelt got us into. Right out of high school, I went to Pensacola flight school, where they trained me to navigate planes," he told Ella. "We patrolled up and down the East Coast looking for German submarines and U-boats.

"Flying was great. Anyway, serving in the Navy wasn't just working for the government. We were protecting the country. A fine line, I know. Basically, the government's role should just be to protect us."

"My church says we should ask God for forgiveness if we've done something wrong," Ella says. "Even if you don't believe, you've gotta show you're sorry for what you did wrong. So you won't do the same thing again. Or…you'll be back here."

"That won't happen," Vern says, shaking his head.

"Let's get goin', Ella," Charles says, standing up. "Got hours of drivin' yet."

"Dad, let's call a truce." Vern extends a hand. "We're both far from perfect."

On the wall, a round-faced clock ticks, an awkward intrusion in an awkward conversation.

"All right," Charles grunts, and he shakes his son's hand.

Charles heads toward the door. Ella hoists her basket, embraces Vern, and follows.

"Hope you get time off for good behavior," Charles calls over his shoulder.

———

FOUR YEARS LATER, CHARLES crumples a letter and tosses it on the floor. "You won't believe this."

Ella comes in from the kitchen, wiping her hands on a dishtowel. "What is it?"

"Vern's in the slammer again," he tells her. "Another two years. For the same damn thing."

Enabling

———

"PLEASE, EVELYN," ELLA HAD begged. "Could you come back to Iowa? Your dad's doin' real bad. And I'm not so good, either. My diabetes, you know, and this stress makes it worse. So, I was thinkin', since you had this problem yourself…? You know…."

Evelyn figured she stood on pretty firm ground—fingers crossed—having been sober for four years, three months, two weeks, four days, and nine hours. Still, as she knew only too well, she was just one drink away from…it didn't bear thinking about.

"I'm not sure how to help, Ella," she told her stepmother. "I couldn't have quit without AA."

But Ella pleaded with her, and Evelyn, people-pleaser that she was, foolishly promised she'd try, though she was certain the effort would be futile. Even so, before hanging up, she asked Ella to look for daily meetings of an AA group near their home. Maybe at her church, she suggested.

What kind of insanity was it to take on Ella's problems when she couldn't solve her own? Then again, it was her husband's first affair—that she knew of. Maybe it hadn't been going on long, and she and Joe could work things out. Maybe getting away would give her some perspective.

Evelyn forced her thoughts back to Dad and Ella. Her eighty-four-year-old father had abused alcohol since his teens.

"You can't possibly think it's gonna work, getting Dad to stop drinking," her brother Norman told Evelyn on the phone. "When we were growing up, he couldn't go very long without his beer or harder stuff. And he could be pretty nasty when he drank. Remember?"

"Of course I do," she said. "But Ella sounded so desperate, I didn't know what else to say."

A week later, Evelyn and Norman, who had decided at the last minute to come along, drove the nearly two thousand miles from California back to Cedar Rapids. They had last seen Dad and Ella four years earlier, in 1971, when the old couple came to California for the first time. They'd stayed with Marguerite and Lowell and met Sandy's new husband, Ed.

"Should we just have a relaxing visit and not put pressure on him," Norman asked, "since neither of them is in good health?"

"Maybe you're right," Evelyn said. "Let's see what the situation is when we get there."

Evelyn was determined to try to help Ella, who'd made her dad's declining years such contented ones. Though she had yet to come up with a plan for talking to him about sobriety. What exactly would she say?

When the two arrived, Dad was sitting on the small front porch, both hands resting on his cane. As Evelyn and Norman climbed wearily up the steps, he struggled up from his chair, leaned on his cane, and gave each an awkward one-armed hug. He followed them into the house and plopped heavily into a chair at the kitchen table. In the open-plan living room, they exchanged hugs with Ella. Evelyn sat next to her stepmother on the couch as Norman collapsed into an armchair.

Evelyn studied the dark pouches under her father's eyes, his heavy jowls, the deep lines crosshatching his face. This was what more than sixty-five years of farming, almost a lifetime of guzzling alcohol, and six months of coping with bladder cancer looked like. He still had a barrel chest, probably from all the athletic training, which lasted well into his fifties. As a young man, Charles had chased a professional boxing career. Evelyn remembered him jabbing the punching bag hung on the porch and running alongside a car driven by a friend or one of his sons.

How his weakened state must sadden him.

"How was the trip?" Dad asked as he rearranged his assortment of pill bottles. His thinning white hair had splashes of burnt orange from a bad dye job. He'd always said he couldn't stand white hair and had colored it himself.

"It was exhausting," Evelyn said. "Drove straight through. Thirty-six hours. Took turns sleeping on the back seat."

When she was planning the trip, she'd called Dad and told him she and Norman wanted to come for a quick visit. The timing was good, she explained. Norman had finished a project at his engineering firm, and she still had vacation days from her bookkeeping job.

"Only have three days, so wanted to get here as quick as we could," Norman said. "Haven't seen Iowa for a few years. But mostly wanted to see how you're doing." He yawned and rubbed his eyes.

"Makes me tired just thinking about you two on that long drive," Ella said, twisting an embroidered handkerchief in her lap. "And not sleeping in a regular bed."

Every few minutes, Ella reached over to clutch Evelyn's hand. At the older woman's touch, Evelyn recalled how she had wanted to dislike her stepmom. But Ella had always been so kind and welcoming, especially after Mom died, when the seven siblings had gathered in Iowa for her funeral. She had invited them all for meals at the house she shared with Dad in Spirit Lake. Evelyn had come to love this woman.

Hearing the sound of gentle snoring, she saw that Norman was asleep in his chair.

"We have to get some rest," Evelyn said, forcing herself up. "It was hard to get any real sleep in the car. You know, raising twelve kids, Norman's gotta watch the pennies."

Evelyn tapped Norman's shoulder. Startled, he opened his eyes and looked around, as if confused about where he was. Then he rose and reached for his duffel bag. Ella ushered him to a door off the kitchen that led to the basement.

"Downstairs is a daybed I made up for you," she said. "I hope it's comfortable. There's a little bathroom, too. Be careful going down the steps, you're half asleep."

Ella gestured for Evelyn to follow her. "See you in a little while, Dad," Evelyn said.

He looked up at her with watery brown eyes and wished her a good nap. Maybe she should just aim for a relaxing visit, as Norman had suggested. Her dad looked like he was on his last legs. Maybe she'd never see him again, so she shouldn't pressure him. Let him live his life.

She trailed Ella down the hallway to a small guest room, where her stepmother had made up the sofa bed. Once Evelyn lay down on top of the covers, Ella sat beside her.

"I'm so glad you came," Ella said, her eyes filling with tears. "I'm praying for Charles and trying to be strong. But my diabetes is a lot worse. My doctor says I can't handle much stress."

Evelyn sat up and wrapped her arms around her. Between sobs, Ella said that every day, Charles sat for hours in the basement at his desk.

"He writes in his diary and looks at the pictures of Dale he's tacked on the wall. So sad, the way he keeps blaming himself. It's been nineteen years."

Evelyn guessed her father would never be able to move beyond Dale's suicide, and that alcohol helped him cope. That would make convincing him to give up drinking almost impossible.

"A couple times a week," Ella went on, "he starts drinking down there, and when I go to call him for dinner, he's passed out on the daybed. I can't wake him up, and he's too heavy to drag up to bed." She put her head in her hands. "I don't want to fight with him. He said he had enough of that with your mom."

"I'll try to help," Evelyn said, feeling less confident than ever.

"It's tough, though. After I joined AA, it still took me years to stop. And I had a lot of support." How could she accomplish in three days what took her more than four years? But to come all this way and offer nothing?

Ella stood up. "I'm sorry to go on like this when you're so tired. The bathroom's down the hall. Now you get some sleep." She took her handkerchief from the pocket of her housedress and wiped her eyes. "Oh, I called, and there's AA meetings at my church every day at two o'clock. You can walk there from here."

Ella left, closing the door gently behind her, and Evelyn lay back down. Maybe her best hope was to convince Dad he didn't want to make life more difficult for Ella, whose own health was declining, thanks in part to the worry he was causing her.

Evelyn sighed. And what about her own marriage? A few weeks ago, she'd picked up the phone to make a call and heard Joe on the garage extension, talking to a woman he called "sweetie" as they arranged to meet. Stunned and trembling, Evelyn had barely managed to hang up the phone without Joe hearing the click. She sank to the floor, struggling not to cry. She needed to hold herself together in front of her husband and their fifteen-year-old son. She told Joe and Steve she had a sinus headache and spent the rest of the day in bed, sobbing into her pillow.

She had finally confronted him a week after the call. At first, he denied any relationship, telling her he'd just run into his newly divorced high school girlfriend. She wondered if Joe's unfaithfulness could be her fault. After she'd gotten sober, she focused on staying that way, on doing well at her job and taking care of Steve. Perhaps she hadn't paid enough attention to Joe. He had even told her he felt neglected. A couple times he'd even become irritated when she wouldn't drink with him.

Of her older siblings, neither Dale nor Vern had developed a taste for alcohol, and Norman limited his intake to one small glass of red wine with dinner. And the younger ones? She hadn't seen Bob, four years younger, since he'd driven up from Southern California with Norman and Jean four years ago for the wedding party Marguerite gave for Sandy and Ed. Evelyn hadn't noticed anything particularly amiss. Perhaps Bob had had a beer or two at the party, she wasn't sure. Anyway, he'd looked healthy and handsome in his linen sport jacket and dress shirt but seemed awfully quiet. And Sandy and Ed? She had no idea of their drinking habits when they weren't with her.

Dan, now thirty-two, lived in Austin, Texas, where he was a maintenance supervisor in a chemical plant. Evelyn thought he was also pursuing a degree in engineering and graphic design. He'd made a quick trip to California about five years ago, but she'd gotten no impression of how he handled alcohol. Vern had told her on the phone several months ago that Dan called him every couple of weeks to "check in."

"Maybe he sees me as some kind of a father figure," Vern said, laughing. "I always tell him he's gotta finish college, go for a business degree. And keep off the booze."

Some father figure, Evelyn thought. A guy who'd not long before completed a two-year prison term for tax fraud.

As far as Evelyn knew, she and Dad were the family's only alcoholics. How had she gotten to that place?

When she and Marguerite arrived in San Francisco, Evelyn was just short of seventeen. With money they'd saved in Omaha, they rented a one-bedroom apartment and started waitressing. Evelyn had also attended adult school at San Francisco City College, taking courses for her high school diploma. She had a passable aptitude for math but was not a fast reader and worked hard at comprehension. Taking one or two courses at a time, she earned her diploma in just under three years.

Turning over on the sofa bed to get more comfortable, she tried to remember what her dreams had been then. She'd wanted to get her diploma, earn enough money to rent her own apartment, get married, and have a family. She'd stay home with any children she and a future husband had, which would give her time to sew some of her own clothes and garments for her kids.

She met Joe, who delivered bread from Boudin Bakery to the restaurant where she worked, when she was eighteen. Joe often took her to visit his sister and her husband, who lived in San Francisco's Marina District with their infant daughter. Evelyn savored Angie's scrumptious Italian meals and homemade pasta sauce, her first experience of garlic. Red wine flowed at dinner, and the fruity aroma took her back to the farm and the tangy taste of apples fresh-picked from their trees, which they made into apple butter.

The presence of any alcohol also reminded her of her dad's behavior when he drank. Sometimes he'd throw dishes at Mom. Once, Dad backed his car into the corncrib, where it got stuck. Another time, returning from town, he drove into a ditch. Evelyn recalled Dad telling a friend that in his late teens, he would drive with a neighbor to Manning, Iowa, to get kegs of beer and take them to weekly dances. So he'd started drinking young.

Though Angie and Pete were warm and welcoming, Evelyn had felt awkward and rude not sharing their hospitality. She'd wanted to fit in, so she finally accepted a glass of wine, then another. Over time, she savored the taste of alchohol and, even more, the relaxed feeling it produced.

She and Joe married when she was twenty, Joe twenty-two. A few years later, they bought a two-bedroom house in Millbrae, a suburb south of San Francisco. Like Angie and Pete, they drank wine with dinner, although they added cocktails before the meal. Now she recalled the many alcohol-fueled dinner parties they'd had with neighborhood friends.

Evelyn had initially toyed with the idea of becoming a seamstress but soon realized she was a perfectionist, working too slowly to make any money. After two bookkeeping courses at

San Francisco City College, she got a temporary job in a small company. Pretty basic duties, but she liked the orderliness and precision of the work—adding columns of figures, recording payments in a ledger—and the regularity of paying bills. But the next job, in a pharmaceutical company, was more stressful: preparing financial statements, ensuring employees filed expenses correctly. It got worse when she began to handle the payroll. Drinking had helped her cope.

It also eased her sorrow as she neared thirty and still hadn't become pregnant. Alcohol helped her deal with her jealousy as Norman and Jean had a new baby every other year. On visits to their house, Evelyn was consumed with envy. Couldn't they give her one of their children, when they had so many? Evelyn squirmed now, to think that she'd ever had such a despicable thought.

Then a miracle happened: The adoption agency called. Evelyn and Joe passed the home inspections with flying colors. They brought home a healthy two-week-old baby boy from an affair between a single woman in the neighborhood and a married man.

Looking back, she thought about how she and Joe had celebrated all their momentous occasions with alcohol—renting their first apartment, buying their house, adopting Steve. That was how their friends marked special events, too.

For a couple of months, she'd stayed home with the baby. She loved having time to sew and to be with him but couldn't manage the boredom of so many empty hours alone. Seeing her neighborhood friends couldn't compensate for the feelings of accomplishment a job produced. She found a neighborhood woman who cared for one baby and agreed to take Steve.

And wonderful as it was to have her son, his arrival added more stress to her life. Balancing motherhood, work, and how much she drank was tricky. Small sips of vodka from a flask in her desk got her through her day—she tried to consume just enough to avoid feeling fuzzyheaded, to stay focused and keep her bookkeeping figures accurate.

Joe could tolerate a lot more liquor than she could, and he never drank until lunchtime. Still driving a bakery truck, he'd commute to work at three a.m., return at noon, have his first beer with lunch, then a second as he mowed the lawn or raked leaves before a nap. When Evelyn got home, they'd have a couple of cocktails as she prepared dinner, then the red wine they bought by the gallon.

She still remembered how the tension in her back from sitting at work all day disappeared, how quickly her nerves quieted. Alcohol was like a magic liquid trickling into each capillary, leaving her relaxed and almost giddy, her veins tingling.

She was never able to stop at one drink, though she woke every day with a woolly head, resolving each morning to quit or cut back. She worried she'd get fired from her job or put Steve in danger. But that resolve always faded, as the stress of everyday life returned. Even though she hated feeling out of control when she drank, she couldn't stop. Now, before Evelyn finally managed to fall asleep, she wondered if, each day, her dad also pledged to give up drinking.

SHE FOUND ELLA SETTING the table for dinner. "You look lovely," Ella said, brushing her hand over Evelyn's short auburn-tinted hair.

Evelyn looked down at her red-and-blue-striped blouse and light-gray wool slacks, then reached up and touched her dangly gold earrings. She would never be a jeans-wearer. She hoped she hadn't overdone the eyeliner and eyebrow pencil. Marguerite was naturally pretty, so she only needed lipstick and barely powdered her nose, while Evelyn had always worked at looking attractive.

"Thank you. Something smells good," she said.

She helped Ella serve the pork roast cooked with carrots and the buttered green beans with almonds. As soon as the men sat down, Dad opened a bottle of beer.

"Now, Charles," Ella said, resting a hand on his shoulder as she put a platter of twice-baked potatoes on the table. "I hope you only have one drink tonight, with your children here."

He placed his hand on hers. "Honeybunch, don't nag me."

Evelyn chuckled as she sat down. Honeybunch. The sweetness of that word. During her entire childhood, she'd never heard such an endearment pass between her parents.

Norman bowed his head, praying silently and briefly, before taking a sip from his small glass of red wine.

"You and your religion," grumbled Dad, staring at the crucifix around Norman's neck. "Guess it ain't done you no harm. How's that good-lookin' wife of yours?"

"Jean's great. Busy with the kids. And 'my religion' helps me be a better person. I try, anyway." He took a bite of potato. "Do you mind Ella going to church?"

"Nah, but she don't need no church. She's naturally a good person. Goes anyway, though." He turned to Evelyn. "Your boy, how old is he now? And what's your husband up to?"

"Steve just turned fifteen," Evelyn said. "And Joe's good. Working hard, of course, while I'm gallivantin' around the country on trips to Iowa. He says hello and hopes you're feeling okay."

She hadn't the energy to tell Dad or Ella the truth. She took a sip of water and sat up straight, on guard. Never could tell what outrageous comment Dad would make about her Italian-American husband, maybe soon to be ex-. She braced for the word "wop." It didn't come, and Evelyn relaxed. How crazy, she thought, that I'm agonizing over a cheating husband while worried about an ethnic slur against him. She thought back to when Marguerite had taken her boyfriend Bill on a visit home in the early 1950s.

"Why, you're a goddamned Jew," Dad had said, upon which the younger man turned to leave. Dad apologized, and Bill stayed. But Dad had mellowed some in his old age. When Sandy had introduced her new husband to Dad and Ella, Dad had said, "So, Ed, I understand you're of the Yiddish persuasion." Sandy told Evelyn that Ed had laughed, convinced his father-in-law was just trying to be friendly.

Around six the next morning, Evelyn awoke to the thump, thump, thump of Dad's cane as he hobbled down the hallway. Unable to fall back to sleep, she considered her plan, vague as it was: She'd try to get Dad to an AA meeting at Ella's church. As old and stubborn as he was, he would probably refuse. But she had no plan B.

Evelyn recalled how hard her dad had been on his children when they were growing up, especially his sons. The boys had been angry when he kept them out of school to work on the farm. And her father often shorted the wages of any farm laborers he hired. She'd heard no regret for any of that. Even if he'd mellowed, Evelyn found it hard to imagine her dad being able or willing to admit he had a problem with alcohol, or to acknowledge past mistakes, then make amends to people he'd harmed—all part of AA's conditions. Had Evelyn led Ella on? But she hadn't promised success, just offered to try. Still, her stepmother would be disappointed in her.

Evelyn wanted to burrow under the covers and escape into sleep, but she put on her robe and went out to the kitchen. Dad was at the breakfast table eating toast and drinking black coffee as he read the *Des Moines Register*. She gave him a quick hug, then followed the aroma of coffee to the pot. Norman must still be sleeping, Dad said, and Ella was at the grocery store after a bad night's sleep.

Evelyn took a sip of coffee. "Dad, you are so lucky to have Ella."

"Damn right I'm lucky," Dad said, putting down his newspaper. "I couldn't have made it through Dale's death without her. But I know she's upset about my drinkin'."

This was the opening she'd been waiting for. "Dad." Evelyn took a deep breath. "I want you to come to an AA meeting with me. There's one at Ella's church this afternoon."

"Hold on. I'm workin' on it, tryin' to drink less, sometimes just a beer a day."

Evelyn fought the urge to say, "Really?" "Most people need help," she told him. "In my meetings, there are some men as old as you. My sponsor is seventy-seven. And I go to meetings almost every day."

"I'm tryin' to manage, but it's mighty tough. My doctor says I need to give up my cigars, too. And chewin' tobacco. But I ain't about to."

"Dad, my sponsor quit drinking at seventy-five. He said he didn't want to die a drunk. And I couldn't have given up alcohol without that man." She placed her hand on his. "Would you give it a try?"

"No." He gripped his coffee cup with both hands. "I tried that nutty AA group in the fifties, when I was picked up for drunk drivin'. I was a pigheaded rascal when I was younger. Did some bad things. But I ain't about to tell a bunch of strangers about my sins. That's between Ella and me."

"Please, Dad." Sweat beaded on her forehead. How far could she push without alienating him entirely?

"No," he repeated. He took a cigar stub from a pocket of his red-flannel shirt, struck a match, lit the stub, and stuck it in his mouth. "Now leave it alone." He exhaled a column of smoke.

She sighed. "Sorry, Dad, I'm just trying to help. You told me your drinking is really hard on Ella, and you know stress is bad for her diabetes."

After a couple more puffs, he took the cigar out of his mouth and looked into the distance. In the ensuing silence, it seemed like her dad was in another place. Was he thinking about Dale? Ella's diabetes? What was left of his time on earth? Evelyn stood up, her body weighted by disappointment. He'd said no, and there was no talking him into it. She didn't want to drive her dad away, so this was it for now.

"Okay, Dad. I'll see you later. Gonna get dressed." Evelyn gave him a halfhearted hug and dragged herself back to her bedroom. Maybe she and Norman should just pack up and go.

Leaving her bedroom a few minutes later, she heard the back door slam and Ella come into the kitchen. Evelyn rushed to grab the grocery bags and help her stepmother unpack.

"Dad and Ella," she said once they finished putting the items away, "let's go sit in the living room and chat. I want to know why you moved here, three hundred miles from the farm."

Norman appeared from downstairs, and he came in to join the conversation. Ella and Dad sat next to each other on the couch.

"Well," Ella said, smoothing out her print dress, "we moved here because my sister and her daughters live on a farm not far outside Cedar Rapids. Near there is the farm where I lived with my first husband, so I still know people. And I missed my church." Evelyn knew that Ella's husband of thirty-some years had died of cancer. "You kids had all left. And most of your dad's friends had died."

"Dad, it must have been hard for you to leave the farm behind, the animals, the machinery, your whole life," Evelyn said. "I guess the tornado…speeded things up a bit?"

"Yeah," Dad said. "In 1968, four years after your mother died, half the house blew down. Lucky nobody lived there anymore. Anyway, I'd been leasin' the land out for a few years. It was time to sell. Almost seventy years of pluggin' away on farms, give or take a few years of boxin' and travelin' around the country when I was a young whippersnapper."

Ella placed her hand on her husband's knee and looked at Evelyn and Norman. "It was hard on your dad, the day of the farm sale. To see everything for the last time."

"The machinery I'd had for years," Dad said, shaking his head slowly. "I'd sold the cattle and hogs already. A farming conglomerate bought the land—a group that already had a thousand acres. It's a goddamn shame what's happened to smaller farmers."

AFTER LUNCH, ELLA WAS napping, Dad was downstairs at his desk, and Norman had gone running at the nearby high school track. Evelyn sat on the sofa reading a small book of AA's spiritual reflections. She focused on the one about respecting other people's personal boundaries. After a few minutes, she nodded off.

Through the haze of sleep, she heard the telltale thump, thump. For a moment, she thought she was dreaming. She opened her eyes and saw her dad shuffling toward the front door. She jumped up as he opened the door, then saw a taxi idling in the street.

"Dad, where are you going?"

"Makin' a quick trip to the liquor store. And it's none of your business." He held up his hand, as if to fend off her objection. Evelyn's body trembled. "I need to get a bottle," he said. "Just to have. I'll try not to drink it all today."

She understood his desperate need, even sympathized. For years, she'd run to the liquor store on her lunch hour, or in the evening after Steve fell asleep, telling Joe she needed something at the grocery store that couldn't wait. She pictured her father clutching his cane and creeping down those concrete front steps, and it set her heart racing.

"Wait a minute," she begged, gripping his arm. "Think about what you're doing."

He shook off her grasp. "Leave me alone," he growled.

"Okay," Evelyn said, taking a deep breath to calm herself. "But I'm coming along." At least she could make sure he didn't fall.

She clutched his elbow, steadying him as he limped down the steps. The driver, a man in his sixties, stood by the cab, holding a back door open.

"Hello, Charley." The man looked at Evelyn. "Hello there," he said, opening the other back door for her. "Your daughter, Charley? How did somebody with your ugly mug get somebody so good-lookin'?"

"Damn lucky, I guess," Charles mumbled, then crawled into the cab. "You know the way," he told the driver.

Evelyn saw Norman half a block away, returning from his run. She flinched, then faced forward.

"What's wrong?" Dad asked. "You afraid he'll see you goin' with me to buy booze and get after you?"

Did she detect a sneer?

"I need to have some hootch around," he said in a quiet voice, glancing at her. She saw the pleading in his eyes. "Just for backup. Don't always need to use it right away. Bet you squirreled away a bottle or two when you was drinkin'."

Evelyn flushed. Of course she had. During the five-minute ride, she looked at the ordinary-looking one-story houses and wondered how many people in them were slaves to alcohol. Why couldn't Dad have more self-control? And spare Ella. She caught herself. How hypocritical, to judge her father and the strangers in these houses, considering her own wretched history.

When they reached the state liquor store, Dad said, "You comin' in? You came this far."

"No." She refused to look at him. "I'm never, ever setting foot in another liquor store."

The driver helped Dad out, then waited near the car. Evelyn felt relieved she didn't have to make conversation with someone who clearly drove Dad regularly to fetch liquor. She struggled to hold back tears. How would she face Ella? And Norman? Should she have tried harder to stop him? She'd been shocked at his look of desperation. Evelyn drummed her fingers on the armrest. A few minutes later, her father slunk out of the store carrying a paper bag.

The driver helped Dad boost himself inside. Evelyn folded her arms across her chest and ignored him the entire way back. With luck, her stepmother was still napping, because Evelyn had no good explanation for her questionable behavior.

Norman stepped into the living room and frowned as Dad scuttled to the basement, holding tight to the paper bag.

"Let's go in your room," Norman said, sounding annoyed. He closed the door behind them. "What are you doing?" he whispered. "You enable him when you help him buy liquor."

Evelyn winced at Norman's AA language. "Enable" was a loaded word. Her face burned with shame. But there were enablers galore in this story: Ella, because she stayed with a husband who drank too much. Norman, because he consumed alcohol in his father's presence. And she herself, because she'd gone with her dad to buy booze.

"We should make it harder for Dad to get alcohol, not easier." Norman shook his head.

"He's gonna get it anyway," Evelyn said. She was very near crying. "I tried really hard to stop him, but I didn't want to get in a fight. And I couldn't let him go down those steps by himself when he could fall."

"Ella gets so upset when Dad passes out drunk in the basement," Norman said. "I thought we came back here so you could help him stop drinking. And Ella isn't in great health, either."

"I know all that. I feel terrible. But I tried to stop him."

Evelyn escaped Norman and went outside for a walk. An hour later, Ella was up, and, in tears, Evelyn confessed that she'd gone with her dad to the liquor store.

"Ella, I came here for the wrong reason. I'm so sorry. I told you, and even myself, I could try to help Dad stop drinking. I didn't really think I could, because that's almost impossible. I think the main reason I came was to get away from home for a while. Joe and I are having problems."

"Sweetie, I asked you to do something that was really hard to do." Ella wiped her own eyes. "I'm so sorry about you and Joe. Can we help?"

"No," Evelyn said. "We'll get through it. I'm mostly worried about you and Dad. Wish you lived closer."

"Here you have your own problems, and I imposed on you." Ella embraced Evelyn and clung to her for several seconds. "Just having you both here has been such a blessing. I'll pray for you and Joe, that things work out."

They heard the thump of Dad's cane on the basement stairs. Evelyn held her breath.

"Oh, Charles," Ella said as he appeared in the doorway. He was upright and steady, firmly holding onto his cane.

"What's wrong, woman?" he asked Ella. Evelyn listened for any sign of slurred speech. "Stop lookin' at me that way. Both of you. Don't worry. I didn't take a nip. Evelyn, how about fixin' me a cup of coffee?"

***

OVER THE NEXT TWO days, Evelyn initiated talks and walks with Ella and Dad—walks to get Ella outside for some exercise; talks with Dad to smooth over any tension.

"I was sad my first husband and I didn't have children," Ella said on one of their walks. "But you are all such a comfort to me and your dad. In Spirit Lake, when Sandy was home, she drove us around, and Danny and Bobby did any house repairs we needed. Marguerite and Lowell were so nice to us when we visited California." She stopped walking and stared at Evelyn. "But that Lowell…I was so nervous when he served Charles all that fancy liquor."

Yeah, Evelyn mused. Lowell likes his alcohol. Not a good person to be around if you have a drinking problem.

"I was hard on you, Norman," Dad said later that day, "when you was growin' up, like I was with all you boys. But you turned out real well. Got an education and a good wife."

"Yes," Norman said, smiling. "I did great. God is good. You didn't have it easy, either. I know you were just trying to keep the farm going and us fed."

"How'd you feel about me and Marguerite leaving?" Evelyn asked. "Or did you just miss the boys? Outdoor farm work and all that."

"Well, naturally, I hated to see you go," Dad said, unable to resist a grin. "Your mother did, especially. She needed your help with the housework and baby Sandy. I think Bob was only ten or so, but we managed. And you did okay, too."

At dinner on the third day, Dad said, "It's too bad you guys are leavin' so soon. Seems like you just got here."

Norman reached over to pat his dad's shoulder. "We won't wait so long next time. I'd like to bring Jean and some of the kids back. Most of them barely know you. In fact, I talked to Jean this morning, and we want to rent an RV and drive to Iowa next summer."

"Good. I want to see all your rascally kids."

Dad drank just one beer at dinner, sipping it slowly. He must hide his alcohol sometimes, Evelyn thought, apportioning it out over several days. Like she used to do. He'd probably stashed the bottle he bought yesterday. All the places she'd hidden her booze from Joe flashed through her mind.

"What in the hell are you doing?" Joe had caught her one afternoon, rooting in the trash can under the sink for her hoard.

Coffee grounds, meat bones, and other muck littered the kitchen floor. She thought he'd gone on an errand. She was so flustered, she had trouble answering.

"I-I dropped my favorite gold bracelet," she stammered. "It's so loose on my wrist." Had he looked at her strangely, or was it her imagination? She'd hidden bottles at the bottom of the laundry hamper, under her muddy gardening clothes, in her sewing-machine thread drawer. He'd never shown any sign that he knew of her twenty years of secret drinking.

A few weeks later, she attended her first AA meeting. She was making mistakes at work and hadn't been paying as much attention to her growing son as he needed. Too often, she would barely get dinner on the table. She asked Joe to join her, but he claimed his drinking wasn't a problem.

———

ON THEIR LAST MORNING, Dad and Ella stood in the doorway of their home. Ella leaned against the doorframe, looking as if a strong breeze could knock her over. Dad gripped his cane with both hands. Evelyn hugged them both, feeling wetness on Dad's cheek. Ella held her tightly, saying, "It's all right, my dear," then reluctantly let her go.

Then Evelyn and Norman drove off, waving back at the two old people, now leaning into each other.

"You were right," she said to Norman, settling into the passenger seat. "I wasn't any help. As long as Dad can't get over Dale's death, drinking will be a crutch. But then, he started long before Dale died. Anyway, I hope Ella can manage."

"But it was a good visit," Norman said, smiling at her. "We had some great talks. I think it brought us all closer."

As for her own marriage, Evelyn would propose a trial separation. She wasn't ready to share the news with Norman. The gulf between her and Joe.... What had happened to them?

So much of it was her own fault. Even after evenings exhausted from work, preparing dinner, and being with Steve, she didn't always go to bed when Joe wanted her to, relishing some quiet time on her own. In addition, she sometimes attended an evening AA meeting or talked on the phone with a younger person she sponsored. She owed AA for her recovery and wanted to pass on to others the knowledge and strength she'd gained.

All this left little space for Joe. No wonder he felt neglected. Was it too late? Apparently, he thought it was.

"I don't know if I want to stay married," he'd said when she confronted him about his affair. She couldn't stay without a commitment to the marriage. And his continued drinking risked her sobriety. "And I don't need to give up drinking. Maybe you have a problem, but I don't."

Even with the prospect of divorce and a single-life-with-child looming at age forty-six, she was sure she'd never go back to alcohol. She could rely on her AA support system, where she had many friends. AA had helped her give up a twenty-five-year smoking habit, too. Being single would be hard, just like giving up drinking and smoking had been. And Steve would be okay, eventually. He had friends with divorced parents.

As for Dad, he had Ella. And, sadly, his alcohol. Ella would continue to struggle with Dad's drinking, but her church and her friends there would give her comfort. Evelyn was grateful she'd been able to spend time with them.

Not all interventions succeeded.

On His Game

I HEARD BOB'S RAGGED and raspy breathing as I entered his hospital room. A tube snaked into his mouth, and IV lines trailed along the body I could barely make out under the white sheet. It was 1978, and that morning I'd flown down to Los Angeles from the Bay Area, where I lived with my husband, Ed, and our two young sons. My taxi to the hospital had rear-ended another cab, and I hoped the crash wasn't an omen for my visit. But the two drivers resolved the issue peacefully.

Our brother Norman stood up from the cot in the corner, his bed the previous night. He gave me a welcoming hug, then I took a quick look around the bleak, sterile room, with its ugly light-green walls. Alongside Bob's narrow bed, a long table held a pitcher of water and a tiny box of tissues. I coughed at the bitter smell of antiseptic from the bathroom, where a walker stood just inside. My spirits sank. My strong, vibrant brother here?

"The doctors don't know if Bob's gonna make it," Norman said wearily, and collapsed onto his cot. Through the closed door, I could hear the murmur of voices, along with intermittent intercom noise. "I can't get over how he ended up here."

Norman had given me only sketchy details on the phone yesterday. Bob had collapsed in the bar where he usually ate after his night shift in Standard Oil's petroleum fields. Bob and I had lost touch in the last few years. All I remembered about his work was that he helped control the flow of oil from a well to storage tanks in Anaheim, about thirty miles southeast of Los Angeles.

But this business about having breakfast in a bar. That was disturbing.

Bob had been the only one of my siblings who lived in Southern California until Norman and his family moved there from the Bay Area nine years earlier, when Norman took a job as director of public works for the town of Stanton, near Anaheim.

"The bartender called me," Norman said. "I guess Bob had something in his wallet with me as his emergency contact. He hadn't looked good for a few days, the guy said; really tired, very quiet. That morning, he was perspiring, coughing, barely ate any of his breakfast. The guy told Bob he should see a doctor. Bob said he was okay. But when he stood up, he staggered a bit, then he fell down."

On the farm, we didn't see a doctor unless there was an accident. Bob was nine years older than I, and my clearest memories of him were from our farm. He could work all day long: loading cattle onto trucks, digging postholes in the hot sun, or driving a tractor cultivating corn.

Growing up, I'd admired my handsome and worldly older brother. I used to watch him from the window of our house, looking stylish in his neatly pressed khaki pants and blue dress shirt, his straight brown hair slicked back, on his way to movies or drinks with his good-looking high-school guy friends. When he wasn't going out, he'd cloister himself in his room and read through the pile of books Mom got for him from the library, which I liked reading when he finished. Sometimes Mom, Danny, and I watched him play baseball in Lake Park's summer league.

After he graduated from high school, in 1950, he enlisted in the service, as our older brothers had done. I was always excited when he came home on leave from his tours of duty with the Navy, first on the *USS Midway*, then on the *USS Coral Sea*, which made stops in Istanbul and Cairo. He never brought toys or trinkets for me or our younger brother, Danny. He always brought gifts for the family that seemed too elegant for our old farmhouse: a gold clock with a flywheel and pendulum, a colorful leather hassock.

Looking down at Bob now, shrunken and emaciated in his hospital bed, I puzzled over why I had so admired him. He hadn't spent much time with Danny and me when we were young, except to play gin rummy with us now and then. Unlike our oldest brother, Dale, he never took us swimming at Pike's Point or to the amusement area at Arnolds Park. I guessed he viewed me as the pesky little sister.

But in 1963, when I was in college in San Jose, I took a bus to Southern California to stay with friends, and I called him. For some reason, he seemed to finally "get" his role as older brother, and he treated me to my first-ever day at Disneyland. He was the same quiet person who didn't talk much. In a Hawaiian shirt and navy cotton slacks, he looked tanned but a little weathered, with crow's feet around his eyes.

He'd left home for good after Dale died, so by then he'd been working in the oil fields for seven years. That day, he told me, "I'm going for a college degree in business at night. Standard Oil wanted me to work in the office, because I took a test and scored high in math. I tried it for a few weeks, but I like being outside, so I went back to work in the fields."

I asked him what he did for fun.

"Deep-sea fishing with my friends," he said, lighting up a cigarette, "and I sometimes play some golf with them."

"As I told Norman yesterday," the doctor said when he came by that afternoon, "Bob has viral encephalitis, severe inflammation of the brain." He looked up from Bob's chart and patted my shoulder. "That hundred-and-six-degree fever he had at admission did real damage. His body was already weakened from malnutrition, due to advanced alcoholism. And I gather he was also a longtime smoker. He was probably walking around with a fever for days and ignored it, until he collapsed."

Trying to focus on what the doctor was saying, I heard phrases like "mental disabilities," "impaired speech," and "memory loss." My heart pounded as I latched onto one of those words: "alcoholism."

I knew Bob had drunk alcohol since high school. But I never saw it as a serious issue, even though two of our siblings, Evelyn and Dan, were recovering alcoholics, and our father drank heavily up until he died at eighty-six. Maybe I'd not seen it because Bob's drinking hadn't impacted me directly, while our father's led to fights with Mom that scared us kids and sent us fleeing to our rooms. I hadn't seen this out-of-control behavior with Bob. But then, he was often away when I was growing up: the Navy, then college, then Southern California.

I remembered how great Bob had looked eight years earlier, at my wedding reception. I could still see him, in his beige-linen sport jacket, blue button-down shirt, and new horn-rimmed glasses. Over the next few years, Ed and I, and then with our sons, drove to Southern California at least twice yearly to visit Norman and his family. At first, Bob always came to see us. But more and more often, he would promise to stop by and then not show up. Once we drove to his one-bedroom apartment and found him in his dusty, badly lit living room, drinking a beer and watching television. He said he hadn't felt like coming to Norman's that day. I wish we had wondered more about his odd behavior then.

After that, he and I had very little contact, and eventually Bob stopped visiting Norman's family. Norman and Jean were so busy raising their large family, Norman didn't realize how long it had been, he said. And when he called, Bob didn't return his phone calls. More than twenty years ago, Bob had left the farm and driven out to California with Stan, one of his oldest friends, but when Norman phoned him, he said he hadn't seen or talked with Bob in several years, nor had Verle, his best friend. When Verle called Bob's other friends, they also said he'd stopped seeing them.

My brother did not wake up that day at the hospital, but a week or so later, he became stable enough to move into a nursing home not far from Norman's house. I wondered why he needed to live with old people when he was only forty-six. But we'd been warned of potential brain damage from the after-effects of his high temperature.

Did this mean his working life was over? I couldn't imagine Bob without a sense of purpose. He had survived, but how much would his life be changed?

———

A FEW WEEKS LATER, I flew down to Anaheim again. While Bob was in the hospital, Norman had gone to Bob's apartment to bring him some clothes and books. Except for a layer of dust and his high school yearbook, the bookcase was empty. Norman also said he'd found a pistol in Bob's nightstand.

Norman and I had lunch with Verle, who drove up from Escondido, about two hours east.

"I'm so sorry," Verle said, shaking our hands. "Bob and I used to play golf together a lot, even after I got married. Mavis and I invited him to lots of our barbecues. He'd always say yes, but sometimes he wouldn't show up, or even call and say why not. Maybe he felt out of place with our married friends and their children. I don't know why I didn't keep trying to reach him."

Verle and Bob had been best friends since elementary school.

"In our group of guys, Bob was the quiet one," Verle said, "a better athlete than I was. He liked reading, usually had a book in the car. We both liked hunting, and we traded guns. I had a 12-gauge shotgun, and Bob had a 22 rifle, for hunting pheasants." He knew about the pistol, which he said Bob bought because he lived in a rough neighborhood. But he couldn't expand on why

Bob had withdrawn from his friends.

We all wondered how Bob, this formerly social guy, had become so solitary, why he'd stopped reading, and when he'd begun drinking so much.

Had he become depressed like Dale? Our grandmother, too, had had mental-health problems. Yet while Dale had basically stopped working, and our grandmother was institutionalized, Bob had managed to function at his job until the day he collapsed.

After Norman and I said goodbye to Verle, I drove to Bob's nursing home by myself. The blooming petunias against the brick façade looked welcoming. In the main living area, the residents, in their sixties and seventies, sat on floral-upholstered chairs and couches, watching television, reading, or playing games in groups; many sat slumped in wheelchairs. This was not where my brother belonged.

I wondered how Bob would be, living in this kind of place.

When I got to his room, I stood in the doorway and watched him for a few minutes. The room could have been worse, with its pale-blue walls, beige faux-leather armchair, television set on a stand in the corner. The three-shelf bookcase held only Bob's high school graduation photo and a bible, no doubt from Norman. A folded wheelchair sat in the corner. Through a sliding-glass door, I could see a small courtyard and green lawn, the brown Santa Ana Mountains in the distance, which cheered me a little. Bob was sitting at a card table and shuffling a deck of cards.

"Hi, Bob," I said, forcing a cheerful tone as I walked in. "Do you know who I am?"

Norman had said Bob might not recognize me. Sure enough, he looked up with a confused expression and stopped shuffling the cards.

He shook his head, as if I hadn't gotten the message from the look on his face. Then his gaze returned to his cards and, in slow and graceful motions, he continued cutting them. His complete lack of recognition knocked the wind out of me. I couldn't believe he was so far gone. At least he looked neat and clean, in a Hawaiian shirt and faded but unwrinkled khakis.

I motioned to the patio, suggesting we sit outside. When he stood up, I was shocked at how loose his pants were on his thin frame.

He looked at me with a confused expression but let me lead him outside. Nearby, two frail white-haired women sat in wheelchairs, hunched and silent, staring down at the cement.

Bob curled his upper lip in disgust. "I'm not like them," he said. "I don't belong here."

So he could evaluate his surroundings but didn't recognize me.

Staring at the distant mountains, I clutched the armrests of my chair, sick and miserable at seeing this remnant of a man I'd once admired. I glanced through the open door. If I made a graceful exit, within a few minutes he'd forget I'd been there.

I was suddenly disgusted at my spinelessness. How could I be so selfish? Spending time with him was good for both of us. Time for me to develop some empathy, and he, who as a younger man had had such good friends, might enjoy some company. He was my brother, after all. What was I thinking?

Glancing into his room, I noticed a cribbage board on the card table. Norman had said Bob remembered the game.

"Want to play a game of cribbage?" I asked in a too-loud voice. "Norman tells me you're still good." He nodded his head yes.

I took Bob's arm, and we went back into his room and sat down at the small table. He shuffled, snapping the cards, then dealt. I took deep breaths, trying to relax, worried about how he would do. If he couldn't play, would it frustrate him?

As kids in Iowa, we'd played hearts and gin rummy on long winter days and dark evenings, when snow piled up outside. We'd sprawl on the floor, huddled around the floor radiator, nibbling from a bowl of popcorn. Bob would have finished his library books, then deigned to play cards with his younger sib-lings. Mom was grateful we were all occupied.

Once Bob learned cribbage in the Navy, he preferred it to other card games. Now he sat across from me, eyes darting from his cards to the cribbage board. After each turn, he advanced his peg to the correct spot and added up the points. Though he couldn't differentiate between suits or among individual face cards, Bob recognized card numbers and remembered that face cards counted for ten points each.

The tension seeped from my shoulders as I laughed at his intense focus. He grinned in response. His hazel eyes shone, perhaps with a hint of triumph. It was a moment of connection. Soon Bob and I were laughing just as we used to, so long ago. It didn't matter if he remembered who I was or how we used to play card games. It didn't matter that he was no longer young and sporty, with lots of cool friends.

———

WITHIN A FEW MONTHS, Norman and Jean had brought Bob to live with them. His drinking was behind him. With their support, he learned to perform chores for the neighbors. He rode his bike to the grocery store and made small purchases of food, always paying the correct amount.

To the chagrin of Norman's teenage sons, Bob often won their pool and ping-pong competitions. When Bob's doctor said he needed to build up his muscle tone, Norman, my engineer brother, rigged up a kind of resistance machine, with a heavy nylon rope, a baseball bat, and a twenty-five-pound weight. Norman also instructed him in a few daily calisthenics.

After a couple of years, though, it became apparent that Bob needed his own space. And his daily care was taking a toll on Norman and Jean, who arranged for him to rent a small apart-ment on the top floor of a house nearby. Norman handled Bob's finances—his disability checks, stock dividends from Standard Oil, and Social Security payments, all of which provided him a comfortable living.

My family and I drove south to visit Norman's family a few times a year, and Bob would be there. A quiet, almost ghostly presence, he sat on the couch and watched baseball games on television. He still didn't recognize us, but he liked playing cribbage. I wondered how much of Bob was really present.

During one visit, I helped Norman clean Bob's apartment, a weekly task. We also delivered a week's worth of sandwiches and microwavable dinners. He had a decent-size room and a full bathroom; the adjoining eating area, next to a small kitchen, had a card table and three metal folding chairs.

When we walked in, I was hit with the overpowering smell of dank sheets, dirty clothes, and spoiled food. I held my breath as I looked into the kitchen, with its dirty plates and glasses, half-loaf of bread, opened jars of peanut butter and instant coffee on the counter.

My heart sank as I saw how Bob's living standards had declined. At home in Iowa, he'd kept his books in orderly rows, his clothes carefully arranged in his closets, and sometimes even made his bed.

Bob was lounging in a faux-leather recliner, watching television. Above rumpled blue shorts, his wrinkled, unbuttoned plaid shirt exposed his pale and flabby torso. On the wall, in his Navy photo, a young man with a lean, striking face and stunning smile—movie-star handsome—looked back at me. In the photo, his hair was combed back under his white Navy cap. Today, that face was pudgy, lined, and in need of a shave.

Even on the farm, Bob had been particular about his appearance. Once, when I was a teenager and he was home on leave from the Navy, he asked me to iron his dress pants. He soon jerked the pants from my hands.

"I could do a better job with a hot brick," he said, and he grabbed the iron and executed two perfect creases.

Now I greeted him with a pat on his shoulder. "Hi, Bob, what're you watching?"

He sat up and glanced at me with a frown, no recognition lighting his eyes. But I was used to that. In spite of the room's gross smells and Bob's slovenly appearance, I was happy to see him, looking somewhat healthy and engaged in one of his favorite activities.

"I'm watching the Angels and the Yankees," he said, turning up the volume. Here I was again, the pesky younger sister, annoying him. "The Angels are my favorite team," he added, settling back in his chair.

I sat on the couch. "Who's winning?" I asked. Out of the corner of my eye, I watched Norman scrubbing the inside of Bob's fridge. Bob didn't seem concerned that the Angels were behind, so I wondered how much he understood about what he saw. In high school, he'd lettered in baseball.

"Can't tell who's winning," Bob said. His foot tapped against the floor. Then he sat up straight, his shoulders stiff and tense. I wondered if he could sense what was coming. When I got up to strip his bed, his eyes narrowed. "What are you doing?"

"I have to change your sheets," I said. As I pulled the fitted sheet from the mattress, I caught a whiff of rotten food.

Under the bed, I found two plastic bags stuffed with moldy oranges and rancid cottage cheese and yogurt. Mushy bananas at the bottom of one bag caught my eye. This fruit had been such a treat for us when we lived on the farm. As soon as Mom brought home a bunch from the store, my brothers and I would gobble them all up.

Norman called me over and said in a low voice, "Bob scavenges behind supermarkets. I can't get him to stop."

We'd never wasted things when we were growing up, but

I couldn't believe this principle had stuck with Bob in this depressing way. He seemed to be going against everything he used to be: clean, neat, and meticulous. What kind of life was Bob leading? Was it much above mere existence?

"Bob, you can't eat food from dumpsters," I scolded, trying to control my annoyance. "It's dangerous."

He hung his head. Would his foraging be okay as long as we didn't know about it? But it wasn't okay. Obviously, he didn't realize how unsafe it was, so it was our business to intervene. Bob frowned as I threw the food into a garbage bag and tied it closed with trembling hands. We were intruding in his life. But at least we, and especially Norman, were keeping him healthy.

Norman and I continued sorting through Bob's caches of food and organizing his kitchen, storing the sandwiches and dinners we'd brought in his fridge. Doing things for him, whether he liked it or not, was a way to communicate our love. To get through his life, he needed our help. But were we treating him as less than human with all our rummaging and organizing?

The baseball game ended, and Bob turned off the television. He sat down at his card table, littered with bank statements, receipts, and a small pile of photos. I followed his gaze to the photographs, his former life reduced to those few images of people and events he probably didn't remember.

Before we ate lunch, Norman and Bob bowed their heads in prayer. I assumed Bob understood nothing about our brother's Catholic faith, but Norman cared about his brother's soul. Though not sharing Norman's religious beliefs, I respected his innate goodness and loving care for Bob.

Ever since I stopped going to Sunday school, I'd always tried to be a good person without religion. When I was a child, I'd thrilled at singing "The Old Rugged Cross," "Blessed Assurance," and other hymns. Often, I prayed to God. I even accepted Jesus Christ as my savior. In church and at bible school during summers, I learned many bible stories and saw Jesus as gentle and loving. But in my teenage years, the minister who preached to us once a month (a postman in his day job) leaned heavily on the punishments of hell for "you sinners." I grew to believe the church members' open censure of our pregnant, unwed teenage neighbor and their judgment of my divorced mother had nothing to do with a loving God. And the church's restrictions on movies, dancing, and wearing makeup I saw as ridiculous, so I dropped out.

The prayer finished, we unwrapped our lunchmeat-and-Swiss-cheese sandwiches. After his fever, along with so much else, Bob had forgotten how to use some ordinary objects, like a knife and fork. At least those were skills he could relearn. Norman told me that Bob once bit into an unpeeled orange. Another time, he confused instant coffee with peanut butter and spread it on his toast.

After we ate, we looked through Bob's photos. Pointing to the youngest of six "stair-step" children in a hazy black-and-white print, he said, "I don't know who they are, but he said," nodding at Norman, "that's me."

In the picture, a tow-headed Bob, probably about six, wore ragged overalls and had a rifle propped next to him. A pony stood in the background.

"That's most of us kids there," I explained, "the oldest brothers and sisters, without me and Danny."

Bob picked up another picture, this one taken before he left for California. He was standing in front of his 1954 Ford.

"Did I drive that car?" Bob asked, studying the picture, a serious look on his face. I recalled the hours he had spent washing and polishing that Ford, getting it ready to pick up his friends for an evening out.

"Do you remember working as an aviation structural mechanic on a ship?" I asked as I picked up a large black-and-white photo.

Bob was crouched on top of an airplane engine on the deck of an aircraft carrier. "You said you repaired the skin on airplanes."

I hoped the picture would jog his memory about his Navy tours. He'd once told us about a bomb that fell off a plane and was rolling directly toward him. "I was scared shitless and couldn't move. Some other guys ran and grabbed it. Turned out to be a dud."

"Don't remember," he said, pointing at the photo, "but I think that's me."

Then I noticed his high school yearbook, next to his graduation photo on the shelf of an otherwise empty bookcase. Once again, I felt sad remembering how Bob had loved to read. Even Verle remembered that. Mom and I had checked out armloads of books for him. After I finished them, I always wanted to talk about what we read, but I don't think we ever did.

I retrieved the yearbook and sat down again, turning the pages, searching for his picture.

"Pretty good-looking guy," I said in a teasing tone, pointing to his graduation picture. He wore the obligatory smile but had an air of hanging back, as if he feared taking on the world. I'd never noticed that look before.

A few pages on, I paused at a picture of a girl with long, dark-brown hair.

"Remember Janice? I heard she had a crush on you."

Bob regarded me with a puzzled look and shook his head.

Wanting to get out of the past, I closed the yearbook. "What do you like to do during the day, Bob?" I asked.

"I get those things off the ground with that long wood thing for the neighbors," he said, taking another bite of sandwich. I had no idea what he was talking about.

"Raking leaves," Norman said. Oh, of course.

"I take another guy's big buckets out." Bob sat up straight, looking eager to describe his work.

"What buckets?" I asked, confused again.

"You know, those big buckets with all the junk in them." He shook his head, as if I was the dumb one in the room.

"Oh, right, trash cans," I said.

"They let me clean their water, too."

He obviously meant a swimming pool. Bob seemed to talk in a kind of code that I was just starting to figure out.

"And I ride my bicycle to the store. Sometimes I have to buy a few things."

As he talked about his odd jobs, his pleasure and the friendly crinkles around his eyes when he smiled made me smile, too. Clearly, he felt productive. I put my hand on his. He didn't respond, but it didn't matter. We could share special moments, even if he didn't know who I was.

I began to understand that I was the limited one. Until now, I hadn't understood that Bob could carry on a conversation. It just took me a little longer to decipher what he was saying.

"See this?" he said, picking up a sheet of paper covered with names and columns of numbers written in a childish scrawl. "Ben still owes me three thousand dollars. He borrowed three thousand five hundred, and he pays me a hundred and seventy-five dollars in interest every year. And Betsy has to pay me one thousand two hundred dollars, sixty dollars in interest. That's Ben's name there, and here's Betsy's."

He beamed with pride at his accounting system, keeping track of loans to nieces and nephews. Norman had helped him determine a reasonable interest rate, and Bob kept meticulous records in his ledger.

Handing a bank statement to me, he said, "See, I have eleven thousand, two hundred and fifty dollars in my savings account. I bought a bicycle for two hundred and fifty dollars when somebody took mine."

During that long-ago trip to Disneyland, Bob had said he

was working toward his B.A. degree in business. Maybe, in some way, he'd held onto that dream.

I was proud of him, though he didn't need my approval. I felt ashamed that I had ever viewed his life as unimportant. He was trying to manage his life. It wasn't his old existence, and we might never know what had happened to him in his earlier life, but this reality had value.

"That's great, Bob," I said, smiling and blinking back tears. "I'm so impressed. You were always great at math, and you're keeping good records, too." My praise sounded disgustingly patronizing, but I meant it.

We had to finish cleaning. I got up slowly, reluctant to leave this conversation that left all of us smiling. I moved the recliner to vacuum underneath it and heard the rustle of another plastic bag.

"Damn it," I muttered, all those good feelings about to evaporate. Then I saw his determined eyes staring at me. He'd heard the noise and watched me uncover another of his secrets. I left the bag under the chair and vacuumed around it. He deserved this, a little piece of control over his own life.

Just after Bob's sixtieth birthday, Norman called to tell me he'd found our brother dead in his room.

"He was kneeling on the floor, his head on the couch," Norman said. "It was really tough to find him like that. But I'd like to think he was praying."

Wiping away tears, I thought about Bob's life, from his days on the farm, in the Navy, and at college to his fateful move to California, though I knew alcohol abuse might have claimed him anywhere. He'd never remembered that I was his sister. But Bob had created a life that worked for him.

I recalled the day Bob had shown me his bank statement and the list of people to whom he'd lent money. After we finished cleaning his room, Norman and I prepared to leave. Bob changed into a clean shirt and khakis, and we all went outside, where his elderly next-door neighbor was raking leaves.

"Hey, Bob, how about helping me out?" he asked. He came over and briefly put his hand on my brother's shoulder. "I can't do all this by myself."

Bob fetched the man's plastic leaf barrel, then he took the neighbor's rake and began dragging leaves into piles. Norman and I got in the car, and I looked back. Hunched over his rake, Bob didn't give us another glance.

Shattered Idol

I N T H E E I G H T - B Y -ten-inch glossy photo, a pretty woman in her mid to late twenties leans toward the camera. She is dressed in a leopard-skin coat and hat, wears bright red lipstick and dabs of rouge, and brandishes a cigarette holder.

"My sister Marguerite," I told Ed. "Taken during her modeling days, almost twenty years ago."

My future husband and I were looking at my family photos in the living room of our San Francisco apartment. Looking at the glitzy picture, I recalled how I marveled at it when I was an awestruck teenage farm girl. Marguerite had always oozed glamour and success to me. When I first left Iowa and moved to California, I spent as much time with her as possible. She was generous in helping me leave that hick farm girl behind, but she was often sharp and unkind. Now I was a couple years older than the woman in the picture and an independent working woman myself, but she still intimidated me. In the last four years, we'd had very little contact.

It was early 1970, more than a year since I'd returned from living in Germany. Ed and I had been together for six months. He'd gotten to know my other sister, Evelyn, and her husband. We'd even flown to Southern California so that he could meet two of my brothers, Bob and Norman. But I hadn't yet contacted Marguerite, who lived two miles away.

"How can siblings not talk to each other for so long?" Ed wondered, studying the photo. "I know you're nervous," he said, putting his arm around me. "But listen. When I was younger, I was put off by how smart my brother was. Mike graduated with distinction from Harvard, but we talk on the same level now. I'm good with where I am, doing litigation with a good law firm. And think of what you've accomplished—working in a foreign country and becoming fluent in German, a very difficult language, as an adult."

"Yeah," I said softly. I'd always wanted to live overseas for a while, so I moved to West Germany after I graduated from college, in February 1965. I lived for a year each in Frankfurt and West Berlin, employed as a secretary for a German company in Frankfurt and for the British military in West Berlin, while giving private English lessons to German citizens. With friends I made in both cities, I traveled around West Germany and to several other countries, always laboring to become fluent in the language by speaking and reading it.

After returning to the U.S., I visited my dad and Ella in Iowa for a week, then took a Greyhound bus to California to stay for a few days with Norman and his wife. They lent me money to rent a room a short bus ride from the University of San Francisco, where I took evening classes in education. I worked at temporary secretarial jobs before receiving a Pell grant.

After a year of teacher training, including student teaching in English and German classes at Lincoln High School, I earned my high school teaching credential. Unfortunately, a glut of applicants enabled school districts to hire teachers with master's degrees. After a stint of substitute teaching, I began working as an administrative assistant at the Economic Opportunity Council, on Polk Street, assisting my boss in helping low-income people access financial assistance, job training, and housing. I also helped organize meetings with community groups to discuss how best to serve them.

And I was about to get married.

I looked around our furnished apartment, with its commercial gray carpeting and flimsy wood-framed chairs with their shallow beige cushions. It was a world away from my memories of Marguerite's stylish apartments, with their colorful cotton pillows on thick upholstered couches and chairs covered with paisley slipcovers she had sewn herself.

"You should call your sister," Ed said. "She's probably mellowed by now."

Maybe Ed was right. Maybe she had become less confrontational. With my life going so well, surely I could deflect her verbal jabs, even talk to her with confidence now. It was time to act like a grownup.

For days, I put off making the phone call, and the first few times I dialed, I lost my nerve and hung up. Finally, I got up the courage to let the phone ring until she answered.

"Hi, Marguerite," I said, clearing my throat and pacing the floor. "This is Sandy."

"Long time no see," she said after a pause, sounding genuinely surprised. "Where are you and what are you up to?"

"I'm working in San Francisco and about to get married." My clammy hands fidgeted with the coiled telephone cord. I took a deep breath. "I'd like you to meet my fiancé."

"Great. Come down to the factory Saturday morning. Be here at ten." She hung up, and I collapsed into the nearest chair. My heart felt as if it would thud out of my chest. I'd done it. But I could tell she still intimidated me.

The factory at Third and Howard streets was in a scruffy industrial neighborhood, although there were some newly painted warehouses. Just two blocks away, streetcars were moving along Market Street, where during the week men and women hustled to their jobs. Ed and I climbed the three flights of stairs and opened the heavy metal door that led into Marguerite Rubel Manufacturing. Sweat dampened my forehead, from either the three flights of stairs or my emotional state.

Clasping and unclasping my hands, I gazed out at the enormous space filling the entire top floor, at the racks of coats and jackets, the shelved bolts of fabric, the cardboard boxes packed with garments to be shipped all over the U.S. Hearing the hum of sewing machines against a distant wall, I thought back to those many weekends I'd sorted invoices, arranged garments by style and size, and unpacked boxes of giant spools of thread. I was always glad to be interrupted in a mundane task to model a coat for a prospective customer. Helping my sister had made me feel important.

We found Marguerite behind a desk piled high with fabric swatches, cigarette cartons, and rough sketches of coat designs. At forty-seven, she was still attractive, with her now short, curly brown hair showing no gray, bushy brown eyebrows, and just a touch of lipstick. She wore a red-and-gold-print tunic over black stretch pants, and the extra ten pounds looked good on her.

I could see her glancing at Ed's moustache and sideburns when I introduced them. "So, what do you do?" she asked him.

"I'm a lawyer," he said.

She rolled her eyes. "Guess the world needs more lawyers. I hate facial hair, just so you know. But guess that's the style now." She lit a cigarette and looked at me. "How'd you meet?"

"On a blind date," I said. "My roommate was dating a guy who was recruiting people for his law firm in San Francisco. He interviewed Ed at the University of Michigan and invited him out here." I could see her interest waning before I got through the second sentence.

Ed gestured at the space around him. "Tell me how you got here," he said. "Sandy's told me a little."

We followed Marguerite over to her metal cutting table and watched as she rolled out dark-orange canvas fabric and positioned some pattern pieces atop it.

"After I finished high school, Evelyn and I hitchhiked to Omaha, Nebraska. Got jobs in an airplane-manufacturing plant. About a year later, we moved on to California." She straightened up and took a drag on her cigarette. "We were homeless for a few days but then got jobs as waitresses. The war was going on, you know, and people could make lots of money."

"Good for you," Ed said to her. "Probably an exciting and stressful time."

"Yeah, compared to me, you kids had it easy." She laid her burning cigarette in an ashtray on the cutting table and picked up a pair of heavy metal shears. A few months later, she inadvertently dumped a pile of coats onto a lighted cigarette and ruined several garments. Herb Caen, a popular columnist for the *San Francisco Chronicle*, wrote about the incident. "Well-known San Francisco coat manufacturer Marguerite Rubel Kuckenbecker...."

"You're right," Ed said, winking at me. "We had it easy." To help finance college and law school, he'd worked summers on a Ford assembly line in Detroit and driven a laundry truck.

Handing Ed the bolt of fabric and directing him where to shelve it, Marguerite continued, "I got a break in the late 1940s, when I sewed a raincoat for a woman going to the meeting for the United Nations. When a celebrity—can't remember her name—wore the coat, she got lots of attention, and that's how I got one of my coats on *Queen for a Day*."

After about twenty minutes, Marguerite said she was too busy to chat any longer. Outside on the sidewalk, I found breathing difficult, relieved I'd gotten through that conversation with her, still standing.

"She's impressive," Ed said. "And a bit intimidating, too."

———

ABOUT TWO YEARS EARLIER, Marguerite and her husband, Lowell, had bought a large home in San Francisco's Marina District, across from the Marina Green and just blocks from the San Francisco Yacht Club. Marguerite furnished the house with white brocade couches flanking the gold-leafed marble fireplace, colorful velveteen throw pillows, and plush floral-upholstered wing chairs. Gold-rimmed china and crystal goblets gleamed from glass-fronted mahogany cabinets.

Marguerite could be very generous, and after Ed and I married that November, she and Lowell hosted a party for us at their home. Most of my siblings and their families were there, including Norman and his wife, Jean, with two of their daughters, Claire and Teresa; Evelyn, Joe, and their son, Steve; and Bob. Dan phoned to say he couldn't get leave from the Army. Vern didn't say why he couldn't come.

Lowell's son, Richard, his partner in their thriving farm-machinery business in Fresno, was there with his pregnant wife and their two young girls. Possibly not to "waste" a party opportunity, Lowell, an avid sports fan, had invited to our celebration a few San Francisco Giants baseball players and some Major League Baseball umpires he'd gotten to know.

Lowell prepared an enormous pot of crab cioppino and served it over pasta, along with loaves of sourdough bread and Marguerite's Caesar salad. We ate around their enormous mahogany dining table, then moved to the spacious top floor, where Lowell served drinks from a full bar. At the other end of the room, guests enjoyed the view of San Francisco Bay through an immense picture window.

I glanced over at Ed, standing at the bar. Also a sports fan, he was all smiles as he chatted with Hal Lanier, a Giants shortstop and second baseman.

After that, Marguerite began inviting us to dinners and parties at their home. These generally included Lowell's family, Marguerite's friends, and baseball players and umpires. Marguerite would typically hold forth before a group of admiring women, usually about her start in the business.

During one such gathering, my sister described how a coat of hers was chosen as the single American raincoat entry at the 1958 Moscow Trade Fair. When the Russian Premier, Nikita

Khrushchev, visited San Francisco later that year, Marguerite presented his wife with a coat. After that, she said, she got calls from the U.S. State Department.

"I've never had so much trouble giving something away," Marguerite said, and all of us laughed. I never could tell which of her stories was true and which merely exaggerated, but her humorous way of relating them enthralled her listeners.

That evening, a woman my sister's age said to me, "Aren't you proud of your sister?"

"Yes," I said. Of course I was.

But I soon realized I preferred socializing with Ed's and my friends, mostly his lawyer associates and their spouses.

Ed and I bought a home in the East Bay and had our sons in 1973 and 1975. We saw Evelyn every few weeks, but I stopped by Marguerite's less often. While Ed worked his way into a law partnership, I took care of our sons and worked toward a master's degree in public administration at California State College East Bay, in Hayward, a twenty-five-minute drive from home. I hoped this degree would help me later, when my children were older, to find a job with a nonprofit organization.

Most summers, my sons and I flew to Iowa to see Dad and Ella; but in April 1977, Ella called to report that my dad had died while recovering from surgery for bladder cancer. This time, I flew to Cedar Rapids alone. Evelyn, now divorced, couldn't get time off from work, and Norman couldn't comfortably leave his large family. We had no word from Dan or Bob, although Bob hadn't been in touch with any of us for a couple of years. Vern appeared for just two days, saying his tax clients needed him. Marguerite and Lowell drove back in his Lincoln Continental.

Ironic, I thought, the three relatives least qualified to offer solace showed up.

Ella looked exhausted, from misery, from years of caring for my dad, and from her diabetes.

Though I was sad to lose him, Dad was eighty-six and had been ill for some time. We all knew his death was a relief from his suffering, not least his grief and guilt over the suicide of his oldest son, twenty-one years earlier. In fact, a few months before Dad died, he wrote me that had he known Dale was going to kill himself, he never would have left our mother.

Despite his and Ella's loving relationship, Dad wanted to be buried between my mother and Dale in the Lake Park cemetery. It was just six miles from our old farm but almost three hundred miles from Cedar Rapids. Lowell drove Marguerite and me as we followed the hearse. Ella was too ill to attend the burial.

"I'm so glad I left this godforsaken place," Marguerite said, looking out at the dark soil—this year's crops hadn't yet been planted—and the farm buildings, sagging fences, and cylindrical silos in the distance. At fifty-two, she still looked stylish in her colorful clothing, if a few pounds heavier. Her smooth skin showed only a few fine lines under her eyes. "If Dale wasn't so weak, he'd've left, too."

What? Weak because he chose to stay on the farm? Weak because he killed himself?

"Your dad was a strong and resourceful man," Lowell chimed in. "It wasn't easy making a success of farming. But your mom was weak." Lowell had met Mom years earlier when she visited California while I was in college.

I stiffened. My brother-in-law, now sixty, his love handles bulging under his polo shirts and his luxuriant black hair streaked with gray, always sounded so sure of himself. Even at thirty-six, I lacked the confidence to argue against his pronouncements. Or even, it seemed, to defend Dale and Mom.

"When I was about ten," Marguerite went on, "Dad gave me an orphan pig. I spent lots of time feeding it, then Dale got me to sell it to him, for just a little money. Turns out it was pregnant and worth lots more. I think Dale knew, and he cheated me."

I stayed silent. Was she really holding a grudge against Dale for something that happened when they were children? And why couldn't I confront these two?

Ella died six weeks later. She had been such a loving companion to my dad, and I was grateful she was free from her pain and exhaustion.

Occasionally, we visited Marguerite and Lowell when they invited us over for Sunday brunch. Ed and Lowell would watch Giants baseball or 49er football games in their den, while Marguerite and I chatted in the breakfast room about how her business was doing and how my life must be so boring, with small children and no other life.

A touch of the old glamour I'd idolized as a young girl still clung to Marguerite. The paisley- or floral-print tunics she wore over dark tights contrasted nicely with the new silver threads in her hair. And I admired the way she continued to run a successful business.

Though Ed and I seldom brought our active sons to their house, I did want them to know their aunt and uncle, to know all my family.

So one day, we did bring the boys. Alex, age five and exploring, had been ordered not to touch anything. Josh, age three, clutched a boy doll dressed in blue trousers and a plaid shirt as he looked wide-eyed at the giant sculpture of an eagle on the sideboard and the impressive brass telescope by the window.

"Boys aren't supposed to have dolls," said Marguerite, smoking her omnipresent cigarette. Josh furrowed his eyebrows and looked as if he might cry. I put my arms around him.

"A lot of us hold onto things that make us feel comfortable," I told him, "preferably if they don't do us harm. Look at Aunt Marguerite. She smokes cigarettes because smoking makes her feel relaxed, even if it turns her fingers yellow."

Her face colored slightly. She tamped out her cigarette and resumed ripping out a broken zipper on a throw pillow. Then I felt a niggle of guilt. I'd forgotten that not long after I'd moved to California, Marguerite had had a hysterectomy—for a cancerous tumor, I think—and so was unable to have children. I didn't think she'd ever wanted any, or Lowell, either. But I was never sure.

On those Sunday mornings, my brother-in-law usually had a glass of scotch in hand, speaking of objects bringing comfort. After the game, Ed and I always hustled out the door before Lowell became loud and confrontational, mostly criticizing Ed for his liberal politics and general ignorance due to his youth. Lowell never failed to note how, in the first year of our marriage, we had marched in demonstrations against the Vietnam War and gone door to door recruiting votes for George McGovern.

"I tried to get the conversation away from politics, back to sports," Ed said one afternoon as we left their house. "Good thing Marguerite's business is doing well, but Lowell's drinking…that's gotta be tough."

Though Lowell and Marguerite never came to our house, Evelyn visited often. I was impressed at how she navigated life as a divorced mother of a teenager. She had maintained her sobriety, from both drinking and smoking, and taken a less challenging position closer to her home, in the San Bruno Municipal Clerk's office. She'd left home at fifteen, married at twenty, and now was dating again, sometimes bringing a boyfriend to our house. She'd taken up square dancing and was starting to travel internationally with friends.

By now, Jean and Norman were living in Anaheim, so we'd fly or drive to Southern California a couple times a year to see them and visit Bob. The brain damage Bob had experienced from encephalitis a year after Dad died had left him unable to recognize us, but he seemed to enjoy playing cribbage with us. We traveled to North Carolina every two or three years to visit Vern and his family, around stops in Washington, D.C., to see Ed's dad and stepmother.

Then Dan surfaced. We'd occasionally talked on the phone, where he told me he'd gotten out of the Army in 1973, settled in Austin, Texas, but not much more. I hadn't seen him in seventeen years.

He looked a bit like the Marlboro Man now: thick, dark-brown hair, bushy mustache, weathered cheeks, a kind of rugged look. But he seemed a little subdued.

Why hadn't he visited sooner?

"My life was a mess. Never knew how long a job would last. My marriage was unsettled. Guess I was waiting until things straightened out, whatever 'straightened out' meant. You, you did everything in the right order. Graduated from college. Traveled. Then got married. Had kids. And me? I was married, but now I'm divorced."

"I'm sorry," I said. A long period of silence ensued. I felt bad for him, but I didn't know what to say.

"One good thing. I have a stepdaughter, Tara, who calls me Dad." He smiled at that. "She's sixteen. Chose to live with me since the divorce, two years ago."

"That's great," I said. "I—"

"No more details." He almost glared at me, as if daring me to ask for more specifics.

"Okay," I said. "Did you, um, get anything useful from your three years in the Army?"

We were still sitting at the dinner table that first evening. He had just told Alex and Josh, thirteen and eleven, that when we were kids, he threw stone-filled snowballs at me as we frolicked in the snow with our German Shepherd puppy, King.

"What?" I said in a mock-angry voice. "I had no idea."

"And I used to chase your mom and dump icicles down her neck."

The boys chuckled at that, then were excused from the table.

"I learned some electronics that helped me train in how to use a pretty sophisticated tunnel-boring machine," Dan told Ed and me. "It's huge—thirty-five feet in diameter and eighty feet long—and computer operated, and I run it for an international construction company in Austin. And I'm working on a college degree in engineering and graphic design."

During that week-long stay, he seemed to perk up, and I felt we recaptured some of the closeness we'd had as youngsters and when we were both in college in San Jose. After dinner one evening, he brought up our oldest brother's suicide, now thirty years in the past.

"None of us talked about Dale much, did we? I think Mom just wanted to avoid the subject. Dad was usually sad, feeling guilty and drinking more."

"I'm sorry I wasn't more available," I said. "I was so young, and I guess I wanted to put the whole thing behind me, too. Like Mom tried to do, I think. She was sometimes moody, wasn't she? So quiet, like she didn't feel like talking. But hey…I have some weird family news."

I had never told my siblings about Uncle Harold's letter, which arrived out of the blue just after our mother died and included shocking information. I hadn't known how to relay what it said, that our grandmother had been confined till her death in a Hospital for the Criminally Insane in Indiana, diagnosed with "acute mania," institutionalized since our mother was sixteen and Harold was fourteen.

"Wow!" Dan exclaimed. "Who knew? Maybe Dale had some sort of mental disease. Sounds like it could be in our family." He shook his head. "Woe is us."

There seemed nothing more to say, so we changed the subject.

During that week, we stopped by Marguerite's factory. Busy boxing coats for shipment, she greeted Dan with a hug. Then she held up samples of two new jackets she planned to manufacture. One had a patchwork design, with denim and calico-print cotton squares. "Lots of people wearing denim," she said. The other was a cute, slightly puffy red jacket with a high collar and diagonal lines of gathered fabric in front. I wanted to buy the second one on the spot.

"What do you kids think?" she asked, smiling. "Maybe it's time to branch out a little."

"Both are really fun," I said. "Should do well."

"People are still buying the old standby styles, velveteen and quilted designs," Marguerite said. "Mostly older women." My sister looked smart herself, in a purple quilted vest over a lightweight navy-blue long-sleeve blouse. She was about twenty pounds heavier, with chubbier cheeks, still wearing bright-red lipstick, and she'd dyed her hair blond.

She went back to work, and Dan and I wandered over to Lowell, who sat at an oversize desk, surrounded by financial documents and tapping on an adding machine.

"So, how's business?" Dan asked.

"It's okay," he said, standing up to shake Dan's hand. I noted a few enlarged blood vessels on his nose and cheeks. Back in his chair, he lit up a cigarette. "But she'll never get rich. Lucky to make payroll. I haven't the foggiest notion how she managed before she met me. No head for business. Just for design."

―――――

By now, I had completed graduate school but was kept busy driving our sons to school and sports practices. In college, I'd been good at writing papers, so I began doing freelance journalism, mostly for local newspapers but occasionally for regional and national press, such as the Pacific News Service. Topics included social issues, education, and mental health. My article about AIDS was the cover story in an issue of the *San Francisco Bay Guardian*. My essay about the competitive process of applying to college ran in the *Marin Independent Journal* and the *Oakland Tribune*. It made fun of one parent, me, as I pressured my kid to complete numerous college applications. Alex's senior English class discussed that essay as an example of satire.

Dan was writing, too. After our visit, he worked for the next several years on subway- and water-tunnel-digging projects around the country. On a job in Milwaukee, Wisconsin, an enormous machine fell on his hand. He passed out from the pain and almost lost a finger. When he was diagnosed with post-traumatic stress disorder, his employer referred him to individual and group therapy. His therapist suggested he write stories about his life to help him cope with the trauma of the accident, and he occasionally sent them to me. Some dealt with the aftermath of Dale's suicide; others were interesting tales about farm life, in which Dan described the inner workings of a car engine, say, or how Dale discussed how to improve our hog-breeding stock.

"You have great details," I told him. "Could be interesting to some people, but the reader might get lost in those details and lose the thread of the narrative."

In the early nineties, Dan's employer began sending him on jobs in Asia—the Philippines, Thailand, Taiwan; we spent a week with him in Hong Kong—to ensure their tunnel-boring machine worked properly. Dan wrote in an email that he especially liked the teaching part of his job, instructing workers in the complicated electronics and using flow charts to explain the intricacies of this enormous piece of equipment. In spite of these assignments, Dan was always afraid of losing his job and not finding another. But he always did. I couldn't understand why he was so insecure when he seemed to be doing so well. I didn't know how to respond. Was it that he had never finished college? But it wasn't clear any of his fellow workers had, either.

We seldom went to Marguerite's house anymore, but I managed to visit her at her factory every few weeks. One afternoon, she greeted me by holding up a black-and-white sketch.

"We've got a great idea for a jacket," Marguerite said, grinning. "A lot of my friends are traveling. You guys went to Europe last summer, right? So, a map of the world, always with you, and something casual to wear on a trip. Makes sense, right?"

She rolled out on her cutting table some white gabardine cloth on which each country of the world was filled in in red, blue, green, or brown, and the names of countries and major cities were printed in black.

"Nice," I said, peering at the fabric, then the sketch. "Great mix of colors." I hesitated for a second. "That blousy style, though, where it kind of bubbles out above the waist but then fits snugly at the waist...? Not sure. Maybe for older women. I'd vote for a slimmer fit. But you're the fashion expert. It's an unusual design. Where'd you get the idea?"

"Trade secret," my sister chuckled. "But I checked *Vogue* and *Harper's Bazaar,* went to Joseph Magnin and Macy's. Nothing like it. I'm excited. And we're going with the blousy look."

***

In 1995, when Alex had graduated from college and Josh was halfway through, Ed and I moved to Honolulu. Over the years, his law firm had grown from forty lawyers to more than eight hundred. He wanted to be in a smaller partnership and, after twenty-five years of litigation and bond work, to move to a broader practice in a new environment. In Hawaii, he continued with public finance but also worked on mergers and other business deals. And I found the perfect full-time job: writing federal grant proposals for the City of Honolulu's Department of Community Services. We sought funding for programs serving disadvantaged youth, homeless veterans, low-income people lacking housing, and others.

Dan, Evelyn, Norman and Jean, and Ed's brother and sister all visited us. We never saw Vern there or, no surprise, Marguerite and Lowell. Every six or eight months, we flew back to California to see my siblings and our friends in the Bay Area. We'd stay at Evelyn's apartment and rent a car to drive into San Francisco. Norman and Jean would sometimes drive up from Anaheim.

By now, Marguerite's business was dying, partly because she refused to update her garment line, although some stores that had stocked her coats, such as I. Magnin and Joseph Magnin, had gone out of business. Her map jacket had been her most popular item in years, selling in the thousands, but sales were weakening. None of this helped her relationship with Lowell.

On one visit to their house, we walked into the middle of a big argument.

"You're so stupid, you can't even run a business without driving it in the ground," Lowell snarled. "It's not a business, it's a joke." He greeted us curtly, then headed upstairs to their bar. Marguerite's face turned bright red.

"I'm so good to him, why does he treat me so bad?" she whimpered as she hunched forward in her wing chair, dark circles like bruises under her eyes, her hands trembling as she lit a cigarette. Her print blouse showed spots, and her bleached blond hair was disheveled. "My friends say I should leave him."

But her business couldn't survive without his financial investment. And she'd hate giving up her beautiful house.

After my initial shock at this state of affairs, I found myself feeling sorry for her. I had never seen Marguerite so vulnerable and had no idea what to say to her. I hoped the situation with Lowell was a minor setback, and she'd soon regain her confidence. Or was I seeing signs of permanent disintegration?

Stunned by that possibility, I stood up suddenly, unable to hug her, and mumbled, "I'm sorry, I'm sorry, we have to go, gotta meet some friends." Looking confused, Ed also stood up, said a quick goodbye, and followed me out.

"She's barely selling any coats," Lowell told us when we saw him at the factory a day later. In his late seventies now, even with his dyed black hair, bloodshot eyes, and belly straining against his velour tracksuit, Lowell was still handsome. "Hell, what possessed her to use that map design without permission?" He crushed his cigarette out in an overflowing ashtray. "That goddamn lawsuit cost us sixty thousand dollars."

"What?" I yelped. "She copied the design and somebody's suing her?"

I couldn't believe it. Then I recalled how, years ago, when I was first helping Marguerite at her factory, I'd accompanied her to Macy's and each of us bought a coat. Back at the factory, she studied each garment inside and out, then made rough sketches. I assumed it was a common practice among designers, a way to get fresh ideas.

"And she wants even more money from me," Lowell continued. "She'll drive me to the poorhouse. Marguerite has no business being in business. I should have paid attention when we got married, when she said her company never made much money."

For so long, I had wanted to emulate this woman, because of her business savvy, the gorgeous coats she'd created, her style, charm, and confidence. I was sad, now, about her situation, yet had no idea what to think, say, or do.

Around this time, in January 2001, Evelyn was hospitalized with advanced pancreatic cancer. She'd called a few months earlier to tell us about her diagnosis and said she was getting treatment. When Norman phoned us with the latest news, I immediately flew to the Bay Area.

I found Evelyn on a ventilator, oblivious to my presence. Her son had had to fly home to his family in Arizona, but Norman and Jean had driven up from Southern California. Over the following week, Norman and I took turns sleeping in her hospital room. My first evening there, I listened to her heavy breathing and thought about our decades-long bond. Evelyn had taken me into her home for almost a year when I first arrived in California, and I knew there wasn't anything she wouldn't have done for me.

Though my sisters had gone through periods of friendship interspersed with years of not speaking to each other, I telephoned Marguerite every evening to report on Evelyn's deteriorating condition. Marguerite had downsized from her factory to a ground-floor space of about two thousand square feet on the Embarcadero. In addition to two adjoining offices, it had an expansive open area in which she put her L-shaped desk and created a small seating area, the table covered with scrapbooks bulging with ads and photos of her creations. Racks of unsold coats and her old cutting table filled half the space. Though Marguerite was in her mid-seventies by now, she drove there every day.

But she would not drive to the hospital in Burlingame, just ten miles away.

"Come see Evelyn," I pleaded. "It's your last chance. She could die any time."

"It's depressing to be around dying people," my sister said. "And she won't know me, anyway."

You heartless witch, I thought, wishing I had the guts to say it out loud. I reminded myself that her life with Lowell had become even more of a challenge. He'd developed heart disease and macular degeneration and was half-blind. And why was I shocked at Marguerite's attitude? She'd never visited Bob when he was near dying, saying she was too busy. I couldn't change Marguerite. In my late fifties now, I still shied away from confronting her.

On my final evening at Evelyn's bedside, I heard her breathing slow down, then gradually stop. Though I had anticipated her death, it came too quickly. I began sobbing. How I would miss her, this kindest and most loving of sisters.

Marguerite didn't attend Evelyn's memorial service, of course, but later she went to Evelyn's apartment with a dealer hoping to buy some of our sister's antique pieces.

Not long after that, Lowell became confined to a wheelchair. Marguerite eventually wearied of trying to find dependable people to look after him while managing her business. She asked Richard to move his father back to Fresno to live near him. A year later, Marguerite sued for divorce.

———

ED AND I RETIRED in 2006 and moved from Hawaii back to the East Bay. I tutored high school dropouts in language arts and writing, to help them earn a GED, or high school diploma, and wrote grant proposals for nonprofit organizations. Thinking about ideas for family-based short stories, I took classes in creative writing. I'd long wanted to write about Dale and his death, having discussed that topic with therapists over the years. Dan and I shared our story drafts with each other, and he would correct any farm details I got wrong.

He was working in Washington, D.C., now, where Josh and his family lived; he'd joined us at our granddaughter's bat mitzvah. Josh and his wife had three children, and Alex and his wife, who lived near us in the East Bay, had two. Dan had come to both weddings and often spent holidays with us.

After hearing Uncle Harold's revelation about our grandmother, Dan began genealogy searches and found a brief record of our grandmother's institutionalization in Indiana, where Mom grew up. He discovered two newspaper stories about our grandfather's automobile accident and death and learned where

Mom had lived during a brief stint in nurses' training, before she married Dad.

Not wanting to end my attachment to Marguerite after so many years—not out of love, really, but a sense of duty—I went to her showroom every couple of weeks. Slowly, she became ill with emphysema, congestive heart failure, and the early stages of dementia. One day in late 2007, she told me she'd persuaded Dan to quit his job. He was currently operating the machine digging a major water tunnel in New York City, but he would move back to San Francisco to take care of her and help sue the lawyer who'd handled her divorce. Convinced she'd been cheated out of her "rightful" share of Lowell's lucrative farm-machinery business, Marguerite wanted Dan to look through the legal documents and help make the case for a better settlement. How our brother, with no legal background, could assist her in that effort escaped me.

By then, Lowell had died, at age ninety. Marguerite's scrounging for money from his business, and the acrimony of the couple's relationship, had so alienated his son that neither Marguerite nor their forty-five-year marriage made it into Lowell's obituary in the *Fresno Bee*. The article instead referenced his first wife, dead since 1959; Lowell's long residency in San Francisco, presumably alone; and his joy in restoring his 1963 Lincoln Continental, which had taken first place in many classic-car shows.

"So, is this a good idea?" I challenged Dan during a phone call. I reminded him how she had sent Lowell away when he was at his most helpless. "Marguerite never once visited Bob or Evelyn when they were really sick or dying. Why do you think she'll treat you any better than anyone else in the family?"

"She's not the nicest person," Dan agreed, "but this is a business arrangement. She promised to pay me twice what I'm earning now. And she thinks she got screwed in her divorce. She doesn't trust her lawyer to handle things anymore."

"And you trust Marguerite?"

"I can't pass this up. I got other job offers, but this is better money. And I'll be helping her out."

"Please don't do this," I said, whereupon Dan hung up on me. I didn't want to alienate him. He was an adult and could make his own decisions. I desperately hoped the caregiving and financial arrangement would work out for both of them.

In January 2008, Dan moved into Marguerite's house and began driving her to the showroom each day. When he wasn't poring over legal documents, he'd fetch her lunch and ensure her oxygen machine was operating properly, always with a reserve tank. He bought groceries, prepared her dinners, monitored her numerous medications, took her to doctors' appointments, and oversaw her caregivers.

Now eighty-three, she spent her days at her metal desk in the showroom, reading conservative political websites on her computer. Surrounding her were the remnants of her business: paper coat patterns, photographs and drawings of her creations, poster-size photographs of models wearing her coats, her original cutting table, and racks of unsold coats and jackets. Two women with a small sewing business sublet the little offices from her and sewed coats for Marguerite's infrequent customers. One customer was Angela Alioto, a member of the San Francisco Board of Supervisors, although that led to no new business. Former friends and acquaintances visited.

Sometimes a friendly UPS deliveryman stopped by, though he seldom had a package to pick up or deliver. Seeming never to tire of Marguerite's stories, he teased Dan about the care he took with Marguerite's oxygen machine, making sure it was operating correctly and had a full tank of oxygen. "You're almost like a mom," he said.

During one of my regular visits, I took a seat across from my sister at her L-shaped desk. Cluttered around her computer were piles of paper, tiny packets of catsup and mayonnaise from hamburger-and-French-fry lunches, and a milky cup of coffee. By this time, Marguerite had grown obese and hard of hearing. Her black turtleneck sweater sloped over her drooping breasts, and her curly blond wig was slightly askew. As she bent toward me in her office chair, I had an unwelcome vision of Jabba the Hutt from *Star Wars*. So cruel of me. Tubes from her oxygen tank dangled around her neck and extended into her nose, on which rested heavy-frame reading glasses. Smells of sweat, cigarette smoke, and unwashed clothes hung in the air.

"We're going to manufacture that prayer jacket," she said in a hoarse voice, pointing to a rack of garments. "Isn't it cute?"

I walked over and pulled out a jacket in white fabric covered with bible verses in black. "God is Love," "God is the Foundation of the World," and "Husbands Love Your Wives" were written in English, Spanish, and Mandarin.

"For all those religious people who love George Bush in the White House," she said. "I think I can get local churches to buy it. Those good Christians need coats."

The truth was, Marguerite hadn't manufactured more than a few garments in years. But she refused to admit her working life—her identity as a coat designer and manufacturer—had ended. Having loved my job in Honolulu and still struggling with how to be productive in retirement, I understood the pain of losing one's career. On the wall behind her desk hung a poster-size picture of President George H.W. Bush wearing her map jacket, along with his handwritten thank-you note. A few of the jackets hung in the dusty showroom windows. Occasionally, someone came in to buy one, fifteen percent of each sale going to the plaintiff who'd won the lawsuit.

"Marguerite," I said, "do you remember that I wore your map jacket last year when Ed and I were in Tiananmen Square in Beijing? Three young people from Mongolia came up to me and pointed out Ulaan Baatar, their capital. Then they invited us to a tea shop, where we drank tea together. You contributed to international harmony."

"Yeah, it's a great jacket," she said. "Those Chinese, though, they're not very smart. A lot of them worked for me." I winced. She'd hired scores of Chinese women over the years. "I need to smoke," she said suddenly. Bracing her hands on the desk, she pulled herself up, gasping for breath.

"You should quit smoking, like the doctor said. Your oxygen tank could catch fire."

"Oh, shut up. It's my life, my place, and I can smoke if I want."

She hobbled into the next room, dragging her oxygen tank behind her. She fell into a chair, then lit incense candles to camouflage the cigarette smell from her tenants, who objected to her smoking.

I walked around her showroom, traveling back through the more than fifty years of her manufacturing life. Some two hundred coats and jackets hung on the racks, remnants of thousands she had made and sold over those years, some of them glamorous for their time: a cherry-red velveteen cape-style coat with a wrap collar; a metallic rainbow-colored jacket; her dark-orange belted raincoat with shoulder pads and flared skirt, one of which I owned, though shoulder pads were now out of style. Then a black-and-white-checked garment caught my eye—one of her very first designs, the one that had been featured on *Queen for a Day*. She'd sold that coat in a variety of fabrics to upscale stores. Only two of these garments remained, dust layering the shoulders of both.

"Marguerite told me not to tell you she had a stroke," Dan said on the phone in early June. He was breathing hard, and I remembered that his blood pressure had skyrocketed during the last few months. Marguerite fired most of the caregivers Dan hired. She'd accused one of stealing her gold watch, only to discover it on her bathroom sink. "Her ankles are swollen, and she's been sleeping twenty hours a day."

Ever since she'd become too ill to go to her showroom, Dan and I had tried to convince Marguerite to move to an assisted-living facility.

"She needs to be in the hospital," Dan said, sounding exhausted and panicky. "But she gets furious if I even mention it."

"You've gotta call emergency services, right now," I told him, "no matter what she says."

"She was scared, after all," Dan reported from the hospital. "When we got here, she wasn't mad at me for calling 911."

But when I got there the next morning, she snarled at me. "What's she doing here?" Marguerite asked, her eyes narrowing to slits as she looked at me.

Her thin white hair gleamed in the fluorescent light. Without the blond wig, her face looked small, lined, and vulnerable. She'd banished me from her showroom a couple weeks earlier because I'd supported the idea of a care home. "I hope you die of cancer," she'd yelled at Norman, who was being treated for colon cancer. That was after he had driven seven hours from Anaheim to help us convince Marguerite she needed assisted living.

At the end of a long visit, though, she extended her arms to Dan and me for a hug, then said, "I'm really glad you guys came. Can you come again this afternoon?"

A smiling nurse entered, arranged Marguerite's pillows, and asked her how she was doing.

"Fine 'til you walked in," my sister said, and she jerked her body away. The nurse adjusted the I.V. line and left. "She's a Filipino, you know," Marguerite said. "Filipinos aren't honest. I saw it in business."

A week later, Marguerite was well enough to return home. Before that, Dan and I hurried to clean her bedroom. Like archeologists, we excavated layers and layers of artifacts, unearthing two nightstands and ashtrays heaped with cigarette butts, all buried under piles of newspapers. Plastic utensils, old pill bottles, crumpled tissues, candy wrappers, and boxes of half-eaten See's chocolates littered the dingy off-white rug. The paramedics who'd taken Marguerite to the hospital had told Dan her house was a firetrap. But she'd forbidden him from cleaning, let alone throwing anything away.

"Why are we doing this?" I asked Dan as we stuffed plastic bags with years-old business newspapers and fashion magazines. "I have a husband, children, and friends who love me, and I'm helping take care of a miserable human being."

"She was glad we came to the hospital," he said. "And there's no one else."

"By the way," I said, tying a plastic bag shut, "has she paid you for the last six months?" I tossed the bag across the room onto a heap of others.

"No, she hasn't." He sounded angry. "But she promised me the house. And I couldn't just leave her, could I? Took me the longest time to find a caregiver who'd stay more than a few days." Months ago, Marguerite had also told me that she'd leave Dan her house, because, unlike Norman and me, he owned no property.

I studied Dan. His crooked nose, shattered from high school football, had made his face more interesting, people had told him, but now, in his late sixties, his bent-nosed face looked battered, walloped by life. Dark pockets underlined his hazel eyes, and his curly flyaway hair and bushy moustache were almost completely gray. Looking at his belly expanding over his jeans, I was reminded of his high blood pressure.

The doorbell rang. "I sure hope the house thing works out," I mumbled as we headed to the front door.

Four young paramedics struggled to haul Marguerite up her front steps in a wheelchair.

"You guys didn't throw anything away, did you?"

In mid-June, we received news that Norman's colon cancer had worsened, and he was in hospice care. Dan, Ed, and I drove to Anaheim, where my kindest and most generous of brothers mostly talked about his courtship of Jean, the woman he'd loved for more than sixty years. Tragically, she'd been killed in a car accident three years earlier. Six weeks later, Norman died, and we flew to Southern California for his memorial service.

OVER THE NEXT SEVERAL months, Dan called me regularly, lamenting the parade of caregivers Marguerite drove away. Now she was accusing Dan of abusing her and poisoning her food.

"I woke up to a light shining in my face at two o'clock this morning," Dan told me one afternoon. "It was a policeman; he said a person from this residence had called 911, said somebody was trying to murder her. I showed the cops all Marguerite's prescription meds."

I pictured that display of medicine bottles on Marguerite's breakfast table, prescribed for hypertension, congestive heart failure, dementia, schizophrenia, and bipolar disorder by her cardiologist of thirty years and her neurologist.

"A city social worker came by later and checked out the situation," Dan went on. "Said Marguerite was lucky to have me." His sigh was audible.

Every couple of weeks, I visited my bedridden sister and tried to provide Dan with moral support. In the last few months of her life, he found a caregiver, Amy, who looked after our sister with loving attention.

One of the last times I saw Marguerite was on her eighty-fifth birthday, in February 2010. I held her hands and wished her a happy birthday. A hundred pounds lighter, frail and shrunken in her bed, she stared back. I wasn't sure she recognized me.

"It's my birthday," she said, waving her arms. "Yay for me."

Holding her hand, I stroked her head. She died of kidney failure three months later.

In writing Marguerite's obituary for the *San Francisco Chronicle*, I emphasized her creativity in design and her ability to market her coats nationwide. I noted how the fashion press had viewed her as a forerunner in making raincoats that didn't look like raincoats and designing functional, fashionable, and attractive all-weather garments. I mentioned President George H.W. Bush wearing her map jacket on Air Force One en route to a summit meeting in Moscow in 1991.

At the small memorial service, I spoke about her journey from the farm to her triumphs in business. Applauding my sister for her vision and ingenuity, I read aloud from handwritten letters that I'd found on her showroom desk. "I love my paisley jacket and get so many compliments," a woman in Iowa wrote. From Anchorage, Alaska: "The rust-colored raincoat is gorgeous, and the removable lining is great for our cold weather here. Keep making your wonderful coats."

For years, I had glorified her glamour and success and let myself feel intimidated and weak. Silently, I thanked Marguerite for all she had taught me: good manners, how to dress and act in a more sophisticated world than I'd known. And I thought of what Ed said to me all those years ago.

"And think of what you've accomplished."

The Trustee

H ERB COOKE NEVER SAW it as fraud. He had intended to protect a sick old lady from her greedy, unfeeling relatives. The money was just a lucky circumstance. But none of this was on his mind this April day in 2009, when he hitched up his brown trousers and pushed open the back door of the showroom of Marguerite Rubel Manufacturing. He removed his UPS cap in the entryway and shivered as a draft of chill air cooled his bald head. He paused, tensing at a twinge in his gut. Last night had been rough. Out of bed at least three times trying to piss. That goddamned prostate surgery had taken a lot out of his fifty-year-old body.

"Leave me alone!" an angry voice shouted. Marguerite, Herb thought. He inhaled the space's familiar mix of cigarette smoke and musty clothes. "Mind your own business," she snapped.

"It's dangerous," Dan said, sounding irritated.

She sure picks on him, Herb thought. Would drive me nuts. Dan was Marguerite's much-younger brother. He lived at his sister's house and drove her to the showroom every day. He also managed her medications and meals and hired her caregivers. Herb couldn't imagine doing all the stuff Dan did for Marguerite. God bless him. Way too much trouble, and the smells would gag Herb. Thank God for his mom's care home. Twice a month, he visited her. And that was often enough. But the nursing home's latest bill still sat on his desk, one of several he couldn't afford to pay quite yet.

He shuffled along between racks of colorful jackets and coats and a long table stacked with bolts of fabric. The last gasp of Marguerite's dying business. He'd heard from Dave, the insurance guy in an office upstairs, that she'd been successful for forty-five years, mainly due to her wealthy ex-husband's invest-ment, Dave said. Once a brand name, her company was no lon-ger considered fashionable. Over the last six months, Herb had seen that Marguerite's business consisted mostly of dust-cov-ered coats. They looked out-of-date to him, though he couldn't claim to be an expert on women's clothes or the sales thereof. Occasionally, she'd show him a trendier item that still sold, like her map jacket, which was loose-fitting and featured a map of the world with the countries in vivid colors.

Visiting Marguerite gave him a break from his route's monot-ony. Herb detoured here every couple of weeks, even though these days she rarely ordered a package pickup. She was peculiar but sometimes thoughtful, like when she asked about his cancer prognosis. He admired her toughness in starting up her business, and her quirky stories. His favorite was about the time during World War II when she hitchhiked to San Francisco from the Iowa farm where she'd grown up. He'd heard that one many times. But at eighty-four, the woman was allowed to repeat herself. As was Herb's mom, who also sometimes went on and on with her life story. Of course, hers wasn't as interesting as Marguerite's.

The long, gloomy aisle led into a large open space with light streaming in through dirty windows overlooking San Francisco's Embarcadero. The "famous" world-map jacket hung in one of those windows.

"We've sold thousands over the years," Marguerite had said a while ago, "but not so many anymore."

Marguerite sat hunched over a long metal desk, clutching a cigarette. She wore a curly blond wig, and her heavy body was encased in black tights and a white zippered jacket emblazoned with cursive lettering in red. An oxygen tube coiled from a tank on the floor into her nose. Dan was standing near the tank, shaking his head of unruly, wavy gray hair.

"Herb, do I look like I belong in a nursing home?" Marguerite looked up and stamped her foot.

"Of course not," he said, patting her shoulder. "But Dan takes really good care of you. He only wants the best. Hi, Dan," Herb said, winking at him. "How's it going?"

Dan frowned, and Herb could read the frustration in the man's face. Marguerite really was stupid to smoke so close to an oxygen tank.

"Ah, I'm fine." Dan threw up his hands and stomped to his desk, in a corner of the showroom.

Herb sat down on the worn brown couch facing Marguerite's desk, among the familiar clutter: old wooden chairs with padded seats, coffee table stacked with scrapbooks filled with sketches, newspaper ads, and photographs of Marguerite's coat designs. He smiled at the half-mannequin dressed in a garish rhinestone-encrusted denim jacket. Marguerite had told him this crazy style might draw in some young customers.

Marguerite's expression had transformed from a glower to a grin, her hazel eyes bright above the horn-rimmed glasses sitting low on her nose. Under her desk, Herb saw, she wore scruffy white tennis shoes. Once again, he wondered how she might be considered in any way a "Marina matron." Though he wasn't sure just what a Marina matron looked like, unless it was someone who wore extravagant gowns and jewelry to the opera and ballet.

A couple weeks ago, he had checked out her house, because he hadn't believed her when she told him where she lived. Turned out she really did live in a three-story home on Marina Boulevard, in one of San Francisco's swankiest neighborhoods: one of elegant, multiple-story houses with enormous picture windows and manicured lawns across from Marina Green, a blocks-long expanse of grass that attracted weekend picnickers and runners.

Marguerite's house sat on a corner lot two blocks from the St. Francis Yacht Club, with its large sailboats bobbing on the water. Herb recognized her beige Mercedes in the driveway. A John McCain campaign poster hung in one of the picture windows facing Alcatraz Island, far out in the ruffled waters of San Francisco Bay.

What would it be like to live there and feast on that glorious view every day?

"Last doctor's appointment go okay, Herb?"

Herb jerked his attention back to the woman who lived in that amazing house.

"Yeah, still in remission," Herb said, crossing his fingers on both hands. "Thanks for askin'." He stood up and stepped closer to her. "Hey, I like that jacket. The word 'Peace' in different languages. One of your designs?"

"Naturally it's mine," Marguerite said. She rolled her eyes and took a long draw from her cigarette. "So you like it?" Suddenly she bent over, coughing. When she finished, she spat into a paper towel.

Herb's heart skipped a beat. "Are you all right, Marguerite?"

She cleared her throat and sat up. "Yeah, yeah," she said in a hoarse voice, then, looking over Herb's shoulder, said, "Connie, come in. Herb, say hello to my lawyer and friend, Connie Olsen."

Marguerite crushed her cigarette into an overflowing ashtray as the woman strode in. In her late forties, Herb guessed, she had long brown hair and cradled a small white dog. Herb glared at the fluffy animal. He'd been bitten by dogs on his route three or four times. The smallest ones could be the most vicious.

Something about the woman seemed familiar. After a couple seconds, it dawned on him. Jesus Christ. It was Connie Olsen. What the hell? Had to be at least three years. Connie looked up at Herb and smiled.

"Connie, this is Herb. The UPS guy."

Herb flinched. UPS guy. He had a last name, goddamn it. Couldn't the old woman use it? He nodded at Connie and extended his hand.

"Good to see you again, Herb." Clutching the dog under her other arm, she shook his hand. Still a hippie, Herb thought, as he scrutinized her wire-frame glasses, denim shirt, worn blue jeans, and brown suede Birkenstocks. He jerked back as Connie's dog jumped to the floor and scampered toward Marguerite.

"Get the damn dog away from me," Marguerite shouted, rolling her desk chair back. "Why didn't you leave that stupid thing home? It better not shit in here."

"Sorry." Connie grabbed the dog, clutching it tight as she sat down.

"I know Connie," Herb told Marguerite. "She was my lawyer when I thought I'd sold my house. When the buyers backed out. Breach of contract." He'd hired Connie on his boss's recommendation. He trusted Jeremy and considered him a smart guy.

"She's not much to look at, but she does decent work," Jeremy had said. "So my brother says. And her price is right."

Herb was skeptical when he met her. Connie's office, on the first floor of a two-story house in the city's Richmond District, had been nothing to write home about: two chairs in front of a metal desk, a few law books on the metal shelves. He seemed to recall she'd worn a pantsuit at that meeting. He couldn't imagine having hired her if she'd worn jeans, no matter what Jeremy recommended. Connie had negotiated an okay settlement for him, a bit more than the down payment, but he should have gotten more. Her bill was pretty big when it seemed to him she hadn't done much work. He still hadn't sold the damn house, and he sure needed the money.

Anyway, water under the bridge now. No use reliving the whole thing.

Herb looked at his watch. No need to hang around and make

small talk with Connie or hear lawyer chitchat between her and the old lady.

"I better get going," he said to Marguerite.

"You just got here. Stay awhile."

"Sorry, lots of deliveries," Herb lied. "See you next week. Take care of yourself. And quit smoking." He grinned, knowing his comment was futile.

"Mind your own business," she snarled, reaching for her pack. "Go on, get outta here."

He waved to Connie. "Nice seeing you." Weird to see her again. Small world.

As he stepped into the parking lot, he saw Norman and Sandy, Marguerite's brother and sister, talking to Dan, who was leaning against Norman's white van. Once a month or so, Norman drove up from the Los Angeles area to help Dan. He was a lot older than the other two, had to be pushing eighty. Sandy lived in the East Bay and stopped by every couple of weeks.

"I see you're back at work already," Norman said, shaking Herb's hand. Herb greeted Sandy with a nod. "Surgery must've gone well. Are you pretty much back to normal?"

Over the last few months, the two had shared war stories about their battles with cancer. For the last six months, Norman had been undergoing therapy for colon cancer.

"Thanks," Herb said. "I'm feelin' so-so. Got bored stayin' home. How's your treatment going?"

"I'm not sure how much good it's doing," Norman said. "It's not getting any worse but also not much better."

"Sorry to hear that," Herb said, pulling his key ring from his pocket. "Marguerite seems pretty good today. Sometimes she'll tell me the same thing five times. But usually she's in an okay mood. Fun to talk to, but she can get really grouchy." He turned to Dan. "You have your hands full."

"She's getting pretty difficult," Norman said. "Accuses her

caregivers of stealing. Fires them for no good reason."

"Sometimes they deserve firing," Dan said, shaking his head. "One guy stole money from my wallet. Of course, I shouldn't have left it in plain sight. But it's a hassle trying to find competent people who'll stay very long."

"Didn't you tell us your mom's in a nursing home?" Norman asked.

"Yeah, Redwood Care Center in Oakland. They're great."

"It's a chain, I think," Sandy said. "In fact, there's one a few blocks from where we live."

"Check 'em out," Herb said. "At least they wouldn't let Marguerite smoke there." Was she really ready for a nursing home? He nodded goodbye to the three siblings. Seemed like good people.

In late June, when Herb walked into Marguerite's showroom, he found the chair at her desk empty. Maybe she'd finally given up her business. The place looked the same, just more forlorn, with no one there. Too bad. He'd looked forward to bullshitting with her, killing some time.

"Hello, Herb." He turned around and saw Marguerite's brother walking toward him.

"What's going on, Dan?" Herb asked. "Where's Marguerite?"

Dan leaned against the filing cabinet. "She's probably not coming in anymore. She had a stroke and went to the hospital for a week. Congestive heart failure, the doctors said."

"Oh, that's too bad. I'm sorry to hear it. Will you say hello for me?"

"She's home now and likes visitors." Dan opened a file cabinet drawer and removed some folders. "Just call the house when you want to come by. I'll write down the number for you."

Nah, Herb thought. One sick old lady in his life was enough. But he took the number, just to be polite.

HERB FOUND A CORNER table in the Jang Li Tea Shop, on the Embarcadero. Damn tea. He hated it. But Connie Olsen wanted to meet here. What could she possibly want with him? All she'd said on the phone was that she had an offer for him, and he'd like it. Could it be about his house? God, he needed cash. The bills from Redwood Care Center just kept coming, and it was damned expensive. Would he have to hump packages until he turned sixty? Herb groaned, then ordered English Breakfast tea, the only kind he'd ever heard of.

When a dog yapped, Herb looked out the door and saw Connie tying her mutt to a parking meter. She came in and walked toward his table, sandals flapping, stopping to place an order with a waitress. Connie wore what looked like a man's white shirt, shirttails hanging out over her jeans.

For a few minutes, they made small talk about the gloomy July weather. When was the sun ever going to come out? A waitress placed two cups of tea on the table and left.

"So, Herb, how well do you know Marguerite Rubel and her family?" Connie asked, stirring a spoonful of honey into her tea.

"Pretty well, I guess." Why was she asking? "Up until June, I was going into Marguerite's showroom every couple weeks, just to say hello and chew the fat. Sometimes I'd see her brothers and sister. By the way, do you know how Marguerite's doin'? Dan said she'd been in the hospital."

"She's pretty sick but still alert," Connie said. "I've seen her a few times since she got home. She's pretty stressed out that her siblings are trying to force her into a home. But I was wondering how well you know the family."

"I just told you," he said. "Anyway, why're you askin'?" He rotated the teacup in his hands, relishing the warmth that seeped into his fingers.

"I'm really worried about Marguerite. She says Dan abuses her and is just after her money. She says he hires incompetent caregivers who steal her jewelry. And the house is a firetrap. I believe what she's telling me. He just wants her money."

"You can't be serious," Herb said, setting his teacup down hard on the saucer. "From what I saw in the showroom, Dan takes good care of Marguerite. Drives her everywhere. Always makes sure she has oxygen in that damn tank. Always fiddlin' with it. She can't be the easiest person to take care of. If anybody tells her to stop smoking around her oxygen, she bites their head off. Anyway, what's it got to do with me? Or you?"

"I'm her lawyer." Connie took off her wire-rim glasses and cleaned them with her shirt. "I drew up the original trust agreement appointing Dan and Norman as trustees and heirs. Now Marguerite wants to change it and disinherit her brothers. Sandy's not an heir, because Marguerite says she's better off financially than the other two."

"I don't believe it. Norman drives up from L.A. every month or so—an old guy with effin' cancer. Sandy sees Marguerite a lot. Anyway, it's none of my business." Herb looked at his watch. "And why is it yours?" Fifteen minutes left on his parking meter, and Connie still hadn't gotten to the point.

"There's a new trust agreement. I had another lawyer draw up the paperwork to avoid a conflict of interest. In this one, Marguerite leaves some money to me, some to whoever the new trustee is, and the rest to the SPCA."

"The SPCA?" asked Herb. "No way."

"Marguerite doesn't like little dogs, but she and her husband had a German Shepherd for years." Connie leaned forward. "Here's where you come in. Someone needs to be the trustee. It would help Marguerite out, and there'd be some money in it for you."

"What the hell are you talkin' about?" Herb felt warm all over.

"Marguerite likes you. She appreciated your visits to her at the showroom. Wonders why you haven't been to the house. She trusts you, Herb."

"I don't believe this." Sweat gathered in his armpits. "You gotta be joking."

"I'm deadly serious," Connie said. She stared into his eyes. "This is the time to act. Marguerite is going downhill, but there are moments when she's lucid. When she's able to sign papers."

Herb looked away. This was crazy. But Connie saw Marguerite a lot, so she must know if the old lady was being mistreated. And Marguerite had asked for his help. Even if she'd asked through Connie. He couldn't let her down, could he? If Dan was hurting her, he shouldn't get away with it. Her brothers and sister had seemed so nice—if what Connie said was true, they'd sure fooled him. Yes, he would have to protect Marguerite.

"How much money we talkin' about?" Under the table, Herb's hands trembled.

"Well, in this market, the house is probably worth about two million once it's fixed up. A real estate friend showed me comparables for the neighborhood. Divided three ways between you, me, and the SPCA, we'd each get about seven hundred thousand dollars, subtracting the real estate commission."

"My God," Herb whispered. "Let me think." What the hell should he do here? He drummed his fingers on the table for, it seemed, a long minute. "Let's say I do it. You're sure I wouldn't get in any trouble? That is, if I said yes." He wiped a napkin over his damp forehead.

"If anybody gets in trouble, it'll be me. Trust me. I know Marguerite, and I know the law. That's why I got the other lawyer to draft the revised document."

"What would I have to do?" Herb pressed a hand over his knocking heart.

"As trustee, you'd manage the estate, pay the taxes, and

distribute the money to the beneficiaries, like the executor of a will. But don't worry, I'll handle all the details."

"Won't Dan and Norman challenge a trust that gives money to a bunch of dumb animals?"

"Leaving money to a charity looks good," Connie said. "Charities hire lawyers and fight like hell. Her family might challenge the new trust on the grounds Marguerite wasn't competent, but they'll have a hard time proving that. You saw how alert Marguerite could be."

"Jesus." Herb took several deep breaths. What was he getting himself into? If this was illegal, he could be in deep shit. But Connie wouldn't commit fraud and risk losing her lawyer's license. Would she? And if Dan really was abusing Marguerite, he had to do something.

"If you're not interested," Connie said, pushing back her chair, "I can ask someone else." She drained her teacup and grabbed her bag from the floor.

"Wait," Herb croaked. "I guess I'm in. What do I do next?"

IN MAY OF THE next year, Herb grabbed the telephone and yelled hello over the noise of a televised baseball game. That idiot Giants pitcher. Couldn't throw worth a damn.

"It's Connie. I hope you're sitting down." She paused. "I've got news. Marguerite Rubel is dead. Your life's about to change... Mister Trustee."

"Oh, m-my God," Herb stuttered. Marguerite was dead. Jesus effin' Christ. How should he react? Sad for at least a few minutes. His hands shook. Was he now the trustee of Marguerite Rubel's estate? Would he really soon pocket seven hundred thousand dollars? All because he'd been friendly to an old lady? And Marguerite's fancy house. Maybe he could even live there until it sold.

"I'll be in touch," Connie said and hung up.

Feeling as if his heart would pound out of his chest, Herb put the phone down. After a minute, he picked up his half-empty beer. He set it down again and switched off the game. What had he done? Cheated an old woman's heirs out of their rightful inheritance? Or saved her from elder abuse?

But Marguerite's brothers? Would they give him any trouble? He'd heard from Connie late last year that Norman had died, but Dan was still around.

Herb tried to remember when he had last seen Marguerite. Late last year. Amy, her caregiver, had answered the door. He'd managed to avoid Dan, whose back was toward the door as he sat in front of an assortment of pill bottles at the breakfast table. He couldn't tell if Marguerite recognized him. Amy had held her hand and stroked her thin white hair, still damp from a sponge bath. No more blond wig. After a half-hour, Herb couldn't wait to get out of there. Away from that withered body, the smell of medicine and dust, the piles of newspapers, the dead potted plants. He hadn't been able to stomach another visit. How had Connie gotten Marguerite to sign the new trust agreement? Now she'd have to show what kind of lawyer she was.

A few days later, a UPS truck idled on Fisherman's Wharf in an illegal parking spot behind Cresci Brothers Crab House. Between bites of a crab sandwich, Herb ran his fingers over the embossed lettering of the business card taped to the center of his steering wheel: "Herb Cooke, Trustee, Estate of Marguerite Rubel."

Connie had laughed at him. She'd never known a trustee to print out business cards, especially before they'd gotten the final paperwork. But Herb didn't care. He would do a great job managing the estate and paying taxes. He'd do everything Marguerite had wanted, including making damn sure Dan and Norman's heirs didn't get anything.

Several weeks later, Herb watched Gus Ferguson climb the ladder to a second-story window of Marguerite's house on the side that faced a quiet, narrow street. Herb wiped sweat from his forehead, pocketed the damp handkerchief, and checked his watch. Five minutes since they'd arrived. Afraid of heights, he'd hired a private investigator to help him get inside the house.

Herb paced back and forth. It would take weeks to force Dan's eviction. Until then, there was no telling what the guy would steal. Connie said the court had yet to decide if the amendment naming him trustee was valid. But Herb had seen the trust documents and all the signatures, even Marguerite's squiggly one. The papers had to be valid. He needed that cash.

The friend who recommended Gus said the guy was willing to tiptoe around the niceties of the law. But they had to hurry. Dan's Mustang wasn't in its usual spot on the street, but no telling if he was coming back or had parked it somewhere else.

"Hey," a voice called from across the street. "What're you doing?"

Shit. The blond biddy who lived around the corner. Over the last couple of weeks, while Herb sat in his car spying on Dan, he'd seen her walking her poodle. Now she glared at him.

"That's not your house," she yelled. "Marguerite's dead, but her brother still lives there."

"I'm the trustee of Marguerite's estate," Herb shouted, "and Dan doesn't have a right to live here anymore. He's been stealing Marguerite's money."

Herb looked up at Gus, who stood on the ladder opposite the window. "Get that window open," Herb yelled. Ten minutes gone since they'd started. That stupid nosy neighbor had disappeared, but she might be calling the police.

It took Gus several minutes to pry open the decaying window with a crowbar. Paint chips and wood slivers fell to the ground.

"Okay, Herb," Gus called. "It's open."

"Climb in, damn it," Herb hissed. Almost fifteen minutes since they'd started.

Herb went to the front door and waited until Gus opened up.

"Dan's not on this level," Gus said as Herb rushed in. "But I'll check the top floor."

"Shit, shit, shit." Herb checked his watch. Twenty minutes gone. He and Gus should have finished and left by now.

The doorbell rang. Oh, God, who was that? Herb took several deep breaths, then opened the door. A policeman stood on the top step.

"Sir, we got a report of a breaking-and-entering at this house," the cop said, nodding at the nosy neighbor at the foot of the stairs. "What's going on? May I see some identification?"

"I'm the trustee for the estate of Marguerite Rubel, the lady who used to live here," Herb said, reaching for his wallet. "Here's my proof."

The cop studied Herb's card and driver's license. "You may be the trustee, but that doesn't give you the right to break into someone's house."

"My lawyer has the legal documents." Herb found Connie's card and showed it to the cop. "The previous trustee is living here illegally, and he won't leave. In fact, I'll call my lawyer now."

He hadn't told her he planned to break into the house. Connie answered and, suppressing his fear, Herb explained the situation.

"Don't try another stupid thing like this without checking with me," she said. "You're lucky you didn't get in big trouble. You still could. Now let me talk to the cop."

"Here, officer." Herb handed him the phone, his hand shaking. "My lawyer wants to talk to you." After some back and forth with Connie, the cop hung up.

"I'm filing a report," the policeman said, pocketing Olsen's card, "and we'll let the District Attorney sort it out. You better make sure all your documents are in order."

Herb closed the door and leaned against the wall. What if being the trustee wasn't enough? What if he really didn't have a right to get in the house? But he wasn't going to steal anything, just make sure Dan wasn't. His legs felt wobbly.

Just then, Gus came downstairs. "Looks like nobody's around," he said.

"Good. Okay, Gus, call that locksmith who's open on Sundays. Now that we've got possession of the house, Dan won't be able to ask any questions."

Herb strolled into the dining room, peered at the gold-rimmed china and cut-glass goblets through the glass of the fancy wood cabinet, then moved into the living room. He plopped down on the white couch facing the window. As he looked out at Alcatraz, he shivered with excitement and couldn't stop grinning. Wow! Can't believe I get a part of this.

***

"THERE'S BEEN A HITCH in our plans," Connie said a couple weeks later. She'd asked Herb to meet her at Crissy Field, a wide area of green grass gently sloping down to a beach at the edge of San Francisco Bay. The Golden Gate Bridge loomed in the distance above Fort Point, and the sun glowed reddish gold. It was late June, and Herb pulled his thin jacket tight against the late-afternoon breeze.

Connie threw a tennis ball onto the beach, and her dog darted after it. "But no need to worry. I can handle it."

"What kind of hitch?" Herb asked, his chest tightening, as the dog came running back.

"Dan's filed a lawsuit," Connie said, throwing the ball again. "His lawyer claims Marguerite wasn't competent when she signed the second agreement. They say they have statements by three doctors. One's a forensic psychiatrist who examined her before and after she was in the hospital. Another's the doctor she's been going to for twenty-three years. Of course, it's to be expected they'd fight back. But we'll fight, too. The real news is that Dan's suing you for slander, because you told the neighbor he stole money from Marguerite."

Connie picked up her dog and started walking to her car, calling over her shoulder, "I'll be in touch. Paperwork's on the way."

Herb's shoulders sagged. Shit! Shit! Why had he made that stupid comment to the neighbor? And all those doctors. Jesus! He had trusted Connie. Had she committed fraud? If so, that meant he had, too. He was close to pissing his pants. His greed had gotten the better of him. And Connie had never confirmed she'd represent him if there was any trouble. When she said she'd handle it, what did that mean?

With a shaky hand, he reached in his pocket for a "trustee" business card. It looked like he'd have to hump packages until he was sixty. Another Ten. Goddamn. Years. As a brilliant sunset blazed behind the Golden Gate Bridge, he tore the card into little pieces. He watched them flutter downward, then blow away in the chilly evening breeze.

Dan's Story

D EAR DAN,

That Sunday morning, your cell phone rang and rang. I sat in my car across the street from your apartment building, wondering what to do. You always answered your phone. I had called you at nine from my home in Oakland, forty-five minutes away, to let you know I was coming to see you. You didn't respond then, either.

Perhaps you were out for a walk. But you never left your phone behind. Maybe it had run out of power. Maybe you were in the bathroom.

Ed saw you just yesterday. Together, you drove along the Great Highway to look at the Pacific Ocean, then past the Cliff House, a restaurant perched on a bluff with a glorious view across San Francisco Bay to the Golden Gate Bridge. Ed dropped you off at the grocery store at 12th and Clement. You said you needed bananas and yogurt and could walk the two blocks home to your apartment.

Six weeks earlier, as San Francisco's cool summer fog disappeared in October's heat, you told Ed and me you had metastatic prostate cancer. You'd known since June, when you disclosed it to John, your investment advisor and friend. John had begged you to tell me, but since Ed had suffered a stroke in mid-May, you didn't want to burden us. Ed had been hospitalized for two days and was still recovering.

Once you did tell us about your diagnosis, Ed and I took turns visiting you every day. We drove you to doctors' appointments at the Veterans Administration hospital, to the grocery store, to your bank.

But you were sure no treatment would work. *I'm going down-*

hill. I used to care about my health. I just can't go on like this. I don't see any way out.

Two weeks after you told us about the cancer, which had metastasized to your lymph nodes, you gave us the keys to your life. Copies of three house keys. Your car keys, and the car itself, because you didn't feel safe driving. You put me on your checking account. You, Ed, and I met with John and listed me as your beneficiary. You signed a will.

But most important, you gave us your two pistols and a box of ammunition, which we promptly turned over to the Oakland Police Department.

So I didn't consider any kind of rash act on your part. Our brother Dale had taken his own life when you were thirteen years old, and I was a couple months short of fifteen. You and Dad had found Dale, dead in his car of carbon monoxide poisoning. And I was darn sure there wouldn't be two suicides in our family.

However, over the last few weeks, you had started speaking in the past tense.

"I had a good life," you told us. "I was going to the gym every day. Saw my friends from there on weekends. Not bad for seventy-six. Did animation on my computer." And, you went on, "I had plans." Those plans included flying to Taiwan, where you'd worked years ago, to visit a woman named Grace Liu. Just last summer, on a visit to Taipei, you met her and spent two weeks together exploring the city and the surrounding countryside.

I was with you when you ignored your friends' calls and texts, though you always picked up when Ed or I called, or when one of our sons, Alex and Josh, rang you.

You asked me why you should keep in touch with your friends. *I won't be around much longer. And don't you tell Liz and Philip and them.* You didn't want our nieces and nephews to know you were sick.

Last Thursday, I took you to your oncology appointment at the University of California at San Francisco Medical Center, on Geary Street. After you'd undergone a CT scan and an MRI, your oncologist told us that even with high-risk prostate cancer, your chances of remission, with radiation therapy, were at ninety percent. At home afterward, you scoured the Internet for information about radiation, which predictably showed all kinds of horror stories. Worse than death, you must have thought.

We kept encouraging you. Ed and I insisted that we would take turns driving you to the five weeks of treatment, which would begin in mid-November. Alex, who visited you weekly, also offered to drive you. In addition, half a block from your apartment was a bus that stopped every twenty minutes and traveled all the way down Geary to the U.C. Medical Center, where you'd get the radiation. You had lived and worked all over the world. We knew you could take a bus twenty blocks.

You begged us to cancel our Thanksgiving trip to Washington, D.C., to visit Josh and his family. We did. Josh immediately booked a trip out to see you. You may have been nervous because we were going on an international trip in early January, even though you'd be done with your five weeks of radiation by then.

Sitting in the car, clutching my phone, I kept looking at your windows. Your blinds were always closed. Whenever I entered your apartment, I'd open them and let the light in. Lately, you'd given up reading. You stopped doing your computer animation, creating houses and rooms filled with furniture and people. These days, whenever I arrived at your apartment, you were sitting in the dark.

I called you again from my car. You had probably overslept—you had terrible insomnia. Or you had traipsed down two floors to the laundry room.

Of course you were depressed about your situation. Anyone would be. In June, you had received immunotherapy, an injection that lowers or blocks the body's ability to make testosterone. In researching it, I learned that men over seventy who received this therapy were "twenty-three percent more likely to receive a diagnosis of depression" than those who hadn't gotten the treatment and had a "twenty-nine percent increased risk of having inpatient psychiatric treatment."

You had worried constantly about the two handguns you gave us. One was never registered when you left Wisconsin, almost fifteen years ago. The other, given to you by Marguerite's husband, our now-deceased brother-in-law, Lowell, was also not registered.

Whenever I visited, you'd walk to the window every few minutes and peer through the blinds, looking for the police.

I'll go to jail. No question about that. Right now, ballistics is checking those guns. The SWAT team'll be here by the end of the day.

You were convinced you'd be evicted from your apartment. *I'm gonna freeze to death here. Space heaters are illegal, and I burned a hole in my bedroom carpet. Mark my words, the landlady's on her way.*

I contacted the rent-control board and learned space heaters were not illegal. Most people have them, I told you. You haven't missed a rent payment, and they can't easily evict old people.

"I don't believe you," you said.

Worst of all, you feared our abandoning you.

You know what you're gonna do in a couple days? You'll drop me. This Thursday or Friday, you'll call me and say I'm on my own. You'll drop my car off and skedaddle.

Then you would ask, "Why are you here?"

"Because we're family," I said. "Remember how you took care of Marguerite for years? We're doing the same thing. We care about you."

But I didn't tell you I loved you, though I say it often to Ed, my sons, and my grandchildren. No. Because we'd grown up in a family that never uttered the words "I love you" or even hugged one another. You didn't "do" hugs now, either, although Josh would strong-arm you into a tentative one-armed embrace when you two met.

Your V.A. doctor referred you to a psychiatrist, who prescribed an antidepressant. The first night on the medication, you said, you experienced frightening hallucinations and barely resisted the temptation to throw furniture out your window. I had never seen you so frightened. No more antidepressants, you insisted.

At another appointment, your doctor told me, with you sitting right there, that perhaps you should have a psych evaluation, that we should consider a stint in a psychiatric hospital. You are hard of hearing, and I don't think you heard this. She determined that that wasn't the right course now, and we'd see how things developed. Later, after we left, I was afraid of raising this issue with you, fearing you'd get upset. Anyway, I doubt you would have agreed to a hospitalization. But how could I have known that for sure?

I took you to see two shrinks at the V.A. and sat in on those sessions. The first psychiatrist was young enough to be my granddaughter. After looking over some paperwork, she asked you how you felt about having cancer.

"I feel like I'm facing a firing squad," you answered, tapping your foot and looking around her office, anywhere but at her face.

"How does that feel?" she pressed.

"How is it supposed to feel?" you responded, shaking your head, as in "What the hell are you asking me?" Then you walked out. She had no clue how to reach you. But then, neither did I.

Two days later, the second shrink, a few years older than the first one, took extensive notes on your mental-health history. Yes, I had individual and group therapy over a couple of years, after an accident that smashed my finger, fifteen years or so ago. Yes, there's mental illness in my family. My brother killed himself when I was thirteen, and my grandmother was in a mental institution for thirty years, diagnosed with acute mania. Busy completing her notes, she asked no other questions. You got up and left.

Three days ago, John, your investment advisor—your friend—called me to find out how you were doing. He said that in June, when you called and told him of your diagnosis, you'd said you were sitting with a gun in your lap. I was in such shock after that conversation, I have no idea what else John said. But after I hung up the phone, I thought, it's okay, because you no longer have your guns.

When I drove you home from your oncology appointment on Thursday, you asked me to come up to your apartment with you to make sure no one—meaning the police—was there. But it was 4:30, and I was facing rush-hour traffic home to the East Bay. I waited in your driveway, engine running, and after a few minutes, you peered down from your window and said all was okay. I waved goodbye from the car.

It was now 10:15 a.m. Time to see why you were not answering. As I crossed the street, I felt the sun's warmth and looked up at the clear blue sky. A beautiful day on a Sunday morning in San Francisco. I walked up the cement steps of your apartment house and unlocked the outer door. My footsteps were quiet as I climbed the long flight of carpeted stairs to your door. I knocked several times. No answer. After squinting in the dim light to get the right keys, I unlocked the two deadbolts. But I couldn't push the door open more than a couple of inches. The chain was on. I called out to you. No answer. I reached around and slid the chain off its slot.

Entering the gloom of the hallway, I saw what looked like a man-size scarecrow hanging at a grotesque angle from the top of the door to the kitchen. Puzzled, I looked at the face. It was yours. I felt a violent thumping in my chest. You were hanging by a double electrical cord, and blood had pooled at the corners of your mouth. The worst sight I have ever seen. I raced past you into the living room and, sobbing, called Ed. I had to be told what to do. Ed said to call 911, and that he was on his way over. The 911 dispatcher told me to cut you down. He might still be alive, she said. But I knew you were not. My heart pounding and on automatic pilot, I stumbled back to the hallway and found some scissors on a table. Forcing my eyes away from your face, I sliced through the black cords. The soft thump of your body crumpling onto the wood floor was the most horrible sound I've ever heard.

I rushed out of your apartment and collapsed against the wall halfway down the stairs, wailing. Soon, a parade of paramedics, police officers, and firefighters trooped past me up the stairs. After a few minutes, I stood up unsteadily, feeling dizzy. Leaning against the wall, my legs leaden, I slowly felt my way downstairs. Emerging, dazed, into the bright sunlight, I gazed around the familiar street. My world had been turned sideways, so how could the surroundings be the same? Your pink apartment building, the narrow strip of park across the street, the Jewish synagogue four doors down, with the enormous gold half-moon over the entrance.

Maria, the friendly grandmother in the apartment on the ground floor, came out and took me in a comforting embrace. "I do healing massage," she whispered in my ear. I relaxed a little as she gently kneaded my spine.

Ed arrived from Oakland within half an hour. I felt secure with my face against the soft fabric of his flannel shirt. Alex was soon with us. In his embrace, feeling his rough cotton T-shirt, I was surrounded by love. Sheltered from the horror upstairs.

Dan, how you must have missed the comfort of touch in your last days.

The three of us waited on the sidewalk for what seemed like

an eternity for the medical examiner to arrive. I struggled to get the sight of your body out of my mind.

A San Francisco police officer in a dark-blue uniform introduced himself and said he'd stay with us until the medical examiner arrived. Ed mentioned to him that Dan still had some bullets upstairs. Dan had shown them to us a few days after he'd given us his guns. But we'd forgotten about the items until now.

The cop said he'd take the bullets for use in officer training. Then he added, "Be glad your brother didn't shoot himself. That really leaves a mess." I walked away, dumbfounded. As if how I'd found you was easy.

A few minutes later, the medical examiner arrived and expressed his condolences. I told him I wanted to see my brother once more. When he came back downstairs, he said he had found no suicide note. I trudged upstairs, Ed and Alex silent behind me. You had been placed on your bed, and the blood I'd seen around your mouth was gone. The corners of your mouth even showed a slight curl upwards—was that the barest hint of a smile? Your eyes were closed, and I saw no anguish in your face. You looked at peace.

Your demons had finally been routed.

———

A FEW DAYS AFTER your death, it was time to handle the details of what you left behind. The relics of your life. Back in your apartment, I felt your absence hang heavily. We had been there with you so many times in the last six weeks. You had sat in your brown faux-velveteen upholstered chair, facing us and the two windows. Dust coated your living room table and had settled on your wallet, your V.A. statements, your loose coins. Boxes of papers in manila folders and black binders hulked in the corners of the room.

Your cell phone, on the table, was still connected to power.

I walked over to open the blinds and glanced out at the park across the way. You had once said to Ed, I should just go and sleep there tonight, because the police are coming. Your black-leather wing chair was next to one of the windows. That's where I sat when I visited. You said that was where you watched for the police and for the landlady, who was going to evict you.

Turning around, I flinched at the sight of an open plastic bag on your computer chair. Had you planned to use it to speed up your dying? I shook my head furiously to banish that thought.

Pawing through your things felt like an invasion of your privacy—your thoughts and actions exposed. I thought of a timely sentence I had read in a novel recently: "Why is it that looking through someone's things is…somehow so sad and also endearing, as if the deep fragility of the person becomes exposed in their absence, through their belongings?" (From *Lost Children Archive*, by Valeria Luiselli.)

For the last fifteen years, we'd seen you once a month or so, at family gatherings at our home or Alex's, or had met you for lunch or dinner near your apartment. Now, in looking through your things, I realized how little I knew you—how you had hidden so much of your inner life from us.

As I rummaged through your possessions, I had to make decisions about what to keep and what to throw away. And this meant the erasing of a life. Your life.

Those decisions broke my heart.

Discarding some of your stuff was easy: bank statements from years past; a box with hundreds of business cards from car-rental agencies, insurance companies, and miscellaneous individuals, some printed in Chinese characters. Copies of documents from your long-ago lawsuit against Marguerite's lawyer and the UPS guy, who'd swindled you out of much of our sister's estate. During the months-long trial, they testified that Marguerite was competent, even though she was on medication for serious dementia prescribed by her neurologist. You and Norman were the original trustees of her trust, but the two crooks somehow conspired to have Marguerite sign another trust document. They also accused you of abusing our sister. After the trial, you gave up your incompetent lawyer, and I think you agreed to settle for about a third of what you should have gotten from the estate, though you never shared with me the exact amount. Years later, the bitterness and stress still lingered, as indicated by your hanging on to several boxes of trial documents.

Digging through your box of photographs was shattering. A Chinese New Year's parade with flower-bedecked floats in Taipei. Random pictures of Chinese people of all ages. Distant agricultural fields in irregular shapes. From the variety of images and landscapes, I saw how you loved that country and its culture and had fun exploring on your small motorcycle. I remembered that once, in the countryside outside Taipei, your motorcycle broke down. Unable to get the engine running, you flagged down an old man in a small, ramshackle pickup truck. He took you and your bike to the nearest small town—some forty miles away—where you had your motorbike repaired.

Sadly, most of the photos had no meaning for me. So they went into the trash can.

But I kept the pictures of you and me, one when you were about five and I was probably seven, perched on tricycles on the sidewalk that wound around our farmhouse. Another in which we were scrambling on our spacious lawn with King, our German Shepherd puppy. And I hung onto photos of you at the high school you attended in Lake Park for your senior year, after our consolidated country school closed. Even though you were new at the school, you were elected prom king. I'd never seen these pictures of you and your queen.

Most devastating were the photos of your estranged step-daughter. You married her mother when Tara was eight months old. We never met her or Helen, your ex-wife of thirty years. But I recognized Tara at various stages of growth, from about first grade into her twenties, a blond girl with a fair complexion and freckles, her hair lengths and features changing over the years. You were wounded and bitter when Tara dropped you. You had been the parent who attended her parent-teacher conferences and sporting events.

"Helen didn't have a maternal bone in her body," you said. "She ran around on me, too. But she couldn't make the house payment by herself."

Over the years, you bought Tara at least three cars and supported her in numerous apartments. You last saw her at her wedding, ten years ago. She had not been in touch since.

From the beginning of your marriage, your ex-wife discouraged you from caring about her daughter.

"She's not yours," Helen told you. "Nobody wants to raise someone else's child. Soon she won't need you anymore." How cruel her words were. And how prescient.

Among your photos were some, I guessed, of Ellen, your lady friend when you lived and worked in Hong Kong. One showed a slim Chinese woman with short black hair in a flowered dress, hand resting on her hip in a coquettish pose. In another, she was tugging her skirt above her knees as she stepped from a rock-strewn beach into the water. I gathered from your comments over the years that you had broken up because she continually wanted money from you and often wasn't around when she said she would be.

Moving away from photographs, I grinned as I looked through your "life in T-shirts," the twenty or so garments folded neatly in squares and stacked in a large plastic container. You and I both loved to take trips, preferably far afield. These shirts were a partial map of your travels: Hard Rock Café, Makati, Philippines; the Golden Triangle, at the crossroads of Myanmar,

Laos, and Thailand; the Trans-Siberian Railroad, which you rode from Beijing to Moscow; "Celebrate Sandhogs, Tunnel Diggers in New York, Local 147."

And one from the San Francisco Police Department.

The carefully folded and spotless items contrasted sharply with the dirty underwear, socks, and gym shorts on your closet floor. During my visits to you, I always cringed when I saw pots and pans all over your kitchen counters instead of in the cabinets, the doors of which hung open. You didn't use a sponge to wipe crumbs off the counters, you'd brush them onto the floor.

Your vacuum cleaner and broom stood in the corner of your living room, used only once, when you thought the landlady was coming to evict you because of your "illegal" space heater. Sometimes I'd nag you to clean up. Now I understand why you did not. Why vacuum when you had no future?

Scattered among your papers were a few typed diary entries, dated and printed out on yellow sheets. Should I have read them? I wanted to understand why you had abandoned life, so I scoured your most soul-searching and agonized thoughts.

The diary entries provided sad insights into your hidden life. Two typewritten pages were from 1999, when you lived in Hong Kong. You described your struggles with alcohol, cigarettes—I never saw you smoke—your weight, depression, and loneliness.

"[I am]…irritated at myself for the addictions I cannot or do not want to control. I need to take care of myself." You never mentioned finding any mental-health therapy in Hong Kong or Taiwan—perhaps you didn't look for any.

And you obsessed about the stock market, wanting your portfolio to grow large enough so you could retire. It reminded me of how our dad fixated on accumulating more and more farmland, even though our family seemed to have very little cash to spend on non-land purchases.

In your diary entries, you wrote that you were often frustrated by your job operating a tunnel-boring machine. You worried about getting fired. When one job ended, you weren't sure when you'd have another. But you always did. You had so much self-doubt.

What came as a special shock were your appeals to God: for a job to continue, for help to stop drinking, smoking, and over-eating, for help in finding a life partner. "I prayed for this job to continue and lo and behold they told me they wanted me to stay…. Thank you, God…. I am really getting lonely."

While we were growing up, Mom took us to weekly Sunday school and summer bible school until we were teenagers. In high school, I'd sloughed off religion, but I had no idea you hadn't. Again, this was something we never talked about.

Taking a break from this painful reading, I looked through your ten boxes of books, which we had removed from your shelves. You were always a reader, as I am. I gave you books for Christmas. A paperback of *The Best Short Stories* of that year, because I knew you were writing stories about growing up on our farm. A novel about a Montana sheep farmer, by Ivan Doig, which I thought might remind you of another kind of farm life.

You recommended Ha Jin's novel *Waiting*, which won the National Book Award in 1999. I read another of his books, *War Trash*, on your suggestion.

You also owned many classics, including *Middlemarch* and *My Antonia*, two of my favorites. And *House of Mirth*, by Edith Wharton, another I loved. But we never talked about what we read. Was I a literary snob, because I had a B.A. in English lit-erature and you had only an A.A. degree in engineering design? Did I assume you read few serious books, because I'd never seen your book collection? But then, we'd never been to your apart-ment before early October. You lived there ten years, but you never invited us over. Instead, you treated Ed and me to meals in restaurants.

Now, in looking through your books and your diary entries, I learned so much about you that I never knew. We had danced around each other's lives. Although we'd talked often about Dale's death and our parents' divorce, we'd avoided deep conversations about other things that mattered.

Some of your books reflected your struggles. *Why Your Life Sucks: And What You Can Do About It*, *What Should I Do With My Life?* and *Life's Little Instruction Book: 511 Suggestions, Observations, and Reminders on How to Live a Happy and Rewarding Life*. You questioned your path in life, just as our brother Dale had done. You could recite from memory the note he left behind: "It is most appalling to note that ninety percent of people drift aimlessly through life, without the slightest conception of the work for which they are best fitted."

And your drinking. AA had helped you stop—three times, you had told me, barely keeping a straight face. Some of your books dealt with this topic: *Drinking: A Love Story*; *Under the Influence: The Literature of Addiction*; and *Alcoholics Anonymous: The Story of How Many Thousands of Men and Women Have Recovered From Alcoholism*. In *Those Drinking Days: Myself and Other Writers*, the author described his struggle to gain control by looking at famous writers consumed by alcohol abuse, from William Faulkner to Tennessee Williams.

You and I often talked about how our family history was saturated with alcohol. Dad never stopped drinking and hit the bottle harder after Dale died. Bob couldn't quit, which led to a serious disability and a too-early death. Evelyn managed to stop by going to AA meetings daily for twenty years.

What an uphill battle you had, cursed with our grim family history of alcohol abuse, mental illness, and divorce.

Seeing your books about depression was painful: *Touched with Fire: Manic-Depressive Illness and the Artistic Temperament*, by Kay Redfield Jamison, a clinical psychologist with expertise in bipolar disorders, and *Darkness Visible*, by the novelist William Styron. Styron experienced such darkness, he came close to committing suicide. Halfway through this long essay, Dan, you marked a page with a Post-it note. Perhaps it was this line that spoke to you: "The pain is unrelenting, and what makes the condition intolerable is the foreknowledge that no remedy will come—not in a day, an hour, a month, or a minute."

I read Styron, too, during one of my own bouts of depression, which I've experienced at least five times over the years. The first was when I was in college, at age nineteen and at such a low point, I had trouble getting out of bed. I went to the Student Health Service center but got no help. Then, in later years, I was prescribed antidepressants and got individual therapy many times. I never told you any of this, did I? I'd experienced what it was like to have mood swings and still function.

But apparently, you never received any help beyond the therapy in Wisconsin after you smashed your hand.

Sadly, you and I never talked about your despair. Did I not want to hear it? We often discussed Dale's behavior before he died and concluded that he must have been bipolar. Why didn't I assume that you, too, had experienced serious depression? Mental illness was part of our family history, going back at least as far as our grandmother's almost thirty-year institutionalization.

Was appealing to God a kind of sharing or therapy? A total surprise to me was that some of your books reflected your continuing faith in God: *The Power of Now: A Guide to Spiritual Enlightenment*; *The Case for Christ: A Journalist's Personal Investigation of the Evidence for Jesus*. You had a copy of *The Holy Bible*. You had either kept your faith or found it again. Something else we didn't talk about.

I was distressed you had hidden so much from me. Was I so preoccupied with myself and my immediate family that I didn't show enough interest in your life?

But I did find some humor. I smiled at some book titles, such as *Making Out in Chinese: Friendly Chitchat, Lovers' Language and Fighting Words—All the Slang You Need To Sound Like a Native*. And *Love in a Fallen City*. I shouldn't have smiled, because after your divorce, you were always looking for another relationship. You told me you'd wanted a large family, but Helen didn't want any more children.

And you tried to learn Mandarin. I paged through the *Elementary Chinese Reader*, which looked like lessons for schoolchildren; *Reading and Writing Chinese*; and a Mandarin phrasebook.

You had several books on writing: *Writing from Within: A Guide to Creativity and Life Story Writing*; *Writing About Your Life: A Journey Into the Past*; and *Description & Setting: Techniques and Exercises for Crafting a Believable World of People, Places, and Events*, and other similar titles. It was clear you wanted to write about your family experiences.

I was so glad we shared our work with each other. And your genealogy searches provided invaluable background to family stories I began writing in the nineties. Though I quibbled about the many details in your writing, I would have been lost without the particulars about farm life you gave me.

One of your richest and most painful stories happened on the job in China. You were operating your tunnel-boring machine in a subway tunnel when a young co-worker jumped from one moving muck car to another. You had been five meters away and yelled a warning to her, "*Qui, qui,*" which means "Hurry." But it came too late. You wrote:

"I watched, paralyzed and in horror, as she was crushed between the two pieces of machinery and killed instantly…. She was a short girl with a pixie haircut, unusual for a Chinese girl, she had a slight gap between her two front teeth and wore hoop earrings…blood covered the entire front of her torso…she left a husband and one child…."

When you visited her family, you gave them five thousand yuan, though it's not clear if that was your own money or the company's. Her family told you she loved her job but perhaps didn't take seriously how dangerous it could be.

Walking to the windows I looked out again and wondered: Did you consider the fact that I might find you? As you discovered Dale? In that last moment, you must have been so consumed by agony and fear that you just wanted out of life.

Dale had methodically planned ahead. He set up the tube leading from his car's exhaust pipe to the hole in the floor behind the passenger seat. Then he filled the tank with gas and drove to the alfalfa field.

Did you have that in mind when you gave us your car? And signed me onto your bank account?

Among us eight siblings, the oldest and the youngest, dead by his own hand. Now I'm the last left, since Vern, age ninety-seven, died from internal bleeding six months after you.

Why didn't you and I talk more deeply? We often discussed what might have driven Dale to take his own life. But not what you were going through.

I see now how the seeds of this tragedy were scattered throughout your life. Now it is time to tell you, even though it's too late: "I love you."

Sandy

Acknowledgments

I'M GRATEFUL TO SO many people who believed in and encouraged me, without whom I would not have completed this book:

My chief editor, Pamela Feinsilber, pushed me to include the stories of all my family members, when I was ready to stop at five and had no thought of a book. She urged me to dig deeper into telling the stories, gave me ideas on shaping the text, and edited the final manuscript.

My dear writing friends, Carolyn Matson and Cheryl Bowlan, perused the entire manuscript early on, made suggestions, and spurred me to finish, insisting this project was meaningful. Others who offered suggestions early on include Frances Lefkowitz and Nina Schuyler.

My brother Norman wrote his own family history, some of which I referenced. My brother Dan provided specific details of our farm life and conducted extensive research into our parents' histories as well as into institutional records. My nieces, Liz Oliverio and Maggie Dunning, and nephews John Rubel, the late Philip Rubel, and Steve Patti recounted family memories. Anita Flint-Early, my friend since elementary school, refreshed my memories of small-town Lake Park.

My earliest writing "buddies," Susan Domingos and the late Margaret Romweber, with whom I began writing thirty years ago, deepened my interest in writing, got me started on this effort, and stimulated my latent creativity.

The Lafayette writing group—Gloria Lenhart, Jack Champ, Lenka Glassner, Chris Lavin, and Laura Loomis—offered great suggestions to the earliest versions of these stories.

Over the last ten years, other treasured friends have nudged me to finish the book. After listening to me read some of the stories, Ann Alderman, Susan Chamberlain, Lynn Saunders,

Jean Johnston, Nancy McHugh, Janet Saalfeld, Bonnie Stack, Ann Chandler, Marcia Vastine, Bahareh Nemani, Suzanne and Larry Fuller, Sue Woodward, Joyce Kelly, Linda Goldstrom, and the late Leslie Henriques all told me they wanted to hear more.

Jacqueline Gilman, graphic designer, helped me choose the cover image and designed the book's cover and interior.

Finally, I'm grateful to my husband, Ed, who wouldn't let me drop the project when I struggled, and to my sons, Josh and Alex, who supported me throughout. Along with Ed, my sons and their wives and children show me every day what healthy and loving families look like.

About the Author

SANDY ROGIN WAS BORN in rural northwestern Iowa and grew up on a farm six miles from the nearest town. After graduating from high school and dropping out of secretarial school, she followed three of her older siblings to the San Franciso Bay Area, where she graduated from San Jose State University with a B.A. in English and later earned a master's degree. She spent the next two years in Germany, working and studying the language, becoming fluent in German, and traveling around Europe. Back in the U.S., she worked as a freelance journalist, writing for local, regional, and national press in areas including social issues, education, and mental health. For nine years, Rogin wrote federal grant proposals for the City of Honolulu's Department of Community Services, gaining funds for programs serving disadvantaged youth, homeless veterans, low-income people lacking housing, and others. *Runs in the Family* is her first work of fiction. She lives in Oakland, California, with her husband, Ed.